AFTER I'M BURIED ALIVE

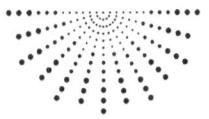

CATHARINE BRAMKAMP

PRAISE FOR CATHARINE BRAMKAMP'S WORK

"Catharine Bramkamp writes with incredible wit, humor and insight into the human condition. She is brilliant and one of my favorite writers and human beings!"

Michelle Gamble-Risley, president, 3L Publishing and author of SMASH and Vanity Circus

"Catharine has a keen eye on the world around her and the rare ability to translate what she sees in life into beautiful prose. Her words are not only witty and acerbic but also insightful and poignant."
    Leslie Wirtley - Runaway Heart (Velvet Seduction Press)

ALSO BY CATHARINE BRAMKAMP

The Real Estate Diva Mysteries

Death Revokes the Offer

Time is of the Essence

In Good Faith

The 380 Degree View

Trash Out

Don't Write Like You Talk

Don't Write Like We Talk

The Journal Book

The Journal Workbook

Ammonia Sunrise (Poetry Collection)

A Good Time Was Had by All (Poetry Collection)

Writing from the Queen's Seat (with Shama Besley)

Writing from the Queen's Seat Workbook (with Shama Besley)

After I'm Buried Alive
Catharine Bramkamp

The characters and events in this book are fictitious.
Any similarity to real persons living or dead,
is coincidental and not intentional.

First Edition: April 2020
ISBN 978-0-9816848-7-1

DEDICATION

To Andrew, who would never bury me alive.

CHAPTER ONE

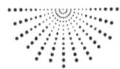

*I*rreplaceable artifacts tend to stay put. More than policy, border patrols or customs, the most important icons of a nation are more often than not pulled home, as if place holds a gravitational field from which it's difficult to break free. At least that's what it looks like from my seat on the couch.

It's more difficult to smuggle ancient artifacts out of a country than you think. My nephew Chris wiggled an inch or two away from me and held up his phone. He had found another article on smuggling. The article explained that a small unidentified group had made at least three attempts to smuggle Egyptian statues, cartouches, and scarabs (provenance still unknown), out of the country. All three attempts had been thwarted. The Egyptian government leveraged the attention and their success as yet another example of how well they were taking care of their own history (no mention of that gravitational pull). That assertion led to the inevitable and evergreen argument over why the Neues Museum in Berlin must return Nefertiti's head. The perpetual demand is popular since so many outlets have ready images of the beautiful sculpture, but the argument never gets very far.

Chris continued to read the feed on his phone. "The authorities are searching for their origin, provenance is everything, we need to know where these come from. I think it's like finders' keepers."

Like Nefertiti's bust. "A great deal like that."

I looked over his shoulder at the screen. From my angle all I could see was a jumble of blue faience ushabtis cradled in shredded packing material.

"That's a lot," Chris commented.

"The old Cairo Museum had so many, hundreds were just stuffed into a glass cabinet, too many to count. The new museum will of course fix all that."

"You need one ushabti for every day of the year." Chris knew most of the story of the replacement workers buried with their masters. If possible, a rich man purchased one statue, one worker a day for the whole year. It was a much better solution than burying the human workers.

"Yes, to do all the work." I had a soft spot in my heart for the little blue figures, made solely for the purpose of working in the after-life fields for their master. Gives new meaning to the term: you were made for this role.

"The one we saw was all alone in a big plastic box." Chris continued to study his screen.

"Yes, it was." I indulged Chris as much as possible since his parents were not as inclined. When the last Tut/Egyptian exhibit came through the De Young, the two of us made pilgrimage to the exhibit: me, for nostalgia, Chris, because he was obsessed. He was right; the De Young displayed only the one blue ushabti, standing in solitary splendor protected in his own purpose-built acrylic box, lit from three sources. Tiny and alone.

"It was precious so they must want to keep it safe," Chris decided.

My sister-in-law bustled into the family room and began to hustle us out.

"Enough!" Tina picked up the remote and aimed it at the massive screen as if commanding a firing squad. "Vic, you need to join the party, people are asking for you. Boys, you need to come and toast your father's retirement."

"Can I have a beer?" Matt piped up. At sixteen he was already more handsome than his balding father and was already skilled in using those bright blue eyes, coupled with an unruly shock of black hair that kept falling into the bridge of his nose, to get what he wanted. Did I want to know about his success with girls? I did not. But while Matt's thick hair was cut and styled for the perfect studied effect, it could never compete with his brother's. Chris, at times, seemed to channel his hero Harry Potter, his hair seeming to grow back days after Tina again spent a considerable sum to get it cut just right.

Tina glared at Matt. "You certainly cannot, young man."

But I wasn't to escape either. She aimed a perfectly French-manicured finger at me. "Come show some support."

"As soon as I refresh my drink." I lifted the empty martini glass and bent to kiss Chris on the head.

"Don't get an olive." His eyes were still glued to his phone. "It takes up too much room in the glass."

I grinned and patted his head.

"You know what else?" He continued without missing a beat.

"Sweetie, what did I tell you about the internet?"

"There is always more." He did not glance up me; he was enthralled and as usual unable to tear away from the images flashing on the screen.

"Come on, big guy." His brother took his arm and lifted

him from the couch. "Stand by me and we'll toast, then get out of here."

"Ride in the car." Chris did not break focus from his phone.

"Yeah, let's take a ride in the car."

Chris obediently followed Matt.

"I just don't know what I'd do without you." Tina sighed. "He does everything you say."

"Not everything." I assured her.

Chosen as the solo ushabti in the box wasn't necessarily a promotion.

I followed my nephews into the living room. For the momentous occasion of my brother's retirement, my sister-in-law had created a tribute fit for a pharaoh. Hothouse flowers overflowed from plastic silver-colored vases competing with random flutes, pinot bowl glasses and shot glasses emblazoned with *Vince Gardner—40 years*. I automatically swept up the silver rented plates and set them in the kitchen sink.

Vince had done well: the beautiful trophy wife, the second family, an impressive home, (close to everything), and he announced as I tried not to rattle the silverware, he was happily anticipating this next chapter of his wonderful life.

I am, of course, paraphrasing his self-aggrandizing party toast. And he cleverly did not describe Tina as his trophy wife. They had probably discussed it ahead of time.

I picked up three wine glasses, edging behind the rapt guests as Vince droned on about his accomplishments. Tina had set up the drinks on the breakfast bar. An attractive young lady stood in the kitchen and handed mixed drinks over the high countertop.

I set the glasses at the end of the counter so they could commiserate with five half empty flutes and two commemorative shot glasses meant to serve as lovely parting gifts.

"Gin martini."

"Oh, I'm sorry, ma'am. We're out of olives."

"And that's how we closed the biggest client in our twenty years." Vince raised his glass again.

Cheers.

"Don't worry, they take up too much room in the glass anyway." With my naked drink I hovered at the very edge of the collective. I eyed a jumble of plates and forks begging to be gathered and cleaned but resisted. I needed to look the part of the loving sister. At least with a full drink in hand, I was safely excused from applauding Vincent's every accomplishment.

The boys slipped out the kitchen door, using the applause to cover the rumble of the garage door opening. It was a beautiful night for a ride. I almost wished I was with them, but Matt's driving was still terrifying. He'd had his license for how long? I counted from his birthday. Four days. The boys were either going up in a ball of flames or nothing would happen at all.

My bet was on nothing. Chris was closely watched over by our gods, his and mine. He would be fine and, by association, so would his brother. I felt a pang as the car roared out of the garage. They would be fine.

Before I could take a sip of my refreshed drink, I was accosted by the person I least wanted to see, a person who, in fact, inspired my escape to the family room in the first place.

"Oh, Victoria, you must be so sad that your mother is finally gone." Beth Ellen Banner took my arm and moved me a fraction away from the crowd, as if that would serve to create a cone of silence and intimacy. She took a tiny sip of her champagne and eyed me speculatively.

Beth Ellen was a dear friend and colleague of Vince and, after a couple of years, friendly with Tina. Beth Ellen and Tina worked out their differences during a company picnic at the historic Empire Mine, the face-off happened in the middle of what used to be tennis courts. Many staff members reported on the outcome. Supercilious, and always fashionable, Beth Ellen used to favor Armani suits embellished with shoulder pads that could block Tom Brady, but now that she was in retirement, she switched it up to a more relaxed wardrobe with Eileen Fisher for volunteer work and playful wardrobe pieces courtesy of Gucci featuring his signature blinding neon green. I was not sure this reinvention was an improvement.

Tina reported that Beth Ellen's retirement party had been held at the Four Seasons and everyone from the CEO to the janitor had been invited. The guest list for Vince's party was more exclusive.

Beth Ellen now devoted her time and her self-reported considerable expertise, to United Way of Sacramento. Even more than Tina, Beth Ellen embodied all the success and security that eluded me. She was thin when I was fat, celebrated when I was ignored, rich when I was poor; she owned two houses, I was technically homeless. And since I was currently all my faults at once, I absolutely did not want to talk with her. I took a deep breath and marshalled all my dwindling resources to appear appropriately polite.

I focused on her brightly colored ensemble that belied her serious expression. With a shock I recognized her dress. It wasn't a Gucci; it was a. It could be a knockoff. It could be a knockoff Gucci for that matter, Max Peters and Gucci were often mistaken for one another. Not the men, the clothes. On Beth Ellen, the slender sheath was flattering, very Twiggy, very mod-sixties, which was part of his second spring collection in the early '80s when Max was just launching his career as one of *Vogue*'s bad-boy designers.

I hadn't thought of Max in weeks. I blinked. I had catalogued this very pattern; the print was bright and loose like a child's drawing or Matisse cutouts, both of which were inspirations.

"Yes, of course I will miss her very much." I patted my natural gray hair wishing I had made time to get a cut and color. But in my defense, I had just recovered from a nasty flu, my third this year. Mom had been healthy up to the end, but I seemed to catch every virus and bacteria available for pickup at the local Safeway. I took a deep breath, happy to not fall into a paroxysm of coughing. I eyed Beth Ellen. I was younger than she but felt a hundred years older.

"Vince says you are just a saint." She sighed. "I wish I had family. I don't know if you heard, but I had to put Mother in a home, the very best, of course."

"Because you are so busy." I offered the expected response; there was little reason not to.

"My work has always been important." She batted her lashes. I resisted a quick retort. My current position was not only tenuous: it was dramatically unimportant, no better than the nursing home staff Beth probably remembered every holiday with a box of See's Nuts and Chews.

I slugged back the rest of my drink. Good thing there wasn't a tooth-picked olive taking up room in the glass, I would have lost an eye. I struggled to compose an acceptable follow-up comment. I had no conversation, nothing interesting to say. Beth Ellen had won again.

The final applause washed over the living room. The crowd broke and made for the food and drink. Before I could escape to pick up those plates and forks, Vince sneaked up behind me, giving me a start. For a big man, he moved with surprising stealth. He grinned at Beth Ellen and threw his arm around me squeezing like an anaconda asphyxiating its lunch. "Vic is going to live with us and help with the boys!"

I gave him a tight-lipped smile. This morning I'd realized I needed to bleach my teeth.

Beth Ellen looked up and down from my best, but dated Calvin Klein black jacket, open because I couldn't button it, down to my low-heeled pumps that, truth be told, were Mom's.

I hadn't been sleeping. I had gained weight. I looked like a vision, a vision of an aging woman on the wrong side of fifty. My sixtieth birthday loomed, and my glass was empty.

Moving from my parents' house to my brother's house was a recent idea. To me. As Vince and Tina marched into our parents' house, it was clear they not only had discussed my next move and my new role: in their heads it was a fait accompli.

They missed the coroner by seconds.

Vince was dressed for work: full Boss suit, shined shoes, the five hairs he had left carefully parceled out over his skull. Tina looked like she was on the way to Junior League. Which she very well could be. Nice they could take time out of their busy scheduled to say goodbye...oh wait, they just missed her.

Vince pulled out a paper from his inside jacket pocket and bade me sit down.

I was already sitting.

I was suddenly overwhelmed. The non-negotiable finality as the coroner zipped up the black vinyl bag wrenched through my gut. I was nauseated, breathless and sweaty and it wasn't from the flu.

I put my head between my legs just to get some blood moving. If it ever would.

Tina, tall and brittle, acknowledged me with a nod and then stepped carefully around the split-level ranch house, assessing; from her body language I could tell she was seeing it all with new more acquisitional eyes. If I thought that afternoon couldn't get any worse, I was wrong.

Vince sat across from me on the matching upholstered chair. He cleared his voice.

"We are both devastated, of course. It is a shame about Mother, but not unexpected, right?" He checked his phone. "Vance and Elaine will be here tonight. But he gave me the go- ahead with our offer."

Tina returned from her initial assessment and perched on the arm of her husband's chair.

We would sell the family house and split the proceeds three ways. Mom left us all a few dollars that, of course, he and Vance would invest on my behalf. In the same breath he and Tina told me I'd be living with them as the best way to preserve my capital, live frugally and not uncoincidentally care for the boys while she and Vince took a well-earned vacation. I was surprised there wasn't an accompanying PowerPoint with slide after slide graphing the cost/benefits of their plan.

I would have my own room and bath, they pitched. Time to myself while the boys were in school. Time off during the holidays if I so chose, but of course, of COURSE! They would rather have me with them during any family gathering and family vacations. I was so important, I was so caring; even as the youngest, I was so competent. Really, what would they have done these last three years? The boys needed someone at home, and you know, Vic. Here Vince eyed me with a jaded expression, as if he knew everything about me, as if I had always acted the caregiver, as if this was my only remaining talent, where else will you go?

Vincent, in his new retirement mode, was already considering consulting offers (I really did miss the PPT deck; I was interested in learning exactly who needed insurance consulting). He and Tina deserved the time to travel. They wanted time with the boys unhindered by homework and school activities. They were not getting any younger, you know.

I was their ticket to a carefree life. They had both worked really hard and deserved this.

I will spare you any more details of that gruesome afternoon. As it finally wound down to its whimpering end, I was hours away from a housecoat, slippers, and daytime television.

I smiled at Beth Ellen, philanthropist, wearer of designer dresses, and carefully extracted myself from Vince's death grip.

"It was so nice to see you again." I dredged up my best party talk. I had forgotten how to make witty cocktail conversation. Three to five years out of practice. Even in his anticipated decline, Max had insisted on witty repartee. Every afternoon of his final two years, he rallied and invited any and all callow young men from the industry and off the street. When I wasn't monitoring the wine, making sure small ornaments didn't wind up missing and anxiously wringing my hands, those afternoons were kind of fun. Max chose death by party—going out with a sigh and half a glass of wine left to go. I turned away for a second so my mascara, old and undependable, wouldn't run with a sudden rush of tears.

But Beth Ellen hadn't missed my expression. She unexpectedly reached out and touched my arm. "I'm sorry for your loss. Both parents in three years, Vince was devastated by your father's death. He couldn't have gotten through it without you. He always said you were indispensable." She reassured me.

I nodded and let her comment stand. Vincent's people at American Interest Insurance were not often given to sentimentality. I suppose it was because they had all heard too many sad stories and were professionally required to make the hard decisions anyway.

Or it was that their nature first and the insurance

industry was the best way to express it?

Either way, I let her be, for a few seconds, human. I nodded and in turn, touched her arm. "Thank you, Beth Ellen, that means a lot to me." That she was helping me mourn another person entirely was beside the point.

I passed my sister-in-law, Tina. She was holding court, gesturing with her half-filled champagne glass. "All the food and drink is gourmet." She emphasized the word, careful to not accidentally pronounce the T. "It's not like those enormous ships with the kiddie slides and the all-night entertainment and the all-you-can-eat midnight buffets." She shuddered. "We will be treated well. It's very exclusive, you know."

I didn't hear the next question. It was pitched below the appreciative murmurs.

"Oh, the boys? Of course, we cannot take them out of school. Vic will take care of them. So helpful! She is indispensable, don't know how we would have pulled this off without her."

I shook my head; it was the first I had heard of a cruise.

I dropped off my glass and more gathered dishes in the kitchen sink. Another compatriot of American Interest Insurance accosted me. "You must be Vic. I've heard so much about you these last few years."

The woman was much younger, probably early thirties and ramping up her career. She wore no makeup; her hair was pulled back in a messy ponytail.

"I'm Mary Sullivan." She thrust out her hand and, out of habit, I took it. She pumped it viciously and leaned in to talk to me, as in confidence.

"What a night, right? Forty years with the same company!"

"He started when he was twenty-five." Same year he and his first wife married. It lasted until Vincent, forty-five, and

Tina, twenty-five, met at a company party. Love at first sight, a chance at a new life, blah, blah, blah. They leveraged their relationship into the perception of the perfect power couple. She was an attorney; he, rising through the ranks in American Interest Insurance one rung at a time. Hardly anyone stays with one company longer than five years, but these two stuck it out, because they always finished what they start. I'm not surprised they have a plan and that it was so quickly executed; they have been talking about retirement since they met. Needless to say, the surprise gift of Matt and Chris, one after the other, derailed the dream. Tina and Vincent were forced to pivot.

But the boys also allowed Vincent into our mother's good graces, Vance already had the girls, precious and precious, now it was Vince's turn.

"Look at your brothers, steady jobs, homes. Those beautiful babies." Mom would lean back in her chair, exhausted by her accolades. "If only you had married, you would know the same happiness."

For my new friend Mary, all that leaning in must have pulled something. She winced and settled back on her low-heeled shoes. "Sorry, I pulled a muscle coaching the soccer match yesterday."

"You have children?"

"Yes, two girls. They just made senior-junior varsity team. It's a traveling team, you know? Every weekend in the car, I barely have time for myself." She was cheerful about it, I credited her for that.

"Do you have children?"

I shook my head and uttered the same phrase repeated ad nauseam during the last three years. "I haven't been blessed."

She frowned, like being child free was a personality flaw. "That's too bad."

No, it's too bad I had gin for dinner last night.

CHAPTER TWO

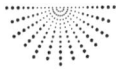

*S*uddenly, everything changed.

I've always wanted to say that.

Not that life hadn't presented those moments in the past. The day I met Max, the day I met Miranda. The day I locked eyes with Nic, the day my father fell and broke his hip. But Miranda was not a hip, something that wore out, something that could be surgically removed and replaced. Miranda was for always. She was indomitable and unstoppable. A beauty in her youth, she was one of the lucky ones who gathered up her fifteen minutes of fame and parlayed them into a career. She had class, charisma, and two mornings ago, extra color.

"You look a little green around the edges." I squinted at my computer screen.

Out of the blue she had pinged me and set up a Skype chat. She looked like she too had been drinking gin for dinner. Who do you think I learned it from?

She twirled something just below the camera and seemed to scrutinize her monitor as closely as I had.

She ignored my comment about her appearance. Models

needed to do that; otherwise the criticism is so crushing it's difficult to get out of bed.

"How are you? Wasn't last night Vince's retirement party? And," she rushed forward as she did. "Shouldn't it have been yours as well? We discussed this." She frowned, but after years of Botox, it was hard for her to make a really intense scrunchy face.

We had. She was one of my first calls after Mother died. What would I do? I think I asked that question in a reasonable tone, but I wouldn't swear to it. I was pretty strung out. It felt like not only was I abruptly an orphan, I was abruptly unemployed.

"You can come back here darling." Miranda immediately offered.

"But you always take me in."

"Of course, for an old lover there is always a bed." She batted her full eyelashes. I did not take the hint.

"I can't. The boys need me. And I'm not sure I should just return. Wouldn't it be like moving backwards?"

"The place is the same. Beautiful people, fabulous wine." She tried to entice me. But I couldn't. And I had been right. Vince and Tina needed me to clear out the family home, help show and sell the same and move in with them to care for the boys. Well, mostly Chris.

I explained that again and Miranda nodded as if she hadn't heard my excuses over and over for the last five years.

"Remember that model?" She moved to a new distraction.

"Which one?" As a photographer's assistant, I had managed many, many models.

Miranda shrugged. "Beautiful faces, few names. To keep her in line, you finally had to point out that there were hundreds of beautiful girls lined up to take her place."

"But there are not hundreds of aunts to care for Chris and Matt." I squinted at the screen. Behind her was something rather black and looming, a sculpture? Over her bed? It didn't look like her typical purchase. I opened my mouth to ask but she cut me off.

"Not hundreds of aunts, but you, my love, are most certainly replaceable."

"I beg your pardon?"

"You are replaceable. You were not the only person who could care for your parents, and you are not the only person who can care for those enormous boys. It doesn't need to be you."

"That's not much of a compliment."

"All right then, never mind. You are irreplaceable, one of a kind. And while we're at it, is this?"

She was breathless, her face distorted over Skype. She thrust a blue object towards the camera. It loomed so large I couldn't make it out.

I squinted. "Is that a statue of a hippo? It looks like something out of the National Geographic holiday catalog."

Her eyes widened in surprise. She glanced down and turned it in her hands. "It could be."

She gave me a sunny smile, one that had melted my heart and encouraged participation in too-many-to-count unplanned and ill-advised activities. A smile that still got to me. Why had we broken up? Ah, her girls. Demanding little things. So many beautiful faces.

"You think it's just a knockoff?" She sighed. "I was so sure it was one of those artifacts you and Nic were always digging up in Egypt. Would it be worth something if it were?"

"Were what?"

She held up the item again. It was blue-green, decorated with thin black markings. From what I could tell, it was simply a small blue statue.

"If it were genuine, you know, the real deal? Would it be worth anything?"

CATHARINE BRAMKAMP

I leaned back on the couch and adjusted my laptop to fix the angle of the camera. I looked like shit, but it was early in the morning; I always looked like shit first thing in the morning, what fifty something woman doesn't? I shouldn't take Miranda's calls before my second cup of coffee.

"If it is real." I hadn't used my brain in years; it was disconcertingly slow to boot up. I sipped more coffee and considered her question.

"If it's real, it needs to be authenticated, where it was found, where is the dig? Are there more?"

I pulled my laptop to me and tried to get a better look. "Miranda, are there more?"

Her face sagged, and for a second, she looked all of her sixty-seven years. Not even her two facelifts could disguise the years reflected in her eyes.

"I don't know the origins. And there was only the one hippo, I bought it for twelve Euro. A steal, I'm sure..."

"I hope it wasn't a steal." I was the one who was reassuring and supportive but sometimes in the face of Miranda's constant bargain hunting, it was a challenge to always put a good face on it. She loved to discover soon-to-be famous art and obscure and certainly valuable objects. Like Max, she had the money to purchase anything that caught her eye. Unlike Max, she was often wrong, and we ended up just storing a lot of "precious" junk. Like the "overlooked" Rothko that hung over the dining room table and the tiny Seurat study of the woman and girl from *A Sunday on La Grand Jatte*, which didn't look all that convincing. But the hunt gave her pleasure and purpose. She loved nothing more than to spend a whole Sunday combing locals flea markets, then when those were exhausted, traveling to Paris to shop more flea markets and small galleries. If she couldn't be Peggy Guggenheim in quality, she made up for it in volume.

I had delivered the wrong answer.

16

"Nicholas said the same thing."

My heart jumped. "You called him?"

"I gave this party." Her parties were legendary. Not even the survivors remembered the details: just a whirl of color, light and laughter. I miss her epic parties; no balloons, no streamers, no flowers jammed into plastic vase. Just a lot of booze, and other festive adult substances.

Miranda and I did not meet at a party, we wouldn't have remembered enough to re- connect. We had met on a shoot in Paris. She was the model; I was the photographer's assistant whose main job was to explain the harsh reality of indispensability to the models. We bonded, in more ways than one, and before I knew it, I was Alice to her Gertrude, a seductively comfortable role. Miranda knew everyone, and everyone knew her, and if they didn't know her personally, they knew her photos and her lavish parties. Venice in the '80s was one big colorful fever dream, drugs, sex and rock and roll. It was a lot of fun.

I grew up under the gloomy prophecy that any good time inevitably carries unpleasant consequences, and so it did.

"Nic said it could be from a dig. It could be the real thin, he doggedly insisted.

"That's great right? You have a real artifact." My eyes wandered to take in my own surroundings. The thick wood shelves surrounding the pale brick fireplace were layered with precious collectables treasured by my mother. What would an archeologist think of this stuff? Were blue hippos the Egyptian equivalent of bourbon bottles shaped like turkeys or figurines from the Franklin Mint collection, guaranteed to increase in value? Not even Elaine, Vance's wife, wanted them. In two thousand years will these be unearthed and given their own acrylic box in a museum show? The tiny museum label printed religious object the catch phrase for we have no clue why this was manufactured in the first place.

17

I sighed, I had to clean the house. The real estate agent Vincent had engaged was due here this morning.

I dragged my hands through my curls and almost upset the computer.

"If it is real, it's stolen." I insisted. Don't get me started. While my affair with Miranda was comfortable and plush, my years with the aforementioned Dr. Nicholas Ratzenberg were not. Exciting yes, thrilling, dirty, and sandy, yes. Years of sex and history lectures sometimes simultaneously. With Nic I earned the equivalent of an MA in tolerance. Every third day of excavations I got an earful about stolen artifacts just in case I hadn't been listening the night before. I traded Murano chandeliers and wine for tents, bugs and terror. It wasn't my brightest move, but it was exciting. Anyway. Nic.

"He's still working? I thought by now someone would have shot him or mauled him or buried him in another unproductive tomb."

"He does stick his head into the wrong holes now and, then doesn't he?" Miranda played with the statue, it fit perfectly in her two hands, like an oversized worry bead.

I swallowed. "You saw him?"

She shook her head. "He couldn't get away; had a project he was consulting on in Luxor."

I relaxed, he was nowhere near, and since he was single minded, one could charitably call it obsessive, the odds of me seeing him again were very low. I self-consciously patted my unfortunate hair. Maybe I'd have time today for a mani-pedi. Maybe pigs would fly.

"I really thought you and Nicholas would make a go of it." Miranda looked up at me, meaning something else entirely.

"You and I were a stronger couple." I assured her.

She nodded. There was too much to say. I loved her. I loved everything about her. It wasn't her income, yes Miranda was from money, which was the only way to really make it in Fashion, with a capital F. I was from Lincoln, CA, with a BA degree from FIDM in San Francisco. I was the biggest, more awkward wannabe the fashion industry had ever witnessed. But I worked hard, I showed up and learned the lighting and equipment and by sheer force of will made myself indispensable to both photographers and later, designers. Miranda, for some inexplicable reason, admired that quality. I suppose she exploited me, but at the time, the compensation for such exploitation was not only reasonable, it was fabulous.

But that life was all over. I was back home and incontrovertibly embedded in the Sacramento area. The address was desirable—Vince and Tina bought a house in Sacramento's Fabulous Forties, the nicest residential district in town. Their home was well over 6,000 square feet which engendered their need for my help as well as what they considered an irresistible enticement: my own private suite on the ground floor. Suite. I have lived in larger tents.

The bedroom was small with a minuscule closet (for resale value) attached to a powder room expanded into a full bath by dint of punching a square into the garage and installing a Home Depot fiberglass shower. But it was rent-free. I would never again experience any needs or wants. All I had to do was care for my teenage nephews. A little light cooking. Pick up a bit. The time clock at the top of my screen ticked away. I needed to prepare for the agent's walk through.

"I have to go, what can I do Miranda? It's just a statue, probably just a nice replica. If you don't want it, sell it back to the store. Or post it on eBay or Craig's List."

"Nicholas seemed interested." She held it up so I could see it more clearly. A blue hippo. Well, not that blue, green. Those particular hippos are manufactured by the tens of thousands for distribution all over the world. They all look exactly the same, like the mascot for the Metropolitan Museum. She stroked it and turned it in her hands.

Nicholas. She had shown it to Nic. I didn't even know she kept his number. I drew in a shuddering breath and willed my heart to slow.

"I've never seen you nervous about something so small." I pushed away the thoughts of Dr. Nicholas Ratzenberg, those days too, were over and gone. One could even say abandoned.

"There's just something...," she started.

I had half hour before the appointment. The older you are, the longer it takes to get ready for public consumption.

"Gotta go. Just sell it or toss it."

"You are probably right." She stopped worrying the little statue. "I should just throw it away, right? That would solve everything."

I had no idea what she needed to solve, but I waved cheerfully before signing off. She blew me a kiss.

Twenty-four hours later I was seated in business class on a direct flight from SFO to Venice. It wasn't just Vince and Tina who considered me indispensable. According to her surviving daughters, I was named the executor of Miranda's estate. I suspected it was because I was the only person left on Miranda's favorites list who was willing to pick up her call.

Miranda had been found (I couldn't say body because as soon as I thought about the term body what popped into my brain was my mother in that black vinyl bag) by a friend who stopped by Miranda's apartment first thing this morning to cajole Miranda into a jog around the lagoon. Miranda hadn't answered the door or her phone. The friend, knowing where the extra key was kept, barged right in. Thank the gods.

Tiffany, Miranda's oldest daughter, immediately called me and coerced me into joining her in Venice. Tiffany was like her mother in one thing—she just assumed. Answering the phone at 12:00 A.M. must have been the indicator that I would acquiesce to her demands. I'm not special mind you; Tiffany didn't even like me. But I was the only one available at the last minute.

Retirement is like that. You become available. Maybe even indispensable. Maybe both.

CHAPTER THREE

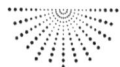

*V*enice, Italy is not Sacramento, California. Not even with the California brand to help Sacramento along, can Sacramento be anything but a small town in a big state. Venice, however, was once a state all by itself. Built on the solid foundation of intrigue, power and trade, the very air is invigorating, artistic. Damp.

Sacramento was traveling soccer and my mother's perpetual and enduring disappointment that I had not been blessed with a real family. Venice was that blessing, something my family never understood. That made it better, that they couldn't understand the allure, the magic.

Muscle memory helped me negotiate the airport crowds. I passed hollow-eyed tourists obediently lined up for buses and jams of guided tours grouped around bulky luggage eyeing the new name tags that would identify them for the next two weeks as aliens. Stay with the class, hold your partner's hand. We are walking, walking, walking.

I skirted around an elderly couple arguing over which vaporetto would take them directly across the lagoon. The woman looked like my twin: gray permed hair, practical tan polyester slacks, blue sweatshirt pulled over a blue and yellow flowered shirt. I quickly glanced down at my attire, my sweatshirt was black. I veered away, dragging my single carry-on, the wheels banging on the divots in the cobblestone walkway shudderingly enough to knock your dentures loose.

I headed straight for the water bus and loaded in, happy to be traveling light. I was trained to carry much more: precious photographic equipment loaded into equally expensive rolling bags. I often packed my own clothes into the light bag, using socks and underwear to cushion the bulbs and filters against any travel disaster. Just rolling one bag along was a complete joy.

I passed the tourists who did not get the memo, nor watched a single YouTube video on how to pack. Public transportation was not for the faint of heart in the best of times, but it can be an unmitigated nightmare if you travel with luggage the size of the average Italian car.

Perched safely on my moral high ground, I watched the same elderly couple struggle towards the boat dragging two purple cases that must have weighed as much as they. The woman hauled a stuffed handbag as well as a duffle-size carry-on. Her husband tried to negotiate the teetering cases; the wheels shrieked in protest. Or at least I interpreted it as protest.

It took two crew members to haul the suitcases on board.

I assumed that the man had not changed his money and so did not have enough euros for an adequate tip. But I was raised to not judge. Unless someone deserves it.

The woman walked up and down the narrow aisle leaving her husband in back to guard the monolithic luggage. She saw ten inches of space next to me and gave me that look.

I sighed and scooted my bag and carry-on two more inches to the left. She took the offered space with alacrity.

"Those flights are so exhausting. What time is it at home do you know?"

I glanced at my watch; I had already changed it to local time. It was 6:00 P.M.—Italian time. Which is relatively meaningless as far as appointments, dinner, or store openings go, but at least it gave me a general idea of how to manage the jet lag threatening even now to take over. I knew, from my former days of travel, that the best way to deal with jet lag is to ignore it. It was evening here. And if I could eat dinner, and last until about 9:00 tonight, I would sleep well and wake pretty much on time and ready to face Miranda's daughter, Tiffany. The other daughter, Lucy, was with her children and couldn't possibly fly out. Tiffany was not happy, which meant I was soon to be unhappy as well.

"You get in at 5:00 P.M. that's plenty of time," Tiffany had protested.

"I will be tired." I pointed out.

"I just flew in from New York, and I'm not tired."

I did not point out that I covered another continent, which doubled the distance and doubled the flight time. I wasn't interested in delivering a geography lesson. Kids don't listen anyway, expect my nephew Chris who, bless his heart, would listen to anything I explained as long as it was convoluted and complicated.

I was about to say, of course, I could come to Miranda's apartment right away. I needed to get this all over with and back to the family. But then I stopped myself. Why rush Venice?

I also recalled that when dealing with Tiffany and Lucy, agreeing with them immediately stopped any argument along with the pouting and protests. It was a terrible way to raise children, but since I was not responsible for their moral upbringing or even for their well-being, I was happy to take the road most traveled. I let Miranda deal with her love children. I was out.

"Tiffany, I just got in." I said as gently as I could.

"Oh, all right. Ten o'clock tomorrow and don't be late. You know where the apartment is?"

"I'll be at the apartment at 10:00." I promised.

"Fine." She clicked off.

The woman next to me was waiting for her answer. "Six o'clock," I offered.

She frowned. I gave in.

"Is this your first visit to Venice?"

"Oh yes, I've always wanted to see Italy, and Henry, that's my husband back there, finally retired, he was in electronics. I still can't believe he actually agreed to a European tour. We are here for two weeks."

"Not with a tour group?"

"We will meet up with the group in three days. We wanted a romantic." She nudged me in the ribs with a well-padded elbow. "Getaway."

"You came to the right city." I assured her.

I closed my eyes. The boat pulled away from the dock and headed across the lagoon.

She did not take the hint. Whatever it was she took on the plane to get through the flight, it wasn't a sedative.

"It's like the Grand Tour, you know the kind where they take care of everything, our luggage, the hotel rooms, the flights. It's quite a luxury affair, five-star hotels, only the best restaurants. We dress for dinner every night."

I nodded.

"Italy, France, Spain, Switzerland, Hungary, Germany, and we fly out of Amsterdam."

Two weeks. Jesus, Mary, and Joseph.

"That will be interesting." I offered. The rocking boat was a natural relaxant. I closed my eyes again, confident that the woman would nudge me when we landed, if only to ask if this was the place.

I wasn't too far off. She nattered on about the relative merits of each country. She read in Rick Steves that they should visit the Basilica first thing in the morning.

"You know, before all those cruise ships dock."

"I know."

"Terrible what the crowds are doing to Venice."

Terrible what the King Tide did too. Terrible about taxes. Terrible about bureaucracy, something the Italians helped invent. I hadn't even heard if Max's estate was ever settled, and it had been three years. Miranda's would not be any easier, or faster. I tried to remember if this was the season for the King Tides or if I would miss them. Some evenings the tide was so strong it inundated St. Mark's Square as if it were in the middle of the Nile. A person could, if they tried, swim from one end of the square to the other. Not something I recommend. The water looks clean enough, but don't swim in it.

The vaporetto docked, knocking my companion against me. I rose slowly so my new BFF could scramble and get out of the way. She rose slowly and stepped into the aisle blocking three people behind her. She then bent over her commodious bag and searched for the hotel reservation. I couldn't walk around her. The backup was five people, six people, seven people deep.

"Paula!" A voice from the back of the boat bellowed out. "Get off the boat, woman!"

She looked up and waved to her romantic partner, gathered up the bag and her duffle and slowly shuffled down the aisle, the rest of the passengers shuffling in her painfully slow wake.

I waited my turn and carried my bag up the gangplank and stepped into the city of dreams.

We looked alike, Paula and me. I struggled with the notion that I could be anything like her, but I was too honest to fool even myself. Retirees. Finally seeing Europe. Badly dressed, sloppily packed and loaded with euros. Why would anyone, looking at the two of us, think any different?

I pulled my small roller and it clattered across the stones. At each of the three bridges between me and the hotel, I picked up my bag with one hand and, without missing a step, carried it up and over. Once at St. Mark's Square I checked my phone that listed walking directions, which in Venice were more a platonic ideal than an actual measure of distance.

I passed Paula and her husband at the first bridge. They were arguing about the best way to haul the luggage up the bridge steps. A few people waited patiently behind them. I hesitated. They were new, they didn't know anything, they were elderly, I really should help them.

A family group, similarly burdened, bumped past me and slowly made their way up the bridge. I glanced down at my own small suitcase, I couldn't carry theirs and mine. I passed them, but not without a considerable amount of nagging guilt.

THEIR VOICES FLOATED over the bridge, him, "What did you pack?"

Her, "No more than you. We are having dinner every night. We need to look nice!"

I would have liked to stay at a hotel on the Grand Canal, or even in Miranda's apartment. Both were impossible. I wasn't sure that Tiffany would welcome me back into her mother's apartment, especially since Tiffany was probably staying there herself.

But the hotel I found was just fine, and apparently,

popular with readers of Rick Steves. I stood in line behind three middle-aged couples, all holding the blue-covered guides. All dressed in indescribably depressing khaki travel ensembles.

I checked in, accepted my plain hotel room card, not even a logo to help distinguish it from any other credit-card-size key, and dragged my bag up three flights of stairs—no elevator. I passed the three sets of Rick Steves tourists, complaining loudly about the absent elevator.

The room was clean. There was a bed. That sums up the decor. I sighed, at least two more hours before I could fall—I tested the mattress, it was firm, damn—into the queen-size bed.

I couldn't bear my outfit, but I had nothing else in my suitcase; all I had was tee shirts and old-lady blouses, practical, fire-proof polyester. Not a single item of my former wardrobe fit. I changed into a tee shirt with a modicum of style and a sweater against the evening air. I descended into the lobby just as Paula's husband wrestled in the last of their purple suitcases through the entrance. He looked on the verge of a stroke. Paula was more ravaged than an eleven-hours flight could explain and, despite the cool evening, they were both sweating. They were also growling at one another. As she rustled through her carry-on bag for the reservations, he plopped down on the largest case and scanned the lobby. I already knew what he was searching for, but I didn't want to crush his brief seconds of hope.

I hesitated. The concierge warily watched the couple as if eyeing rabid dogs.

Paula slapped down the printed reservation with a gesture of triumph. The young man handed over the key cards.

"We're in room 406." She announced.

The husband nodded wearily. They were a floor above me.

"Oh hi!" Paula finally noticed me and tried to smile. "Those streets are just murder on your feet, and all those canals and bridges!"

I smiled and nodded. Four large hard-sided check-in bags. I had carried worse, heavier, more precious if it comes to that.

The words were out before I could stop myself. "Let me help you."

Miranda would have not approved.

To their credit, Paula and Hank (by the third flight of stairs, we were all on a first-name basis. They were from Iowa. First time in Europe. Should they drink the water? Why is the bathroom so small? Why are there no elevators in this country? The usual) did invite me to dinner, but I declined and suggested they rest a bit before venturing out.

Unburdened, I skipped down the stairs and headed out. I did not even bother hunting down the "best" restaurant. I walked out of the hotel, turned left and walked into the first local trattoria I encountered.

The tablecloths were white, I was offered a window table, I was offered wine. Ah, the glorious Italian food and fabulous, inexpensive Italian wine. Everything a woman with a healthy appetite could want.

Full of a fine Primitivo and celebratory Alfredo, I sailed back to the hotel and collapsed into my bed. After a ten-minute rest, I managed to remove my shoes. It was as far as I got. I had stayed awake until nine, I could sleep as long as I liked. And I did.

CHAPTER FOUR

 woke at 7:00 feeling that something was very wrong. First of all, I was fully dressed, my bra wires dug into my ribs, my right shoulder ached. Second, was the noise. Heavy metallic sounds vibrated up from the street and into the open windows. Workers banged on wood and tile, trading insults over their hammers. A dolly heavy with an enormous keg rattled over the cobblestones. A cascade of broken glass fell into an empty bin, the shattered sound vibrating back and forth in the tiny alley.

Yet it was completely quiet.

No news cast, no talking heads. No canned laughter. No obligatory applause (cue the spontaneity of the live audience). No TV. I listened again. Two men argued over how best to work the jackhammer, the keg was the wrong one causing more shouting and, I assume, gesturing. I blinked back tears.

For three years, the TV was never not on. By 9:00 every morning, Mother was in the thrall of her morning programs. She did not move from the couch until lunch. That gave me time to clean, fix the meals, ostensibly have time to myself, but after Vance bought my parents the largest flat screen on the market, there was no escape from the chatter, the swell of music telegraphing alarm and danger, the commercials kicked up ten decibels louder than the show.

"It's like Dr. Phil is right here in the room!" Mom exclaimed with delight the first day she spent a whole afternoon in front of the new screen. It was very much like Dr. Phil was in the room. It was the world writ large, and that world was scary indeed.

Good Morning America—Bunk Beds, are they endangering your child?

FOX News—The President tweeted again to confirm that he is incapable of irony.

Dr. Phil—Next, more platitudes and clichés dispensed calmly to screaming accusatory guests.

In all those years of listening to Jerry Springer, sorry, Dr. Phil, not once did I overhear a TV show about what watching unregulated amounts of daytime television will do to a person's psyche. What was my eighty-three-year-old mother supposed to do with all this information? There were no actionable suggestions, no number to call, just wave after wave of free-floating anxiety.

She certainly took it all in. She worried about border security, she worried about asteroids.

Every fifteen minutes, Mother's thin, querulous voice cut through the TV noise.

Was I was giving her enough Metamucil so she wouldn't feel so weighed down? Do we need metal straws? Should she buy an alert necklace, in case she fell?

"No," I yelled over the opening credits of Dr. Phil, "No you don't need an alert necklace, I will hear you when you fall."

Why couldn't we watch PBS? Brought to us by a cruise company or large corporate insurance group—AIG—still in business. I wouldn't have minded a Mr. Rogers re-run or two. I loved Mr. Rogers because his was one of the few TV shows that did not upset Chris; in fact, the show was calming. Chris watches Mr. Rogers even now, just to get centered.

I stretched in the hard bed. Miranda had insisted, almost from the day I left Venice, that I needed to return, to take a break from the incessant stress of caregiving. But what could I do? I couldn't leave my parents for a mere vacation; I couldn't even leave them to pee. I was on hyper alert, conscious of every sound, every breath, every catch in the oxygen machine. I'd anxiously wait for the beep, the sigh, the call, the fall.

I aged exponentially with every one of their last breaths.

I ran my hands through my hair. The last bottle crashed into the metal trash bin. The beer keg was accepted and bounced over the threshold. The workers took a smoking break.

I was determined to enjoy my unexpected reprieve.

The shower was tiny, little more than a drain and an accordion pleated vinyl door to prevent the shower water from drenching the toilet paper jammed up under the single sink.

But it did the job.

I pawed through my luggage. My keys rattled. I pulled them out. They were shiny from use, which is an odd thing to say about keys. They were my worry beads, a mnemonic device. Here was the key to my parents' house, the key to their safe deposit box, the key to Vince's house, Vance's house. The key to a storage facility, the heavy key fob to my car. I studied it. Key to Miranda's? I had a couple of mystery keys; it was a possibility. Vance always teased me about keys; apparently when I was a young, I loved carrying around an oversized key ring filled with useless keys donated by my parents. When I saw my first school janitor, I admired his heavy key ring, clipped onto his belt. That Christmas, I asked for a belt clip.

"Why you need all those keys?" Vince would taunt.

"They don't open anything." Vance would chime in.

"Maybe I just haven't found the right door." I would always answer. At five.

I tossed the keys back into the suitcase. Tiffany would meet me at the apartment. She had a key because years ago I had mailed her one.

I squeezed into jeans and a shirt that used to be "oversized" but now just fit like a shirt. I was too distracted to worry about my appearance. I was old, I was clearly a tourist. Didn't need to pretend anything else.

The hotel stay included access to a breakfast bar in a small room just off the lobby. I eyed the offerings laid out on three cloth-covered tables pushed against the walls. The far buffet table was decorated with stale pastries and a single bowl of apples. I didn't need food, I needed real coffee, with a real kick.

"The breakfast is included." Paula and Hank were up and on the move. The decision was easy, I ducked out and made my way to Miranda's apartment.

I stopped at an espresso bar. Two older men pushed against me at the counter, but I held my own and ordered a second small cup of straight up espresso while drinking down the first. As I knocked back my drink, the two men, startled, eased back and gave me more room.

I placed my euros on the table and knocked back the second cup. I needed fortification before I took on Tiffany and my deceased friend.

I fingered the tiny espresso cup.

In the rush to respond to Tiffany, pack, drive to SFO, assure Tina I would be right back, assure Chris I would be right back, make reservations, and pack, did I mention pack?,

33

I hadn't allowed much time to consider the reason for all this frantic activity. My dear friend. My friend who never deleted me from her top ten favorites, my friend who was always there for me, was gone.

I glanced out at the square, still relatively empty of tourists. I met Miranda in 1985. A popular model then, her image is now considered an icon of the '80s.

I was working with Deb Friedman, who had the big idea to photograph Miranda playing in the King Tide. We set up, at considerable peril, the lights in the wash of the tide. Miranda frolicked in the water, backlit in red, the wavering image of the illuminated Basilica in the background. Deb's camera whirled. Miranda was beautiful, wet black hair flying, bright white teeth, mouth open in delight. It was a magical, lightning in a bottle moment, and in today's parlance, the images went viral. So did Miranda.

What no one knows is that Miranda sucked down two large swallows of the sea water that included large amounts of unknown particulate matter. She was ill for two weeks.

I nursed her back to health. We then spent the next ten years ruining it again.

I knocked back the rest of the coffee and headed to the apartment. I did remember the way. Both Miranda's and Max's flats were in the same general direction from St.. Marks. I remembered the way, but I did not see a single landmark.

I walked through an altered city. Each time I recognized a facade of an old favorite café or shop, I was shocked again: a Burger King was egregiously wedged into the facade of Trattoria da Acqua. The pizzeria, always changing hands, looked suspiciously like a PizzaExpress. The twinkling glass shop windows displayed carnival glass ashtrays that belied the sign claiming Murano originals. My favorite bakery was shuttered. The display in Señor Vargas's hand-crafted leather shop was not the soft original hobo bags I loved but packed with thick heavy purses and belts that looked machine-made. Small signs by building doors announced Airbnbs upstairs.

Miranda's apartment was on the third floor overlooking the Grand Canal. Not the curve that overlooks the bridge. But the Grand Canal nonetheless. I always thought her place was impossibly romantic: from the deep recessed entrance that looked like it led to little more than a wet basement, to the third-floor flat sporting ceiling height windows (bitch to clean) that opened to a narrow balcony overlooking the water. The fish-rot stench, the mud, the floods, increasing in the last few years—Miranda sent me scary videos. I had wondered about Max's first-floor apartment, still empty, but she assured me she had checked, and it hadn't washed into the canal, (not just yet anyway. It all came rushing back, soothing my dismay at the changes I witnessed in the streets.

The building door was always left unlocked. I climbed the dim interior stairs one at a time. Each step led me up and emotionally back. I had ascended the steps in so many states of mind: my first visit to the magnificent apartment with ailing Miranda in tow; the morning I returned from Nic's hotel to tell her I was leaving for Cairo; the afternoon after a direct flight from Luxor, chastened, heartbroken. Miranda always welcomed me back, sometimes as a sister, sometimes as a lover.

Had I missed something? Had she been ill? It wasn't like her to not list every ailment, every cough, every bruise. I certainly had my own problems in the last month, had she been protecting me from hers? At the last step, standing before her unassuming apartment door, what the hell had happened?

Tiffany had not given me any details during our phone conversation because that would have been helpful. I was in the dark. Literally, it's a dark hall.

"Never have children!" Miranda declared after another acrimonious phone call with one of her offspring.

I was already in my forties. I was good.

It was a thing back in the turn of the century. Have your own babies, pose pregnant and naked for magazine covers, then relentlessly work your body back in shape in record time and climb back on the runway. Miranda was one of the first super models to do it.

But supermodels do not make the most attentive parents. Her daughters, as beautiful as their mother, still resented the lack of attention and presence of their mother. I would think they'd at least be grateful for inheriting Miranda's high cheekbones and flawless skin. But no.

My phone buzzed and I reached for my back jeans pocket. It was a tight fit, my phone barely fit in the pocket and it was hard to wrestle out. I glanced at the screen text from Tiffany. Where are you?

It was 9:58 A.M., Italian time, which means I had a window of about an hour to be considered on time.

At the front door. I texted back. I shifted my sweater over my arm and reached for the door handle. Miranda could be miserly in the oddest ways. Her apartment would be cold. As cold as her daughter.

CHAPTER FIVE

I pushed open the apartment door, bracing myself for the worst. For a second, it was like coming home, the living room fanned out from the alcove entrance and opened to a view of the canal. The water sparkled in the morning sun and threw light and shadow on the dingy ceiling. I paused for a second to watch the play of light. The memories shot through me and I faked a sneeze to explain my suddenly watering eyes.

A figure turned from examining the paintings hanging on the far wall. If I was almost sixty, Tiffany had just crossed to the wrong side of forty. She was rigorously slender; her face was a mask of anger. If she makes that face too many more times, she'll need another face lift.

"Ah Tiffany." I reached out my hand—what else was I supposed to do? I met the girls maybe three times. Tiffany's father Steve was a savvy, undeservedly successful business-man, adept at side stepping disaster which included a pre-nup with Miranda. They had met at a party, she was at the bottom of her weight, he was at the height of his powers. Steve's claim to notoriety was to fortuitously drop all his bank clients in 2007. His hobby was buying California real estate even before the local fire had stopped smoking. Miranda was always surprised he didn't give a TED talk about his techniques. Steve was brilliant, ruthless and for a very short time, married to Miranda.

Tiffany's younger sister, Lucy had a Hollywood father. Mike worked as a photographer just long enough to fall for Miranda and she for him. Theirs had been a love affair, but their careers dragged them apart one too many cross-continental flights and they had to call it quits.

The children looked like their mother but behaved like their fathers.

Steve ended up more rigid than Mike. Blame it on the east coast, blame it on Boston. Tiffany took after the Puritan side of the family. Over the years I watched as Miranda's former in-laws exercised disapproval into a contact sport. Steve secured full custody of Tiffany days after I moved in, calling Miranda unfit and me a bad influence. I was mortified but Miranda was only amused. Even at the time I though Miranda did not care as much as maybe she should. The girls suffered because of it. But Miranda didn't need to care. Her family was old New York money. That's why she could afford to model. That's why she could afford ex-husbands.

"And you are?" Tiffany didn't approach, making me cross the wide room to reach her.

"Vic Gardner." I prompted. "You asked me to fly out, paid for my ticket and here I am." One would think she'd remember my name, even for just this one twenty-four-hour period.

"Oh." She started and peered more closely. "Oh, of course. You and Mother were friends."

I smiled. If Tiffany wanted to revise history, that was her prerogative.

"Yes, friends. You and I have met once or twice, but you and your sister were pretty young. What happened?"

"My sister moved to California."

I looked at her. She flipped back her shoulder-length hair. "Oh, Mother. She had a heart attack." Tiffany put her hands on her hips and slowly surveyed the living room. "And now all this is ours." She looked at me again. "A few things have been left to you."

My phone buzzed. I shot an apologetic look and dug out my phone, which was buzzing like an angry bee.

A text from Chris, I miss Grandma

We all do, I texted back.

Not Mom.

I love that kid.

I clicked off the phone and wiggled it back into my jeans pocket. "To me?" I stepped up next to Tiffany and eyed the art collection.

While Max loved new art, new furniture, new things he at least rotated the old items to the back bedroom, later to a storage facility on the mainland. Miranda just added. Often. Indiscriminately.

I never broached the subject of all the clutter. My job was to push everything it to the walls when we held a party. Once pushed back it only took a couple of days for the glacier of art objects, small chairs, and complimentary gifts once again to encroach the living room. Why do some people have such a difficult time giving away their stuff? Do things have a gravitational pull? Does a rock from the Valley of the Kings exert as much attraction as a bracelet by David Yurman? Miranda believed that things should be kept just in case, the bracelet, even the rock, could be worth something later.

On an unrelated note, can we keep people in storage until we need them?

Tiffany frowned at the wall of art. "In her will, you and..."

she squinted at a scrawled list that looked like it had been written in eyebrow pencil. Expensive eyebrow pencil but sometimes a Bic pen will do the job just as well. "...Rachael Monrovia were to take whatever you wanted, then the rest will go to us." She put her hand on her hips and glared at the Rothko. "How much room does she think I have in New York? I have nothing." She dismissed the Rothko and I almost snatched it off the wall. Fake or not, it was beautiful.

I looked around the living room. What had my old friend come to? She always loved stuff, collecting, saving. But during the years I had been away to care for people, I had obviously neglected my friend. Where her art acquisitions had once been considered charming in a cluttered Gertrude Stein way the walls now looked like the poster displays during move-in day at college. Paintings crowded up against the ceiling as if trying to escape, only narrow lines of wall were visible between the heavy frames. I tipped my head back. Was that a Childe Hassem? Where on earth did she...? I would take that too.

"Do we put colored dots on what we want? Or are you making a list?"

Tiffany frowned at a tiny Pissarro. "We get tax credit if we give these to a museum, right?"

"There's one down the canal."

"They only show Peggy's collection. I'm thinking of donating the lot to the Met. That may give me an invite to the May event."

"That would be generous."

She waved a hand at me. "Dots, Post-its. I have plenty of this stuff. And Lucy has even more. We just want the jewelry and the real paintings. You know, the valuable ones." She pointed to a Cassatt. "Is that one worth anything?"

"Probably." I answered mildly. Worth, when faced with this kind of abundance, is relative.

"And the proceeds of the apartment sale." I pointed out.

"Of course." She was still squinting at the paintings as if she could judge their authenticity and value.

"A heart attack, is that the official report?" The online posts were sketchy; even the aggregators and outlets based in fantasy and conspiracy theories were silent on the cause of death. One blog had featured the Sports Illustrated cover from the '80s, another re-posted the famous Deb Friedman photo shot here in Venice. It had been all about the photos, little copy except for time and place of death. Miranda Banks, popular model in the '80s died of natural causes in her apartment in Venice. No one even made up that she left peacefully surrounded by her loving daughters. Her daughters weren't even listed. No mention of the ex-husbands. Natural causes. But sixty-seven is not old. Plus, there was little left of Miranda's body that could be categorized as natural.

I glanced at the bedroom. She had been found there.

When we spoke, Miranda had been fine, maybe a little hung over. She had exhibited none of the albeit subtle signs of a heart attack: achy all over like the flu, a backache, fatigue. She didn't look particularly robust, but I attributed that to her favorite sport—drinking. Her heart was fine, she rarely used it, it should have survived for much longer.

Tiffany sighed and pointed to a picture of a mandolin. "Is that a Picasso?"

"She loved living with the art." The Picasso was probably genuine, valuable because of the large signature. My eyes traveled back up to the paintings at ceiling height. The ceilings were twelve feet high. When you run out of floor space, you go up.

"Well, good, I'm glad you like it, because the rest of it is yours." She turned away from the wall surveying the jumble of furniture—far too many chairs pushed to the walls. An enormous coffee table that often doubled as a dining space had been pushed under the window. In the kitchen, another dining table stood with five mismatched chairs crowding around. It looked a lot like a post-party configuration. The bar cart was pushed against the oven door. The only two items in the refrigerator would be milk for foaming and a jar of martini olives.

Tiffany headed towards the master bedroom.

"Lucy and I get the jewelry."

"That is only right. Your mother died when?"

"Monday morning."

It was Wednesday.

"And we already know who inherits?"

She impatiently flicked away the idiotic question. "We keep a copy of her will. Sealed, we never opened it. Until Monday." She glared at me. "Of course. There are a few things to negotiate, but right now, we have to move the art."

"Have to?"

"Well, the real estate agent said it would be best."

Points for efficiency. But moving the art, cataloguing it, valuing it, and selling it would be a big pain in the ass. And Tiffany knew it. Tiffany could walk out of the country wearing her inheritance. I glanced at her hand. Sure enough, Miranda's prized emerald flashed back at me. I wondered if Tiffany actually pulled it from her mother's cold dead hand. Ewww.

Not that I had anywhere to wear such a beautiful ring. My own rings, gifts from Max, were stuffed into my parents' safe deposit box. I rubbed my neck and stretched my back. I was not jet lagged, but I could use that as an excuse to gain some time.

"I have to get back home." Tiffany dropped the familiar keys into my hand. "Take your time. God knows you'll have to in this country."

"How long do I have?" Was that a Seurat pitched from the ceiling?

"She was healthy." I said out loud. "I just spoke with her. She didn't seem sick."

"She had a terrible diet, you should see the wine; oh, you need to get rid of that as well. In fact, you need to get rid of everything." She flipped her hand towards the center of the room. "Except the couch, maybe those two end tables. People want something spacious and this is terribly small. That bathroom!"

"You trust me?" I got straight to the point.

"Of course not." She grimaced. Again, careful, your face will freeze that way.

"I don't have a choice. I need to get back home. I have a family. You need stay for as long as it takes to get rid of the art. Pick up the mail and any packages. Our attorney says that the will is very clear: you take care of it all, and we, my sister and I." She looked at me as if daring me to remember Lucy's name. I didn't take the dare. Tiffany and Lucy were named after diamonds, which, next to art, was another of Miranda favorite things. Maybe if you were thin and beautiful, you also have the nerve to extract tribute from your lovers. Had Nic left me anything? Fortunately, no; I got tested.

"Should get half and we split that."

"You don't think that's much, do you?" I looked up at the paintings. She loved them. She loved every damn one. Why else spend so much cash? When you buy one thing, you choose not to favor another. The girls were never really in favor.

Tiffany searched the paintings, still scowling.

Miranda was my best friend; through it all, she was always there for me. I sneezed again. "Of course. I'll do my best." What else was I supposed to say?

The master bedroom (there is another smaller bedroom to the right) was very tidy. Which was very wrong. Because as much as Miranda was a collector and loved things, she was as careless as only the rich can be.

I surveyed the room. "You found her here?"

Tiffany had gathered the Picasso, the Cassatt and a Rousseau and stacked them by the front door.

"In bed. All that eating and drinking finally caught up with her." There was a note of satisfaction in her voice that I left unchallenged.

"She was old." Tiffany insisted. She approached the jewelry box on the dresser for another look.

"Not terribly old." I countered.

There were bits and pieces of memories scattered around the base of the commodious jewelry box—I recognized my gifts, bright pieces from Luxor, fake gold nuggets representing the times I had to leave Europe and help with the boys in California. Mardi Gras beads swayed from the bed post. Ah, that overbearing black sculpture I noticed during our last Skype call. I was sure that if asked, Miranda would swear it was an original Louise Nevelson. Original or not, it cantilevered over the headboard in a rather alarming way.

When I fell for Nic and abandoned Miranda for adventure and itchy sand—because it bloody gets in everywhere, the sand not the adventure—I spent the first year tormented that I had broken Miranda's heart. When I heard she had almost immediately taken up with a new girl—Cheryl? Sandy?—I relaxed and focused on Nic. By the time I returned to Miranda, tail metaphorically between my legs, all was forgiven. The girl was gone, we both had regrets, but I had more sand rashes.

"That thing would be enough to give anyone a heart attack." Tiffany gestured to the sculpture.

For the first time that morning, I agreed with her.

CHAPTER SIX

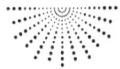

*W*e were not done. "Maria, you know Maria?" Tiffany clutched a string of pearls and started to hunt for her purse.

I'm in Italy, so I must know Maria? "No."

Tiffany hesitated. "Thought you might, it's a small town."

Venice is a small town, but not in the way Tiffany assumed.

"She's the estate agent. She'll be by later. You stay here."

"For the day?"

"No, for the week or however long it takes to sell the place. I read that a house for sale always shows better when someone is living there. You can bake cookies for the smell, that's supposed to help."

I must have looked askance. She retreated, "But only if you want."

I remained silent.

She switched tactics. "Please Victoria, I can't trust anyone else. I don't know anyone here. And the thieves! It's a wonder the place wasn't stripped to the walls. Good thing I got here when I did."

45

She sounded like a woman who listens to too much news. I glanced back to the bedroom. How many people will it take to dismantle that thing?

Tiffany found her purse and gathered up the three paintings. "I'm depending on you."

That sounded familiar enough.

I helped her carry the paintings down the narrow stairwell. Tiffany negotiated the narrow stairs carefully. Her high heels made her sway against the wall and I worried that with a painting under each arm, I wouldn't be able to catch her before she tumbled down the stone stairs. I was quite relieved when we reached the cobblestones all in one piece. She tucked the paintings under her arm, and I directed her to Rachael's place, the closest gallery (at least I hoped it was still there and not a Hanson Gallery featuring authentic hand-painted Disney animation cells), just around the corner.

"Remember," she adjusted the awkward canvases; we had pulled them from the frames to make them easier to carry. "The paintings will need to be removed, and you'll need to clean."

"Call a house cleaner, got it."

She opened her eyes wide. "You can clean."

"I never cleaned." I straightened and looked her in the eye. I was not the maid. I had been mistaken for the maid once, never again.

Alone in the apartment I fired up the espresso machine, another former job, delivering tiny cups of life-giving caffeine to my lover.

I moved five chairs away from the windows. At almost noon, the streets and canal below were coming to life. Boats zoomed by, gaggles of tourists on both public taxis and private tour boats shouted and laughed. A siren in the distance. But here in the apartment, the silence raged. I sat on the couch and sipped my coffee.

Depending on you.

Vic is so good at managing Tina often bragged. She has been invaluable, Vance insisted.

When Dad had his second heart attack, who was right there, calling the ambulance while doing recitation? You know, that Ah, ha, ha, ha, stayin alive thing? My brothers insisted on calling Dad's resurrection a miracle. Then went out of their way to express their devotion and absolute pleasure that good old Vic is in town, ready to take care of everything.

That was two years ago. Yes, I brought Dad back to life but I'm not sure he ever forgave me.

Both Vince and Vance certainly took credit. They were the heroes, keeping Mom and Dad at home, the money and sacrifice they made. They were always so good to them. Vincent even had the temerity to call his weekly visits "a great sacrifice."

Our parents lived for Vincent's shadow to fall over the front stoop. I admit that Vincent did liven up a week otherwise devoted to doctors' visits and prescription purchases. My oldest brother usually stopped by after work on Tuesdays, since Wednesday was golf, and Thursday was Tina's spa day, and then it was the weekend with Matt's sports and Chris's special school projects. Often over the weekend, when Tina and Vince needed some couple's time, they would drop off Chris at the house and he and I would work on his homework while Grandma and Grandpa napped. It was the only time the TV was off because all those voices were too disturbing and difficult for Chris.

Vince impressed Mom and Dad with how organized he was how in CHARGE of everything he was. No matter what my proposed solution to a problem was, it was Vince who fixed the computer glitch, added the tax bill differently (don't ask), or hammered the final inch of a protruding nail. He rolled in late, left early. Waiting for Vince's visit was a full-time job. Nothing else could be done. I dressed Mom and Dad in their nicest sweat suits, practical, ugly. It made me shudder remembering how I used to handle 140,000-dollar designer dresses and made sure every detail of a perfect photo shoot was executed. I had been reduced to helping my mother find her favorite ill-named turquoise jogging suit, adjust her Velcro shoes, help her to her favorite chair.

I made drinks and served snacks, Maui potato chips, artichoke dip from Costco and JB bourbon on the rocks.

"So." Vince would lean against the couch, arms across the back, drink in hand.

"How are you doing today? Vic treating you right?"

Mom launched into her day: the doctors, the traffic, the old people driving badly in the CVS parking lot. The old people making her wait in the doctor's office. What a terrible state the world was in, with all the kidnapping, murders and pedophiles trolling parking lots threatening the elderly. Immigrant murderers walked around Lincoln, California, free and unfettered. It was such a dangerous world: better to stay in, better to be safe. It was an old refrain; I had heard it all my life. The best way to avoid the pain and apologies of failure was to not try at all.

Vincent nodded, taking everything Mom said very seriously. After two bourbons, he'd glance at his watch.

"Got to get home for the boys. They are getting so big!"

Mom knew. She saw Chris every week. But she always nodded, "You do so much Vincent, you and Tina, thank you for dropping by."

I kept my expression neutral and gathered up the snacks and drinks.

Vince nodded to me and quickly exited. His personal land speed record was a 9.5-minute drop-by. His visits averaged twenty minutes.

But those few minutes were well leveraged. For the next twenty-four hours, Vince's visit was the primary topic of conversation. We discussed Vince over our hot oatmeal and decaf coffee. We marveled at his business acumen as we drove to Save Mart for groceries on Senior Discount Day, we wondered how he managed the job, wife and children over our chicken pot pies. Vance, who cleverly lived exactly forty-five minutes farther away, visited on holidays. He too was devoted and would approve of any invasive procedure, any intervention that would keep our parents alive.

After spending thirty-six months, five days, and seventeen hours hovering at "the end" I had a lot to say about quality of life. During my tenure in the fashion business, I knew far too many men who, through no fault of their own, sacrificed quality over painful stupefying quantity.

Max himself was having none of it. He insisted on his own way out. Easier in Italy, not so simple in the States. Max allowed the cancer, helped quickly along by his severely compromised immune system, to take its course. I discouraged him from tattooing Do Not Resuscitate on his chest, assuring him that I understood, I got this. Max focused on quality, my parents, with my brothers' encouragement, volume.

Dad spent his next six "miracle months" visiting doctors. Every other afternoon, I loaded first Mom and Dad, then just Mom slowly very slowly, into the car. The smell and feel of the car triggered car-specific stories, all of which I have heard hundreds of times: the afternoon I threw up in the back, the July Vincent had diarrhea and we had to turn back from the planned drive to the Grand Canyon, the Halloween I broke my arm because I was so clumsy. All stories built about the theme of hospital visits, inconvenience and the expense, lovingly recalled in detail and repeated without variation until I pulled onto Highway 20.

The only bright spot in the week was our Senior Stretch classes for the very old with nothing left to do but spend ninety minutes moving even more slowly than usual but this time under professional supervision. Mom and Dad were very good at Savasana, lying very quietly. I liked the modified yoga class, but it was disconcerting to have so many elderly people lying quietly on their mats, barely breathing. Every day I worried that someone in the class would just stay where they were, forever in the final resting position. I liked the instructor; she didn't allow us to rest for very long and was conscientious about making sure every student rolled over and up off the matt. Losing a client to forever Savasana probably involved a lot of paperwork.

During one of our last Senior Stretch classes, while executing one of my better versions of downward dog, I suddenly understood that my own life was ebbing away under the rip tide of elder care.

I took a breath and shook my head. That was all behind me. Concentrate on the present. My phone vibrated in my pocket, but it took too much effort to pry it out.

Tiffany could leave a message.

What had Miranda shown me over Skype? That blue hippo, mostly blue-green. It couldn't be the real thing, there we too many copies in circulation. Jolly, round and deep blue, that hippo figurine was one of the more charming Egyptian collectables, especially if you don't know anything about Egyptian history. If you've hung out at the Met for any time at all, you know this hippo. He even has a name, William, an oddly formal nickname, but I'm not sure the Egyptians of the Middle Kingdom (or New or Late Kingdoms for that matter) actually gave their gods nicknames. At any rate, William is a particularly good example of beautiful, durable blue faience, the plastic of the ancient world.

I set my cup in the sink and automatically dusted the

counter and the glowering espresso machine. I wrestled my phone from my back pocket and made a note to buy more coffee. And milk. Food. I stuffed it back in my hip pocket and pulled my shirt over it.

I expected to see the little guy on the shelf by the front door where Miranda displayed her latest finds. The shelves were cluttered with porcelain cups and saucers decorated with members of the British Royal Family, stained glass patterned pitchers and plates from Barcelona, a few inexpensive Polish pottery mugs and on the top shelf, two wonderful Italian urns painted with bright blue and yellow lemons. I pulled a chair over and carefully removed the urns and set them on either side of the front door.

I dusted my hands on my jeans and entered the bedroom. The purported genuine Louise Nevelson work looked sharp and precarious. The TV screen was perched on a set of drawers to my left, its big black screen complimented the enormous Nevelson for a decided post-apocalyptic vibe. I loved that the TV was off. I once accidentally turned off my mother's TV.

The falling silence was like those rare mornings when you wake with no electricity and can't figure out why it's so quiet. I used to blame the snow, the muffling of the cars, the forced slower speeds, the soft trees, but no, I now realize it was the absence of that constant hum of electricity, that constant drone of working refrigerators, clocks, the microwave, the ever-ready coffee maker, clothes dryer.

And just like that, the chatter was gone. I stood by the blank TV in a kind of shock, unsure of how to respond.

"What are you doing? I need that on!" Mom shouted.

"Why?" A solitary word, one often left unanswered in my family.

Mother paused as if really considering the question. Then slowly said, "Without it, I'd be too lonely."

I switched it back on and left the room.

Outside, the roar of vaporettos, neighbors calling to one another, the distant sound of hammering and jack hammering in a futile effort to keep yet another building from falling into the canal.

I don't clean, but I do organize. I opened the dresser drawers and automatically made piles of clothes—sweaters and slacks to give away, a few scarves and socks for me to keep. I moved to the nightstand: phone still on the charger, water glass, box of tissues. Missing were the pile of favorite rings and bracelets Miranda had shed at the last minute before passing out in bed. Tiffany had already taken those.

I looked in the nightstand drawer but couldn't tell if someone had raided it or if that was just the usual chaos that was Miranda.

I pressed a hand on the bedclothes, rumpled and cold.

We had been good together, at a time when it was all the more exciting because it was new, part of the bohemian fashion world, part of being forward, crazy.

It had been crazy,

But it was also love.

I smoothed and straightened the bed, making neat hospital corners. I stubbed my toe on the shallow platform bed; it was a pain to make the bed, but the drawers were necessary additional storage.

That was it.

The drawers surrounding the bed were packed with off-season clothes. I pulled out the one under the left side, the side Miranda favored. It moved smoothly. I pulled it all the way out (more sweaters) and reached under the space as far as I could. I grabbed the box, feeling like that opening scene in Amelie.

This box was not dusty. Ah, active to the end.

I sat back on my heels and opened the box. It was packed

with all the latest gadgets. I gingerly searched through the dildos and vibrators, a collapsible whip—that was new. The little blue figure hardly stood out among the rabbits and snakes with articulated battery powered tongues, but there it was. Still bright blue, after what I assumed was a good 4,000 years. We should all be so well preserved.

Hello. You look friendly enough.

William-the-hippo did not look like he'd come straight from the Metropolitan Museums' gift shop. That one was, as the Museum's bulletin read, a "particularly fine example of a type found, in common with various other animal forms, among the funerary furnishings of tombs of the Middle Kingdom". This one was faded, nicked and battered. Too green and too small to be from a gift shop or catalogue. It was only four inches long, with five tiny ducks painted on each side of his light blue hide. I pulled him out rattling plastic, leather and something else.

I unpacked out all the toys. Underneath was a hand full of matching blue ushabtis. Definitely not sold through the National Geographic Holiday Gift catalogue. Not sold at all.

I gathered them up and cradled them in my lap. Your ticket to the good life in the next life. They were nicked, but intact. The Hippo could be fake. A cheap knockoff painted with ducks instead of the typical papyrus fans. But I was sure the little statues were real. And illegal.

I held one up. Hundreds of them littered the workers villages where Nic and I had worked. Only a few survived in the tombs, robbed before anything could really age. I wanted to keep one, just one, but Nic wouldn't hear of it. It was like taking your first drink, your first hit, your first cigarette.

"Don't start, Vic. Everything we find needs to be counted for."

He was so self-righteous. But right.

I had spent years with Nic on worker sites up and down

the Nile. Nic was an on-and-off archeologist, dependent on grants, dependent on his adjunct schedule at UCSB and UC Irvine. Lecture for a quarter or two in California, back in the field for the season. I had followed him back and forth for as long as I kept his interest, and for as long as I could stand it.

I tried to recall the article Chris had shown me, I would need to ask him for the link. I could claim ignorance about the hippo; the faience, not so much. This many? They had either come from the home of an exceptionally enterprising tomb robber or from a tomb. A new tomb. A fresh dig.

I glanced at the toys. Should I remove them and spare Tiffany? Or return them so the person who bothered to stretch-out on the carpet and grope under the bed would be well rewarded, all her worst suspicions confirmed? I opted for the reward system. I dumped the toys back into their box but kept the artifacts. They weren't safe here, not with an imminent move, not with strangers traipsing in and around the apartment looking in the closet, searching the drawers, measuring the shower, reaching under the bed.

Where had Miranda found these? A small shop in town. Around the corner? Not helpful, Miranda's sense of direction was never very good and her vague explanations about where and when she found fabulous things were often not to be taken at face value.

I couldn't explain away my uneasiness. Miranda had hidden these in an excellent place. Except, except. Someone had searched her place. Searched thoroughly, and not found these. Or maybe they had found something else?

Plus, if Miranda had a real heart attack, why hadn't she reached out for help? I returned to the nightstand. Had the phone been moved? I couldn't tell. I picked it up and tried Miranda's old password, no luck. I was a number short. I tried three more times using different numbers at the end of her usual password. I was locked out for my trouble.

I returned the phone onto the end table and regarded the bed. It didn't feel right. Yet I had no evidence, of anything. Why did I think her death was not of natural causes? Had there been a report? I'm not an official family member, so I doubted I would be able to secure the coroner's report. If there had been one. Considering Tiffany's attitude, it was likely there was NOT a report of any kind. There is nothing harsher than the revenge of the living.

I shivered, a dying woman, someone or a couple of some-ones searching frantically through the jewelry, the sweaters, the designer outfits, all in vain. When the apartment goes on the market, whoever had bungled the initial search would free to return. This time there would be considerably less stuff to move and considerably more time to do it.

Deep breath. Think. Miranda was fine when I spoke with her. She looked stressed, older certainly, but fine and alive. I couldn't shake the intuition that she was killed. For these?

I grabbed my purse and slid the ushabtis and hippo into its commodious central compartment.

I held the purse close.

How many people besides me, did she tell? Nic. She would have asked for his opinion, confirming that she had indeed, scored a bargain. And had she? I glanced at the neat room, shivering at its tidy incongruity.

Find the receipt, and search for the store. She didn't find them on a dig. Miranda's interest in Egypt was limited to the song by the Bangles.

Who else would know about this? Everyone else. Miranda was a social creature given to routinely revealing more information that anyone wanted to hear.

Which clearly was a bad, bad thing.

CHAPTER SEVEN

*M*y superpower is I am trustworthy. Back in the day, Miranda signed me on all her accounts. I was the chief signer on all of Max's accounts. I paid all my parents' bills and monitored their assets I retrieved cash from ATMs, I sold art and took the proceeds, no questions asked. I even piled the most precious of Max's collection into an obscure storage facility, so obscure Max didn't even want to know where it was. Now that is trust.

I was better known at the bank than Miranda, but it had been a good four years since I walked into the Republic Bank on her behalf. Would Phillip, junior clerk, still be there? I remembered encouraging him to propose to his girlfriend of six years. And just before I took off for Egypt, he had popped the question. While I worried about his love life, he worried that I was too much at the beck and call by my formidable friend.

"You need your own life, Signora," he insisted every time he opened the safe deposit box for me.

"This is my life." I countered, lightly.

I was like a tiny ushabtis, working away in both this life

and probably the afterlife as well. It was part of the deal, how I earned my keep.

I would deposit the hippo and its attendants into what I remembered was a commodious safe deposit box. Phillip would help me, but no one else at the bank, standing around, working carefully against the pending avalanche of paper and rules, would remember me or remark on what I was doing. Would the typically slow bureaucracy and form filling and delays work to my advantage? It drove Max crazy. He was so acutely aware of time running out that every day was a race to get things down now, today: take the old sample books to storage today, clear out the closet right now, file these papers this afternoon.

The deposit box key wasn't in her desk. I looked in the bright red Murano glass dish on that shelf where we kept the house keys. Nope.

One would have thought, I certainly did, that a safe deposit key was important. Had the thief taken it as second prize? A participation trophy? But the key was devoid of bank logos or addresses. If the thief had taken the key, they would not know where it belonged.

Think, think.

The light on the ceiling wavered and picked out highlights from the paintings. So many. She had been busy while I was away, and obviously no one was around to help her replace, so she just added. One painting hanging above the other.

I wanted to sit on the lanai and contemplate the colors on the canal. I needed a nap. I needed to find the safe deposit key.

What would Miranda do if she knew the next people to look for something like a key or a treasure would be Lucy or Tiffany?

She would screw with them.

I returned to the bed and the hidden drawer. Sure enough. The safe deposit key was taped to the side of the toy box. Oh Miranda.

For this errand I did not want to attract attention. According to my mother, nice girls did not call attention to themselves. I had years of practice doing just that, being invisible; it was a brilliant skill for a photographer's assistant, and it would help me today.

A close friend commented that the bigger he gets, the less he is seen. A little extra weight helps make you forgettable.

I already had the rather long curly gray hair. I bundled that up in a low bun.

I hunted through Miranda's clothes for something pastel, like what that Paula on the water taxi wore. In fact, if I could create that look, I'd be home free.

My own jeans would do.

I found a pale blue sweater, cashmere, but that couldn't be helped, and I topped it off with a blue and tan flowered scarf. Which must have been a gift since Miranda favored black and red.

I was already wearing the low shoes. At least not white tennis shoes, but just short of Velcro fastening.

I've been in fashion my whole career and at no time did Anna Wintour ever announce that Easter-egg pastels are a thing! Tan cargo pants are this fall's must have! Never.

Dressed like this, I could rob the bank. No one looking at the security feed would know what to make of me. The best descriptor anyone would come up with was—she was a little old lady.

It's a perfect disguise. Of course, you must have a boat load of self-esteem to even consider this disguise, which I was a short on, but I needed to do a job, and I needed to be ignored.

I locked the door and hid the key under the fat haunch of

one of the seven plaster cherubs decorating the hall. The landlord saves money by rarely lighting the stairway. The little cherubs are easy to overlook.

The bank, like everything in Venice, was a few blocks away. I didn't want to take the taxi, because I didn't want to wait in line, the bulk of my purse was too tempting. I hefted the purse onto my right shoulder and held it against my hip. The day had turned bright and gorgeous almost like the photos in every cruise brochure, and yes, I peeked into St.. Mark's Square as I passed by. It was packed with men wearing shorts and baseball caps, and woman who looked just like me.

The bank was open, a relief.

I hadn't asked Tiffany if she had already filed the succession paperwork and pulled Miranda's bank statements. If so, I was SOL. The whole enterprise would be shut down and I wouldn't be able to open the safe deposit box, key or no key, because I was not an heir. Did Tiffany even know about the safe deposit box? We had usually kept some cash in the box for buying paintings, or from selling paintings (rarer). Miranda stored some jewelry here, depending on her mood and who was staying in the apartment. But it looked like Tiffany was draped with the best of Miranda's collection, so I didn't know if there would be anything in the box at all.

I hunched my shoulders and shuffled in.

I stood in line and offered up the key as my proof. I surreptitiously glanced around for Phillip. He was not on the floor, which I hoped meant he had advanced to management. I hoped he married and now had an adorable family. He was such a lovely boy.

I glanced at my watch, 1:00, still lunch time.

The young man who could have been Phillip five years ago, who was clearly not at lunch, was a bit put out that I showed up at such a slow time.

He glanced at the key, found the signature card and dutifully checked my signature. I held my breath: had Miranda deleted me completely?

He glanced at me without really seeing me and nodded, leading me to the old-fashioned room with a lock on the door. The young man, still sighing heavily, retrieved the square box and set it on the low counter. He gestured that he would wait right outside the room. I nodded and thanked him.

He just barely kept from rolling his eyes. No respect for his elders.

The box was as empty. I sat down and rested my elbows on either side of the empty container. Was I disappointed? No. I gently placed the hippo and ushabtis into the box. They looked forlorn, with no Book of the Dead scrolls or tiny barcas to keep them company. Hell of a way to end up, so far from Egypt to rest in a foreign tomb.

I hesitated. Once in the vault, the only way to get them back was to be named as the direct inheritor. It could take three years for all that to clear. A long time. Damn. I tried to imagine Lucy, who looked like her sister only brunette, discovering these. What would they do? There would be questions. Accusations. Miranda would be blamed, maybe not for long, people forget. But during the discovery, she would be labeled a thief, and her reputation smeared. Perhaps, because her daughters were disinclined to defend her, a label that could out last even her photos. It would be my fault. I broke her heart once already; there was no need to do it again.

On the other hand. If I couldn't access them, no one could. Like a hot potato, the last person to touch them would be responsible.

The young man coughed.

I took another breath. Okay, not so great an idea. What if

Nic had heard about these? Could he return them? How did Miranda get them in the first place and why? That was the real question: why have these at all? If I couldn't get at them, I couldn't leverage them.

I did not check to see if the taped key had been disturbed. Had someone already cleaned out this box? Did they have better, faster access than me? No, this was a bad idea.

I stuffed the guys back into my purse, adjusting the bag so it wasn't so bulky looking. I thought about draping it across my body, but the strap cut across my boobs like a bandolier, not a flattering look. I checked my phone, secure in my pocket and emerged, handing the closed, but still empty box to the young man who barely glanced up as he took it from me.

I headed back to the hotel, my phone either silent because the battery had cut out or because Tina was between panic attacks. I relished the reprieve.

A group of men passed me and knocked against me. I shouted, but they were out of earshot their voices ringing against the shop walls and cobblestones.

CHAPTER EIGHT

*H*otels will hold things, not well, not necessarily safely, but they will allow you to stash a suitcase or two before your room is ready or after you check out so you can see the city for one more hour before your flight. How safe then would my little workers be? I had to believe they would be safe enough.

I hunched over and as quickly as is reasonable for a woman my age, scurried across the lobby. I whispered bon giorno to the receptionist who barely raised his head.

Took the stairs two at a time.

I always pack a nylon shopping bag. Indispensable for extra purchases, shoes, gifts, books, artifacts of suspicious provenance. I stuffed the six statues into six socks and wrapped the hippo in a tee shirt. One of the socks held extra cash. I dumped the twenties and hundreds back into my suitcase and put the final statute in. The whole round package fit into another tee, then into the bag. It looked and felt like laundry. Perfect.

I brushed the bills to the bottom of the suitcase, checked for my lucky keys and closed it. I had one more night reserved. I checked my phone, no calls. Everyone in California must be asleep. I stuffed the phone back into my back pocket.

I carried the bag back down to the lobby.

"I can't believe this city is so crowded!" It wasn't Paula, but a dead ringer for her. Do we really all look alike?

The woman had her hands on her hips, her mouth pursed as if the crowd in the square was a personal insult.

"It is the cruise ships madam." The desk clerk kept his head down and continued to shuffle papers.

"Well, they need to do something about it, just ruins it for others." She sniffed, took her plain room key and harrumphed away.

"Excuse me." I kept my voice soft and a little high. Little old ladies often develop a higher voice often described as querulous. After three years of that pitch, it was distressingly easy to mimic.

It took the young man a minute to turn from his absorbing paperwork to look up. I smiled and pushed the oddly shaped bag across to him.

"Can you hold this for me?"

He gave me a look as if waiting for me to start complaining as well. But I kept my head down, my eyes on the precious bundle.

"It's for the girls, gifts you know. I don't want to leave them in the room." I tried to look as guileless and as naive as possible. He seemed to buy it.

He swallowed, eyeing the package that didn't look like much worth stealing. But who knew what was going on in an elderly brain?

"Certainly madam."

"Room 416."

He took a tag, wrote the room number and tied the tag to the floppy handle.

"Don't let anyone pick it up but me." I winked.

He rolled his eyes. "Of course."

I watched him casually stuff the bag under the desk. Soon it would land in unclaimed luggage.

Perfect. As long a young clerk doesn't fling a hard-sided check in case on top of my bag, we were good.

I KNOW I shouldn't compare. But my years spent with Max in his luxury apartment were very different from the years with Miranda which in turn were different from my years with Nic in the desert.

I ricocheted between living in the cover shoot for *Elle Decor* and extreme camping. In fact, I remember back when I first met Max, the flat actually had just been featured in House Beautiful or Architectural Digest. One of those. The fame, such as it was, gave you bragging rights only for the rack-life of the magazine, no longer. It's tacky to keep bringing it up.

Miranda's place was in no danger of becoming obsolete because no photographer or editor, no matter how drunk, ever thought it was a great idea to create a magazine feature of the former model's Venetian digs or, unfortunately, the former model herself.

"But why not?" Miranda always gestured with the hand holding her drink. The carpets needed to be replaced yearly.

"Darling, it's just so white."

Miranda looked up at the white walls, little more than Mondrian strips between thick gilded picture frames. "It's not white at all."

Whomever she had taken on, would lean back, blink at the overwhelming number of paintings cantilevered from the top of the walls and drop the subject as quickly as they could.

Not to say that Max's home wasn't just as filled. But he knew when to jettison the tired and dated. Miranda couldn't let go of anything. Max had style. Miranda had stuff.

Max told me stories about redecorating, cleaning the mold, replacing the wallpaper, troubleshooting the original plumbing circa 1684. His apartment on the canal forced rotating upgrades every few years. It was expensive, but the result was that he learned all sorts of tricks and had many, many friends in the construction business. Max's apartment was on the ground floor and always in danger of flooding. Miranda's was on the third floor, which I assume made it more impervious to the ravages of Venice's tides and weather. At least according to Miranda, it was.

The last time I lived with Max, right when he passed, the living room was lined in navy wallpaper outlined in silver. He had replaced the carved Moroccan settee and matching chairs (inspired by Saint Laurent's place) with mid-century modern, a vintage Eames chair and a low-slung upholstered couch in silver and chrome. It contrasted beautifully against the blue walls, which of course complemented the patio blue chairs and the canal outside. We replaced all the pictures frames, silver for gold.

And where did the old stuff go? Even though Max wanted to save the gold frames, I had a better place for them. I hauled the frames over to Rachael's brand-new art gallery. Rachael, like many of my acquaintances, was a former model. I met her at one of Miranda's parties. Rachael had been as slender as her cigarette. Clutching a flute of champagne she entertained a group of guests by unerringly pointing out which of Miranda's paintings were fake and which were real. Miranda was not amused. But I liked the girl, and immediately knew that Rachael should use her skills for good. Months later Rachael appeared at our door. The stories of her career ending defeat preceded her. During what was her last runway show, she had indulged in a particularly acrimonious and unfortunately, memorable, shouting match with a designer over his use of real fur. From the runway she announced she was out of the business.

But not out of luck.

Max came to the rescue. He funded the perfect gallery space for Rachael, and I loaded her up with all of Max's rejected gold frames to class up the place and attract tourists and high rolling locals.

I insisted the frames were a loan since Max typically redecorated every three years. I also knew that Max did not have three years left.

"You are too kind." Rachael had quit smoking, not because she was no longer modeling, but because of a special boy. She was nervous and paced up and down her bare gallery unsuccessfully searching for something to do with her hands.

"No, Max would want you to have them. You can use them for the time being."

She finally paused and started to sort through the frames. "Are you certain? These are lovely, some are antique and valuable."

"All the better. You can pay me back later. Us later." I quickly amended.

She raised her perfectly arched brows.

"Miranda will need more paintings, you can help, how's that?"

She nodded. I left with Rachael still holding a frame, squinting at the gold leaf.

No more gold in Max's apartment, it was all silver then, maybe still. Silver and navy in the main room, the powder room was lined in silver wallpaper with navy touches.

We had three bedrooms (so different from my years stuffed into a single flimsy tent jammed against the half-excavated wall of an ancient village hut). I had my own room, decorated in peach, a color popular back in the day for walls, not, as we discussed, for slacks. Max never changed his beloved emerald green complemented by a brilliant fuchsia, yellow, and pink-pattered bed spread and, courtesy of Rachael, original art. The third room was the work room, and, in a pinch, a place for various pretty, pretty boys that he called friends to land when they were in need.

Many were in need. Since I was familiar with the type, as well as the average half-life of a lovely young thing in residence, I developed a system: fewer bathrooms than people. Give a girl or a boy their own bathroom and they will never leave. Max's apartment had one full bath, one half bath. To shower, the pretty boys had to wait their turn. It was the perfect organic way to keep guests in full rotation.

Max's place was so perfect, why ever leave?

Why indeed.

St.. Mark's square was bright and glittering in the morning light. The spires of the Basilica glowed gold against the blue sky. I would say something poetic about the cobblestones and the pigeons and the small chairs gathered around the edges of the square, but the only beautiful thing I could see were those tall domes of the Basilica; the rest of the square was packed with tourists—shoulder to shoulder. They all looked like me. Which was quite enough to stifle any emerging poetic impulse.

I automatically checked my back pocket for my phone and pulled up my now feather light purse onto my shoulder.

I should sling it across my body, but it was too depressing a sight, a round woman with a purse across her chest emphasizing her stomach and drooping breasts. The only item less flattering was a black waist pack cinched around the thickest part of a body. The waist pack only worked if wore ironically. And even then, only if you are a very thin, very young girl. I am neither.

My encounter with Tiffany must have depressed me more than I realized. My feet were heavy as I laboriously made my way back to the apartment. I put one foot in front of the other—Chris loved that holiday song; we watched Santa Claus Is Coming to Town almost every month.

Hundreds of patient tourists stood in a line that snaked around the Doges Palace, hours under the hot sun for the chance to admire the wavy tile floor and the stunning wall mosaics that lined the interior of St. Mark's. Grateful I had already toured the church, seen the Doges Palace, climbed the bell tower. I was guilt-free as I ducked into a side street. I planned to snake my way around the main square which was faster than struggling through all the bodies clogging the square.

When my mother wasn't parroting the latest from FOX News, she discussed how hard my brothers worked and how they deserved more—more money, a bigger inheritance, more love because they were men. I didn't have much to contribute to that announcement, so I switched to discussing the headlines of the day. I felt a bit guilty that my last conversation with Mom was to disagree that the Nile was being dredged to accommodate big ocean liners that would sail from Luxor to Cairo. It was preposterous and I said so. But Mom remained adamant. She had heard it on the news; therefore it was true. Don't listen to me, I had only lived in Luxor for two years.

I was so relieved to finally turn off the news that I never did learn if the Nile story was true.

I automatically turned towards Max's apartment but after a block realized my error and turned back towards Miranda's. There must be a flotilla of docked cruise ships. Even the side streets circling the square were crowded with tourists.

Locals avoided the crush by ducking into cafés, tourists wandered into shops packed with brightly colored pottery in yellow and red. They invariably reemerged not with that beautiful vase, but with a small commemorative coaster. I noticed countless women toting bags emblazoned with cruise logos—Celebrity, Princess, Holland America, Royal Caribbean. All here.

It had been so long since I moved through this kind of humanity, I was unprepared.

I was bumped and jostled but kept a grip on the shoulder strap of my purse. I watched where I was walking, over sensitive to my footing. I didn't want to fall and break a hip or twist an ankle. Even as I braced myself against the push of the crowd, I chastised myself for acting like my elderly parents instead of a woman who still had some life, who still could easily roll with the punches or a random shoulder bump.

As if to make a point, a man bumped my shoulder and I lost my grip on my shoulder strap. I gasped in pain, but quickly grabbed my strap. But my fingers encountered only empty air.

It was like a head butt to the stomach.

I stopped. My heart pounded; my ears filled with a roaring sound. Three people pushed into me and mumbled obscenities as they detoured around me.

I blinked rapidly and turned to scan the crowd. Heads bobbed and weaved as people barely avoided colliding with me. He was gone, or she was gone, let's not be biased. They could have ducked away anywhere. I would never find them and calling out wouldn't help my cause. I couldn't catch my breath. I should have cross-strapped the purse, ugly or not. I should have clutched the strap more tightly. I should have taken a different street. I blinked back sudden tears. For a second, I didn't know whether to be upset about the purse or upset that I clearly looked like an easy mark. Damn, Damn, Damn.

My phone pinged. I resisted pulling it from my pocket waving it aloft yelling, "You missed this!"

I took a deep breath and blinked a few times to clear my vision. Tourists jostled me; locals jostled me. I was alone in a crowd of indifferent people. I sniffed. No tissues. They were in the purse.

There are a few things I credit to muscle memory. I used to travel, I lived abroad. I spoke rudimentary Italian. I should be able to tap back into all that. I touched my back pocket; the phone was still secure in my pocket. I had aged out of the grab ass phase, so the phone was safe from harm. I glanced at my old watch. One o'clock. The American Embassy would either be closed for lunch or closed for the day.

I took a deep breath. Police? No, I did not want the police. I had just spirited away six unidentified and possibly valuable statues from my dead friend's house and hidden them. No police.

I pushed out of the crowds and wedged into a doorway, away from the streaming pedestrians and tried to calm my breathing. In Senior Stretch class we learned to breath. I know. I was skeptical, but deep, long oxygen sucking breaths were exactly what I needed. The door was damp, and I sucked in the miasma of urine with each ragged intake.

The extra key to the apartment was secured under a cherub. But Tiffany had given me a key as well. The key was in the purse, I hadn't had the time to thread it onto my lucky key ring. Who else had a key to the apartment? Tiffany had taken it on faith that her mother died of natural causes. There was no reason to be suspicious. Except that Miranda's bedroom was unnaturally tidy, which was always suspicious. There were only two reasons for an organized bedroom: new lover who hadn't yet become inured to the mess, or a bugler with OCD. Which was it? My head hurt and my heart hurt, and my stomach still protested the violation of the theft.

I bent over, my mouth felt foul, would I throw up right on the street? Like during Mardi Gras? I gulped air and tried to clear my head.

Wallet, passport, hotel room key.

The room key. Did it have the hotel logo? No, and it didn't have my room number. Okay good. I'd need to apply at the embassy for another passport. Get another credit card. I wondered if I could apply for another life while I was at it. If all the thieves wanted was my identity, they were welcome to it.

I jumped as my back pocket buzzed, jarring me out of my head and back into the street and the situation. I touched it but didn't have the heart to pull it out. Besides, it was the only thing I owned that was clearly secure.

HOTEL FIRST. I needed to re-group and extend my stay.

Which was not to be.

"I'm sorry, signora, we are full tomorrow night, I have you checking out this afternoon." Fortunately, I was not faced with the same young man who took my "laundry" bag. This desk clerk was a young woman fashionably dressed, eschewing the typical front desk uniform of blue blazer and narrow skirt, for a pink sweater and black leather jeans. She stood remarkably steady on her spike-heel boots. I nodded, more to acknowledge her style than her disappointing news.

Okay. I took a breath. Okay. I can do this, I'm an adult. There is no TV blaring to distract me so it's much easier to think and make good choices. I trudged up the stairs to my room.

The phone buzzed. It was Tina. I turned it off.

Okay. I banged open the door and regarded the nondescript room.

"Okay." I said it out loud to emphasize that it would be okay, okay, okay. Breathe, breathe, breathe. I never thought that class would do me any good outside of the gym. Who knew?

I grabbed my suitcase and dumped the contents on the bed. I pulled the phone charger from the wall and tucked it into the suitcase. I pulled out the euros, thank the gods; dinner money.

Something jangled. My keys. I set those aside.

I regarded the small pile of clothes. The packing had not been well considered. I had been in a big hurry, more interested in avoiding Vince, Vance, and Tina, especially Tina and escaping to the airport as quickly as I could. If they had offered even a single protest, my resolve would have crumbled, and I would have cancelled everything and stayed where I belonged. But I couldn't abandon a friend in need, even if she was past help, I felt responsible. I had missed something, something critical about Miranda and her little blue hippo.

I even felt sorry for Tiffany, who for the very first time since we met, sounded like a seven-year-old. It was midnight. Her voice was small, even scared. I tried to refuse, but the no stuck in my throat. "I'll be there."

"Your ticket will be at the desk. SFO 6:00 flight."

I nodded even as I pulled out my carry-on. I was used to packing light; all the photographic equipment I shipped, checked, and hauled around the world took priority. Clothes we check, cameras we carry. All those practical thoughts ran through my head as I rolled and stuffed anything that fit into my old suitcase.

I planned to text Vincent just as the plane lifted off. The perfect getaway.

It was even kind of romantic. My first adventure in years. But now I had a disaster on my hands. I probably deserved it.

I picked through my wardrobe: polyester slacks, sensible short sleeve blouses, an extra pair of tennis shoes.

I had worn nothing but tennis shoes for three years. That's the kind of neglect that can creep up on you. When was the last time I dined out in a real restaurant that demanded suitable clothes? When was the last time I wore heels? I didn't even wear heels to Vincent's retirement party. What had been the point?

I fully intended on being in Italy for only twenty-four hours, forty-eight tops. I would fly in, comfort Tiffany, eat pasta for breakfast, lunch and dinner and fly home before my whole family fell apart in hysterics. That was the plan, that was what I promised Tina as the plane launched into the rising sun. 24 hours, I texted, I'll be back before you know it.

I lied. I would be here for a bit longer. At least long enough for another pasta dinner. I counted the euros, and wine. I studied the clothes and packed three pair of under-wear and two bras into the suitcase with the keys and money.

I left the rest of the clothes on the bed.

The suitcase was so light it rattled and bounced behind me sounding like a fast approaching skateboard. I was starving, even though it was only 7:00 P.M. Had all this happened that fast? I was not used to fast. I was used to slow. The slow walk to the car. The slow unfolding from the passenger seat. The slow approach to the store/office/Chili's. Older people move like wind up dolls winding down, down, down. No wonder I was depressed.

When she was in residence, Miranda rarely locked the apartment door, because on the third floor, why bother? She was a fixture in the neighborhood, everyone knew her, most looked out for her, which was why she was found so quickly. Which was why the door had been unlocked. Had it been unlocked? But neighborhoods change, the locals were leaving Venice proper for the mainland and cheaper apartments and homes, away from what was increasingly only a tourist attraction not a real working town. Who wants to live in Disneyland? Don't tell me, probably a lot of people.

Speaking of living in town. I assumed Max's apartment had sold or was by now leased as an Airbnb. Miranda told me she had run into one or two of Max's pretty boys, some were still hanging around in town.

"But never at one of my parties. I didn't like the way they treated Max."

I nodded. When Max was healthy and generous, the boys were there, pretending to be helpful, pretending to be loving. As soon as Max's illness became obvious and scary, all boys disappeared, and it was left to me to care for my friend. The cowards.

Over the last few years I considered looking up the address to see what happened to the estate, but I didn't have the heart.

Miranda had always insisted that this was my forever home, that I was always welcome. She was right about that. In the state I was in, re-entering the apartment was like coming home; for all the mess, it was a welcoming space. The light reflected off the canal water and illuminated the living room making it look like it was underwater. The growing purple shadows hid the cobwebs and delivered depth as well as the comfort of strong memories.

The phone beeped and buzzed. Feeling a little safer, I finally answered.

"Vic."

"Hello Tina, you know my data plan doesn't cover calls, can you text me instead?"

"We'll pay the difference." She offered magnanimously.

"I've been trying to call you all afternoon. The boys start school on Wednesday and we really need you here."

"I have a small problem."

"We all have problems Vic."

"My purse was just stolen. My passport and money are gone. I haven't even been away for twenty-four hours. Are you willing to help expedite the procedure and wire me cash for the next few days?" I'd have to extend my plane ticket as well. Need to do that right away.

The phone was silent. I quickly followed up. "I'll email you when it's all sorted out. And Tina, Matt is sixteen, he has his driver's license, he can get Chris to school easily enough." Horrified that I said that out loud, I quickly disconnected and put the phone on mute.

The last of the evening sun highlighted the dust covering the glass coffee table. The white couch looked dingy. The life of the apartment had left the building. I sighed and plopped on the couch, a little pouf of dust rose and settled.

Money. I had enough cash for a couple of days, but not enough for any unexpected expenses.

I scrolled through the apps on my phone. I changed my flight to an open-ended ticket.

I called to cancel my single credit card. The nice man offered to issue a new one.

"Unless you can overnight it, I'm not interested."

"For a fee, of course we can overnight you a new card."

I held the phone temporarily speechless. It had been a long time since I depended on the kindness of strangers. It was not a habit my poor parents endorsed. In their world all strangers were predators, and considering my recent loss, they may be right.

The stranger from Chase paused, waiting for my answer.

I let out my breath. "Yes, please." I rattled off Miranda's

address, firmly embedded in my hard drive. I took another breath, then another.

I scrolled through the phone. I kept a picture of my passport and for good measure, my California Driver's license, as well as a picture of my AAA card and Costco card. Don't ask about the Costco card, I was on a roll one morning photographing everything in my wallet.

The embassy opened at 9:00. I'd hike over first thing, back up photos in hand.

I took a breath and regarded the paintings. Five were already gone. Tiffany had mentioned donating to the Met in the hopes it would be her fast track to the First Monday in May. I worked that event one year. It looks more fun from the outside.

The late afternoon sun washed the far walls of the living room illuminating the remaining paintings and turning the empty walls gold. Tiffany had taken the Rothko, but not a small painting of a hummingbird which was likely a Church. I scanned the grouping. If we were showing the house, some paintings would be necessary, but not, contrary to Miranda's proclivities, all of them. Their value was in their beauty, not their re-sale value.

My brothers were all about re-sale, they were all about value. Vance estimated that the family saved tens of thousands of dollars because I was able to care for Mom and Dad for three years. All that effort, all that savings. The boys promised to proportionally increase my share of the estate but in the end, they didn't. My parents' estate, such as it was, ended up divided evenly between the three of us. I did see that coming.

I glanced at my watch. They hadn't stolen that, HA. It was a wonderful old Rolex that no one recognized because it just looked like a watch. It was still early, 7:30, if Rachael was even still in business.

I pushed out the couch and pulled five paintings from the wall.

It was not easy wrestling the paintings down the narrow stairs and out into the street. Fortunately, most of the cruise tourists were gone, all snug in their tiny rooms in the bowels of the enormous cruise ship dressing for their included gourmet dinner.

It was more muscle memory than any conscious memory that led me back to Rachael's shop. Both Miranda and Max were consistent customers helping her get her start. I hoped she was still in business.

I passed by the familiar buildings with new and unfamiliar store fronts. Venice had changed. We all need to change, but as I passed one new shop, another new café, an old family business replaced by obvious and obnoxious international chains, I couldn't help feeling blue, feel a little of their pain.

To my great relief the gallery was still intact and open for business. Even better, Rachael was in.

"Vic!" Rachael, dark hair, dark eyed, still looked like a former model. She glided across the polished gallery floor, her high heels making no sound. How did she do that? I thought of asking, but not now. "You look," She kissed me on both cheeks.

"Like a middle-aged woman? My purse was just stolen, my best friend just died suddenly. And all I have are these." I handed her three of the of five canvases. By the time I struggled down the stairs, I had to leave two just inside the front door. I hoped they'd be stolen just so I wouldn't have to haul them back up the stairs.

But seeing beautiful Rachael, recognizing some of the Max Peters gold picture frames still on display, calmed my nerves. I didn't realize how much I needed to see a friendly face. How I needed a friend.

Rachael pulled from me and regarded the paintings.

"You want to sell these?" Rachael picked up and held out the Chagall and tilted it one way and then another as if uncertain which was the top and which the bottom. And she was a trained professional.

"Yes, and I have more."

"Miranda gave you the paintings?" She stopped. "Oh, I am so sorry. I heard the news of course, but it's so."

"Difficult to believe?"

"She was so alive, that last party. It was an Egyptian theme. She covered the floor in sand."

That would explain the dust and disorder.

"Did you go?"

Rachael shrugged. "I hadn't seen Miranda in a long while." In other words, yes.

I nodded. "Her girls are selling the apartment. I plan to stay for two more days to get things organized, then I need to return to the States."

"For?" She raised a perfectly arched eyebrow.

"I need to take care of my nephews."

She narrowed her eyes. "Your nephews? They are how old? What happened to you Vic?"

I shrugged avoiding her gaze. I was hungry, I was cranky, and I would need to find clean sheets before I could sleep tonight. Sleep sounded like an excellent idea. "Life happened," I muttered.

She didn't say any more. "I'll take what you have, I know the collection. Do you want me to send someone around for the rest of it?"

"Yes." With limited time here, I didn't want to squander Venice on trips up and down those treacherous stairs balancing awkward and occasionally valuable paintings.

"You need cash now?"

I nodded.

"You need also." She gestured at me.

I nodded, not meeting her gaze. My round toed tennis shoes looked like cruise ships docked next to her pointed toed leather sling backs.

"You know Nic is in town." She dropped that bomb, oh, so casually.

I jerked out of my slumping posture. Shit.

"Is the beauty shop still open up the street?"

"My cousin just bought it." Rachael said softly. She pulled out her phone. "She will stay."

CHAPTER NINE

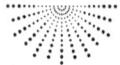

*R*achael's cousin looked just like her: fabulous. I love the Italian style, the insouciance, slender legs encased in tight jeans or leather pants, thin sweaters worn year-round in defiance of the damp. Unapologetic breasts loaded into La Perla push up bras.

The effortlessness that is the Italian brand. It looked easy, but it took hours and thousands of dollars as well as the right lighting and good postproduction Photoshopped fixes. But if you are all alone in a small split-level ranch house bristling with wheelchair ramps and endless news stories predicting the end of the world, why color your hair?

Francisca was comfortable in her own skin and even more comfortable critiquing mine. She declared we would stay at the salon for as long as it takes. Which meant we worked into the night. She cut, colored, and made calls. While the color and highlights set, my head a UFO-deflecting halo of foil, her niece blew in: tight leather slacks, baggy sweater with a deep V that showed off her tiny perky breasts barely contained in a matching leather bra. She flipped her long black braid over her shoulder, took one look at my nails and almost burst into tears.

"We fix." She declared. And did.

She threw in a quick pedicure and I let her, not wanting to make her to cry again.

We ordered pizza, the thin crust, fresh ingredients, the Italian kind. Francisca pulled out a bottle of red and we continued. The wine and pizza helped my mood, as did the emerging new look.

By the time I was declared finished and fit for the street, I was hundreds of euros into the program, but Francisca, the salon owner, refused my cash.

"You pay later, I know." She looked at my outfit, now completely at odds with my hair—colored a dark auburn with dark gold highlights, very high maintenance. My nails were short and gelled blood red. The cut was short, but not old. If I didn't straighten it, the coloring and conditioning would keep it to a short wavy look. It took ten years off me. So much for my cloak of invisibility.

On the other hand, I no longer looked like an easy purse-snatching mark.

"Now." Francisca tapped her lips; her own nails were the same color as mine. "You need clothing, no? Is everything." She gestured to my ensemble, carefully curated from the perpetual caretaker collection.

I nodded.

"You need new." She decided. She glanced at her watch and made another call.

"Simone will open for you."

"It's already nine o'clock."

Francisca shrugged. "For emergencies, she will open and you..." Her eyes traveled up and down taking in my sensible polyester ensemble.

"Are an emergency." I finished. Very well, If I was going to do this, I may as well go big. The very real possibility of encountering Nic in my present finery was gut-wrenching. I'd rather have my purse stolen again.

I took Francisca's business card and over her protests, promised to pay her back.

Simone's shop was located a street off the plaza in a tiny area crammed with designer shops, all too expensive for the average tourist, but perfect for those in the know.

I knew, I just didn't have the wherewith all to follow up.

That was about to change.

"Simone?" The woman, like me, was older, wiser around the eyes, but the same, oh yes, very much the same.

"Carina!" Simone emerged to the front of the store. In full light she looked her forty years, but for a second, I was looking at the young model from Aix-en-Provence, determined to make it in the business, eating tissues and smoking a pack a day, thin, beautiful and really angry.

During those first few months, I talked Simone into eating food, pulled her from the front of the camera to wardrobe where she proved to be a brilliant stylist. We spread the word and between her beauty and her family contacts, she quickly became the in-demand stylist for most major photo shoots. For the next ten years I read her name in the credits for most of French and Italian Vogue spreads. She could make even the oddest bleeding edge fashion look good, even on increasingly hanger-like models. She was a vocal supporter of the European model rules. She sparkled with energy.

"So, this is where you are!" We kissed, we hugged, we hugged again.

"I am so sorry about Max."

"Thank you."

"You were so good to him."

"He helped me." An understatement.

"He helped us all, you would think he loved girls." She twinkled as she said it.

I smiled. As a photographer then designer assistant, I worked with hundreds of models. Most were hard working and naturals for the job, but enough were in the wrong place: the wrong agency, the wrong man, the wrong business. What do twenty-year-olds know about anything? I was determined that they would get the same help as I. Max had taught me everything about the industry, the ins and outs. He introduced me to influencers, helped me make a game of it, and gave me permission to eat again. I wanted us to do the same and Max agreed. We invested in people found them, burnished them, and sent them on their way, better, stronger and in his words, able to make the world a better place.

He was a fashion icon who hated the fashion world and what the careers did to people. That's why I was with him. That's why I was there at the end. He deserved that much.

"How did you end up here?"

"One does not end up in Venice." She chided. She flipped on the lights and locked the door. "Tourists." She sniffed.

Most stores on this street were devoted to one thing or one designer or one designer of a single thing. Think leather purses, think shoes, think fur. Think a single mannequin complete with alert nipples, a single tiny purple cross bag displayed over the plastic shoulder.

Simone's was not that store. The small outlet was lined with racks of clothes. I did not immediately recognize the styles or the designers. Leather skirts shared space with wool jackets. Silk peeked out between heavy tweed. I wasn't sure if the stock jumble was on purpose or accidental. Sometimes shoppers think they have found a bargain simply because the blouse was so difficult to free from the rack

"Consignment." She correctly interpreted my expression. "Like walking into your big sister's closet. Of course, in

Venice. We trade, we drop off, we borrow. I take some seconds, I take some designer, but not small, never size two, never size zero."

"Venice?" I couldn't let it go. What was she doing here of all places? She could be in Paris, living off her considerable talents and reputation. She could be in Milan, at the heart of the action. For her world, Venice was quite literally a backwater.

"Ah," she sighed. "You remember the Milan show of 1995?"

I nodded.

"The organizer, Maurice?"

Maurice was talented, even brilliant. A portly man given to bright blue suits and navy cowboy boots; he was as wealthy as the Gucci family but was not disposed to good works. He liked the models in his shows to be so thin they were constantly on the verge of passing out and falling from their shoes. No size zero indeed.

"Remember his son Andre?" Maurice had one son, flamboyant, handsome. During his school breaks, Maurice spent all day behind stage. He loved to flirt and was good at it. Drove his father to distraction. Which I am sure was the point.

I frowned trying to recall the end of that story. Did Andre inherit his father's title and more important, business?

She read my expression. "Yes, Andre. Remember you told me to flirt back? Remember you coached me on how to flirt?"

I nodded, that sounded like me.

"He lives here in Venice."

"And you live in Venice with Andre."

She grinned, "Maurice doesn't like me. I'm too vocal, have too many opinions, but Andre, he is a catch. I flirted, he flirted. We live on the island." She held up two fingers. "Girls.

They love science, refuse to wear anything but jeans and hoodies."

I was delighted and a little lightheaded. It was probably the good wine. It was all like a dream. That's a stupid thing to say because in a dream you don't get hungry, tired or drunk. I suspected I was also a little drunk and more than tired, how else to explain turning over my whole image to strangers? But they were not of course, strangers, they were friends, old dear friends. That was something I had missed. In California, I had family. In Italy, I had friends.

She waved to the colorful garments crowded onto the rods. "We will dress you, how many days?"

"I'll go to the embassy tomorrow. I should get my new passport by Thursday." It was Tuesday, still. I think.

As if to emphasis the point, my phone pinged again. I pulled it out and make a mental note to return Tina's call.

Simone moved to the first rack and pulled out three pairs of slacks. "You'll need clothes for at least a week."

By 11:15 P.M., I was beautiful—unlike myself as possible. With a wave to Simone and a promise to reimburse her once the credit card arrived, I had no desire to waste all this good work to a lonely night in Miranda's apartment. I had cash in my pocket and an appetite that would make the perfect dinner companion. I headed to the quay off the lagoon and found a charming trattoria offering dozens of versions of homemade pasta and a table by the front window.

I was treated far better than even twelve hours ago.

My waiter explained that this trattoria was one of the few survivors of the changing gentrification of the city.

"We hold on. But all the young people, you know." He shrugged.

I did know.

And after life-altering a

Alfredo made with genuine organic, fresh ingredients: eggs and cream and bacon and everything bad for you, I was ready to forgive Venice for stealing my purse.

I even slept well under the scary Nevelson sculpture. But really, it did have to go.

CHAPTER TEN

I woke with nothing on my agenda except making an appointment with the embassy at 9:00. It was more expedient to make the apartment livable for me and call a housekeeper later. Every other minute I checked the phone for a return call from the embassy confirming my appointment, a missive from Chris that all was well, a text from Tina assuring me it was not. I moved the couch to the center of the room to take advantage of the view and carried two thirds of the chairs to the spare bedroom to wait for the next gathering. I swept out the last of the sand from the Egypt party. Maybe I could make a career of styling homes for sale. This was my second one. Did that make a career?

I needed help with the sculpture over the bed, I didn't want to break it. How had Miranda managed to get it up the stairs?

I admired my manicure as I texted Rachael to ask for a cleaning service recommendation. Tiffany promised to send over help, but I didn't believe her.

Once the small apartment was clean and ready for its close up, I focused on clearing out the rest of Miranda's drawers and closet. I pulled out arm loads of clothes: the thin designer outfits; the impractical event dresses, many, many fat jeans. She had a great deal to donate. I found a Max Peters duster from his last collection—2005. I slipped it on against the morning chill.

While digging out all (except the one notable one) drawers, I discovered the perfect purse. It was made of bright green patent leather, structured and elegant. And also covered in stamped MP logos. I considered it a tribute and liberated it, replacing the heavy travel bag.

It made me feel more Italian.

I also discovered more jewelry. I remember Miranda's delight at finding the necklace and bracelets at the Paris Flea Market. Big handfuls of shiny things. The gilt had worn away, exposing the base metal but the long necklaces of paste rubies and emeralds complemented the duster. I layered all four, they clanked and caught at the pile of clothes I hauled down the stairs, but I didn't care.

I felt more fabulous by the minute.

I would love to report that I discovered a clue to the blue statues in the lining of Miranda's purse. But I didn't. I did find a Kate Spade wallet though.

Even loaded with clothes, I felt an old swagger creep into my walk as I made my way to Simone's.

Simone assured me that the first delivery of clothes I brought from Miranda's closest was fair trade for what I wore today. Rachael was delighted with the additional paintings. I explained they were doing me a favor by taking all this stuff, they pretended to believe me.

By high noon, the apartment looked more restful than I ever remembered. Miranda was many things, none of them calm. I would have taken care of Miranda, even in her exuberant clutter. If she had asked me to come, to help her, and nurse her through a damaged heart, I would have hopped on a plane and been there. Funny, staying with friends felt like an act of compassion, a calling. Staying with my parents dug out my soul like a melon baller taking scoops out of a cantaloupe.

The locksmith gave me a once-over before settling down to change the locks.

I tipped him just for the lascivious look in his eye. I left the old key under the cherub and threaded both new keys onto my lucky key ring. If Nic was at large, the least I could do was prevent him from bursting in while I was in the shower.

I was on the verge of making a comeback as a competent adult.

Nic. Nic was not to be faced on an empty stomach, I indulged in my promised lunch, finishing it off with two scoops of gelato. Is there such a thing as too much gelato? No, no, I do not think so. Paris may always be a good idea, but gelato is an even better one. Especially if one is stranded in Italy.

And the texts.

My nephew Chris, my special guy, is the only reason I even hesitated when Tina and Vince suggested I care for the boys. Matt, the oldest, may be the boy who could get his brother to and from school, but Chris is the guy who helps Matt stay in school. I never considered Chris difficult, he simply focuses on one thing at a time. To the complete exclusion of everything else. Including showers and meals. This focus comes with a price. For instance, to my everlasting chagrin, Chris was completely obsessed with Egyptian digs, both past and present. If I thought I could ever forget Dr. Nicholas Ratzenberg, my unaware nephew would remind me. He always asks if I knew about this dig or that discovery, was I there? No, Chris, I was not there, not anymore.

The first text of the day was from Matt—Do we have a fire extinguisher?

I typed in the location.

He texted back—what time was it back home? I didn't want to know.

Found it— crowbar?

I had no answer. I should go home. As soon as the passport came through, I would board the next plane.

I'll be back soon.

Hurry. Now that sounded like Tina, not Matt.

Can't hurry Italy.

I finished my gelato and licked my fingers. Nic. How would I face Nic?

Nic was one of those men unmoved by emotional displays. I could beg, I could scream, I could cry, but he would just shake his head and comment on how emotional and fragile women were. It drove me crazy and eventually, drove me back to Miranda.

No crying. Be strong. Man up. Be solid.

By the time Tiffany dropped by, I was back to contemplating the sculpture over the bed.

Tiffany parked her white hard sided case and matching travel bag at the door. She was dressed for travel in head-to-toe Lululemon looking very Vogue International.

"You can take care of this now?" She glanced around. "Looks good. We'll be in touch." She didn't offer her hand, she didn't thank me, though I didn't expect she would. She just nodded and backed out of the apartment. At least she had the courtesy not to ask me to carry her bag back down the stairs.

I resisted saluting. There was little else to say, and I had the Nic thing to deal with.

Absently rubbing the small of my back—is there an ergonomically sound way to wrestle large canvases down narrow stone stairs?—I walked to the kitchen. I had put off opening the small refrigerator. It only takes a week for anything kept in this ancient piece of crap to disintegrate into organic matter than only eight-year-old boys can appreciate. I hadn't wanted to face it.

I held my breath and jerked open the door.

Nothing but three bottles of Prosecco, a desiccated lemon and a small jar of caviar. Are there any large jars of caviar? There is an item I have not seen at Costco, then again, I could have been shopping the wrong aisles. I shut the refrigerator and opened the casement window and leaned on the gritty windowsill. I knew enough to snatch a peaceful moment when I could. The canal glittered beneath me. Speed boats passed the vaporettos that in turn sped by the larger flat boats lumbering with tourists. The air was clear, and the stench of low tide hadn't completely overtaken the breeze.

I was different in this city. I was a caretaker here as well as in California, but here was different. Max had a strong emotional bank account from which to withdraw. He had taken an interest in my career, helping me with contacts and industry secrets so I had a leg up even though no one wanted to photograph my legs. He never berated me for my choices, it was all about support and I suppose, love.

The doorbell buzzed and the voice on the intercom bellowed. "Vic! I know you're up there, let me in."

After Simone and Rachael, I should be used to opening up a door and greeting my past. But I knew, Chris's relentless updates aside, that I would never be prepared for Nic.

"Vic!"

It was bad enough growing up as part of Vince, Vance, and Vic. But Vic and Nic? We could never marry.

Nic did look the same, although not as looming. As he stepped across the threshold, I was surprised that he did not fill up the whole world, he did not even suck all the oxygen from the room. Probably diminished lung capacity.

Despite his permanent tan, he looked a little pale.

"Nic." I stepped back to let him into the apartment, but I did not get far.

He grabbed me in a bear hug so strong that my back cracked in three places, which felt pretty good.

"Good to see you too." My voice was muffled against his chest. "Let me go."

He released me and shoved his hands in two of the seven pockets attached to his travel pants. "Sorry. I miss you. You look fantastic!"

"You look like you should have used more sunscreen over the last twenty years."

His eyes crinkled into a smile. "See, you would have been good for me."

We would have been terrible. I worshiped him and he took advantage. I cried; he was stoic. He was a generous lover; I would give him that. But like many people of genius, everyone and anything else took a back seat to his main passion. I accepted that, because everyone I loved fell some-where on the Spectrum.

Nic was over the sixty- year hump and must be closing in on the end of his career. How was he doing really? He still lean, but as we age, that's not such a great look. His hand-some face fell into long creases, white laugh lines fanned into his temples. He was still lively, still charismatic.

With a flourish of my Max Peters original I led him into the newly cleaned living room. When I say living room, what I mean is the area left over when the kitchen and dining area are through. When we entertained, Miranda and I pulled out a huge folding table that replaced the coffee and end tables that were in turn stashed in the windowless extra bedroom. The party always took over the whole apartment. Didn't matter where we put people, the public space overlooked the canal through floor to ceiling windows so there wasn't a bad seat in the house. The windows, however, needed professional help.

Nic obediently sat on the couch.

"You cleaned," he observed.

I raised one eyebrow and stepped over to pick up a bottle of red wine.

"You saw Miranda?"

"Oh, no." He raised his hands. "Just the hippo over Skype. But I could see the apartment behind her of course, she was never very tidy."

"I can't remember if you're tidy."

"I'm a disaster, especially after you left, couldn't find my notes for days." He said it with a smile, but I suddenly knew it was true. Nic was more Belzoni than Petrie. Belzoni was a circus strongman who searched for treasure using the expedient technique of blowing impediments up. His best stunt was to ship an intact obelisk to England to grace the private estate of William John Bankes. Petrie on the other hand, was an eccentric scholar devoted to exacting process, cataloging pot shards under the relentless Egyptian sun. Like Petrie, Nic was a scholar and a careful, academic excavator, but like Belzoni, Nic loved treasure, he relished the big finds, the press, the attention. Nic was able to bundle up all his hubris and deliver spectacular, well-attended lectures at UC Santa Barbara where, when he did show up, he was treated as minor royalty.

I didn't even mind trailing behind him on campus. I loved that campus, I loved the beauty of Santa Barbara, the opportunities offered by one of the largest university systems in the world. I even forgave myself for not taking some of those opportunities, my choice, my consequences. And look, here was another consequence.

I handed him a wine glass. He seemed smaller and I was quite aware that in contrast, I was much, much larger. Maybe over the years we had exchanged mass.

I sat next to him with my glass in hand.

"To old times."

"To old times."

He drank and looked at me over the rim of the glass. "Did you see it?"

My mind shot back to the secret drawer filled with toys and games. Those were the Oreo years: Miranda was dark chocolate, hard, crumbly. Nic was the creamy stuffing in the middle. Yes, really go ahead and extrapolate that creamy middle metaphor to its logical end. But like delicious cookies, neither was sustainable, nor nourishing.

I took a shuddering breath and tried to keep my hand steady. I gave up and set the glass on the coffee table.

Max had insisted on hearing all my Nic stories. The finds, the fights, the gritty sand. Heady intense experiences rendered more and more harmless in the telling.

Nic covered my hand with his. "It's been a long time. Sorry, I didn't mean to make it all about the hippo."

"But it is all about the hippo, isn't it?"

He shook his head. "You've been away."

He made it sound like I had been in prison and just got sprung for good behavior.

"Not so long." Five years.

"Long enough."

He glanced at his watch. "Come, the tourists have all retreated to their ships by now. We have a fighting chance."

"It's a little early for dinner."

"Drinks then, out in the world."

Damn, he was still handsome, rugged, worn and decidedly beat up. But the blue eyes were the same, the sardonic expression that only soften in that five minutes window of post-coital sentimentality. That was the look I fell for. And the look I worked my damnedest to inspire over and over again.

Have you made love in the desert during a sandstorm protected only by flimsy nylon? Very romantic. Sand everywhere. Took me a week and seventeen showers before I could walk without pain.

I stood and took his empty glass. "Of course, we can go out." Miranda's room was tidy; the object of his desire, that hippo, was safe and far away. Okay, safe in a hotel across the plaza. On a crowded Friday night, that was far enough away.

My phone buzzed. It was Tina. I didn't answer.

"Will you take a photo with me?" I gestured for him to come close and held up the phone for the most flattering angle of me, I wasn't worried about Nic. He obligingly smiled and I quickly sent the image to Chris, texting that I had met up with the great man again.

"My nephew thinks you are the bomb. He follows your career slavishly."

"A rabid fan?"

"Not unlike the undergrads at UCSB." I punched his shoulder. "Come on, I lost my purse, so you're treating."

The cruise ships had gathered their unruly guests and had all just disembarked. The plaza was lively with locals clearly happy to reclaim their city. Few people were ready for dinner, so we had our choice of tables to relax and order over-priced wine while we basked in the reflections from St. Marks. I figured I may as well have one final grand outing. Nic didn't protest and obediently followed in my wake as I snaked through the tables on the square and chose one with an unobstructed view of the Basilica.

I talked the waiter into allowing us to remain for dinner even though we occupied a table clearly marked reserved.

"I promise we will be finished by 9:00 for the next group."

Either the maître d' was enchanted by my new look or that I could speak a little his language. He put on a good show, he frowned, calculated and finally nodded. "Not a minute longer."

I nodded and smiled. "Not a minute longer."

We sat at our lovely table until ten, mostly because it took half an hour for our waiter to produce the bill and another twenty minutes before he popped back to run Nic's charge card.

We worked through a second bottle of wine, taking our time. Nic fiddled with his fork and knife. He glanced around. He was restless and not because he was appreciating the young women parading around the square, laughing and taking selfies. He caught me up on his digs; he was still located in Egypt. I caught him up on my parents. We both discussed Miranda.

I ate and fended off questions about Miranda and her estate. He was using me, of course, but that wasn't such an unusual thing; it was, in fact, comfortingly familiar. I basked in his direct attention, his blue eyes, the expensive wine I kept ordering. We drank and talked of the old times: when he was young, and I was foolish. It was so grand to be led solely by stupid crazy love. We only regret the sensible decisions.

Nic, for all his intelligence was a man driven by hope over experience. You have to, he pointed out, in order to keep digging. Each new day could be the day you discover the artifact, the statue, the mummy, the mummy case that will catapult you to fame and solvency.

Every goddamn day.

After a couple years of all these days strung together in endless succession, I was exhausted emotionally and physically, seemingly suffering from perpetual sunstroke. Or suffering from an overdose of Nic. Miranda, who took me back, claimed it wasn't the sun; it was Nic in all his attractive neediness. At one point she called Nic my Egyptian curse. Maybe.

My brothers often parroted my parents pointing out that there is always a price to pay for pleasure. I've lived abroad long enough to know, deep in my bones, that isn't true. I wanted to take a photo of Nic and me at dinner, floodlit St. Mark's in the background. Just to make Vince's weekend that much more stressful. Already paid the price—here are the pics.

Nic noticed me fingering my phone. "You really must stop, you know."

I set the phone face down and tried not to look at it. "Stop what?"

"Caring for others, you are always caring for others instead of taking care of yourself."

"I cared for you. You didn't seem to mind."

Cheshire cat smile. "I'm different. I give back."

So did Max, charming to the end, lively, grateful. So did Miranda, brittle, fascinating. So did my parents...my parents were family.

While we waited for the second phase of paying for our meal, Nic circled back to the whole point.

"The hippo may be the real thing, but I couldn't tell over Skype."

"And what exactly does that mean?"

"It could mean a major dig, a major find." His eyes lit up, but it was just because the waiter was finally returning to take Nic's payment.

"Or it could mean someone did not take good care of their souvenir from the Met."

He nodded, "That would be better."

"Why better?" I poured the last of the second bottle into my glass. "That's not like you, turning down an opportunity to discover something new."

"Not as easy anymore. The digs are hellishly expensive and the government, at least the group in charge this week, is not interested in more artifacts, they are interested in progress, taxes,"

"Graft." I supplied. I wasn't naive. Promising discoveries, promising digs were routinely re-buried so as not to disrupt a housing project or building large retail establishment. That the Sphinx was directly across from a KFC outlet only proved the point. What made more money? The chicken.

No woman with a solid education in romantic comedies and paranoid newscasts would have taken Nic at face value tonight. We had met at a party, me looking fabulous, Nic, working for the Cairo Museum to track a ring of smugglers, looked exciting. He was following a lead; I was trailing a long Ralph Lauren. It was all very James Bond, which appealed to me so much I only asked general questions to which he replied with vague answers. Within hours of meeting, Nic had swept me and a small overnight bag out of Venice and into adventure in the grand desert. I do not regret a second.

I sipped my wine and smiled at him, thankful for what we had. Thankful I had one more chance to thank him.

A good Nebbiolo will do that to you: help you forgive. "If we can't find the hippo, then what?" I had locked the apartment as we left, but there was no reason a determined person couldn't just smash the door. We were eating very early likely, so the thieves had more light for their search. Did Nic ask them to be sure to return everything back where they found it? As neatly as possible? I spent the better part of the day making sure the place was presentable, I didn't relish cleaning it again.

I leaned back and grinned at him. He was still handsome. I was still attracted at least to the idea of him. I was not yet dead. Game on.

I asked Nic up. Whatever I would find, I did not want to

find it alone. He hesitated, but dutifully followed me up the stairs.

"Oh, no!" It was almost difficult to sound surprised.

The apartment was once again, trashed, this time more obviously since I had straightened up everything before the robbery. I hurried to the kitchen to make sure the espresso machine was unharmed, then hurried to the bedroom to make sure Miranda's hidden toys were undisturbed. The closet was rifled, but there wasn't much to rifle. My suitcase had been opened, but again, not damaged; none of my things were disturbed.

I had already added the locksmith to my favorites list and left a message.

Nic's eyes darted around the living room as I emerged from the bedroom. "Anything missing?"

I shook my head. The only things in my suitcase were recent acquisitions from the store. My key ring, cash and phone were secure in my tiny green purse.

"Do you even have it?" Nic's tone was casual, credit for keeping his voice steady.

The locksmith pinged me back. Tomorrow morning, first thing.

"No." Completely and totally true. I did not have the hippo.

He needed to ask a different question if he wanted a different answer. I smiled. "Is that what you think the thieves were searching for?" Point for me.

As if they hadn't been in the house before, as if this wasn't the second time in a week the house had been tossed. As if they didn't figure that with a new person, there was a new possibility the hippo would emerge. Because they knew where I was and exactly what I was doing.

"I told you I hadn't found it; did you really need to do this?" I turned on him, hands on hips as if he were Matt still holding a smoking fire extinguisher. Nic looked just as guilty.

He let out a sigh as he massaged the back of his neck. He didn't even bother to deny it, too much trouble.

"We need it." He held out his hands in supplication. "I need it."

"It's not here." I repeated. "I only saw it on Skype as well."

"Some very important men want to find the hippo," he finally admitted.

"You can order one on-line." I held my ground. He rubbed his face, then carefully circled the room picking up the cushions, righting the end tables, retrieving the pieces of a broken lamp.

"And why you?"

"Because I know Miranda and I know you. And they thought it would be easy."

"But it wasn't."

He shook his head.

"You were here the night Miranda died?"

"No! Yes, but earlier, she was alive, I asked her for the hippo, but she wouldn't give it to me."

"She liked it."

"She said she didn't trust me." He clutched a cushion to his chest.

"I wonder why." I took the cushion and replaced it.

"Look, we parted on good terms. Mostly good terms," he amended.

"Mostly." I confirmed. "But she is my friend and I am feeling rather protective right now. Do you blame her for not trusting you? You were the one who bounced me out of the tent to make way for a younger and, I may add, thinner woman. She had to pick up the pieces and I wasn't as easy to re-assemble as one of your finds." It was possible I was at fault as well, but this wasn't about me.

"How did you know?"

I sat on the newly replaced cushion and gazed out over the canal. The lights from the hotel across the canal lit up the water in undulating yellow squares. Black figures strolled the quay below.

"No one eats at 6:00."

"Jet lag?" He offered.

"Lame." The mess wasn't bad; his work had righted most of it back to show-worthy order. The wavering squares of light were mesmerizing. I rose and retrieved the wine and the glasses. "They left this." I poured him a glass and poured the rest into my glass.

Nic took his glass, offered a silent toast and almost downed the whole thing.

I sat down, feeling superior as the wronged one. I had morals and ethics on my side. As well as danger. Damn.

I sat forward resting my arms on my legs. "I can't stay here, and I can't check into a hotel without my passport."

He sat next to me mimicking my position. "You can stay here, no one will be back."

"Comforting from the bad guy."

"I just need to know where it's from and how she got it. All she said is she found it here, at a shop in the city. Where?"

"The shop or the dig?"

"Both, we need to stop the flow. If there is a new dig, and it's producing artifacts, we need to know."

"You don't know there's a new dig? The country is not that large."

"But it's a vast desert. The government is small, and not necessarily on board, UNESCO and the Ministry of Antiquities can only do so much. If I had a small clue, if we could trace the hippo back to at least the end of the supply chain, we could find the origins."

"You have enough men to invade Miranda's home, steal my purse, rob the place again."

He waved his hand. "Locals."

"Call them off?" I looked at the lock, still intact but useless if someone could pick it.

He followed my gaze and immediately took a dining table chair and shoved it under the doorknob.

He sat back down and pulled out a rumpled photo. It was the hippo, my hippo since I inherited it. The glass had either faded or this was a greener tinged hippo in the first place. I had seen it, held it in my hands. But I was not about to admit that. I had the one thing he needed; it was not necessary to give it up to soon. Not even for love. Not even for sex.

I looked up hippo images on my phone. Those were all of William; some but not all were the same color as the printed photo in Nic's hand.

"Still could be a fake." I insisted, scrolling through the photos to find a match. Chris still liked playing the matching game, it soothed him. And he was damn good at it, sometimes, okay, often; I wished for his brand of focus.

"Look at his head."

I studied the photo again. Twelve years fell away. I was almost forty and, in the desert, feeling it. But we were still passionate, still together in a singular focus of discovery. The days were brutal, hot and disappointing, but the nights, the nights had been magical. I touched his hand to get a closer look at the printout. My fingers lingered on his. It wasn't electric but it was jolting enough.

"See?" He pointed to the figures, blurry.

"Where did you get this photo?"

"Took it off Skype."

"Great."

"Can you make out the decorations? The black lines."

"Papyrus. All the hippos were decorated with images of papyrus, that's where the hippo lived."

"Yes, except these." He traced the photo. "Are ducks."

Yes, they were.

"Armana?"

"Possibly, likely."

"Then what's the problem?" Armana, the city created from scratch by the heretic pharaoh Akhenaten who was devoted to a single true god—the sun, Aten. Husband of famous Nefertiti, father of even more famous Tutankhamun. The city site, built well outside of Thebes (Luxor), was not only known for separating from the old school of priests and for building its own city, it was also known for encouraging artists to experiment with more natural style. Palms bent, plants swayed, ducks flew.

Ducks replaced papyrus decorations on a hippo's back.

"You don't have any leads? How many outlets for stolen goods can there be in the city?"

"A lot. A lot are Chinese knockoffs, but those fakes usually travel the Silk Road route."

"Makes sense."

"Yes." Shadows crossed the windows across from us. People going about their business, readying for the weekend.

"Want to help?"

"If it keeps me safe and prevents more break-ins, yes." I searched the walls, remembering where all the paintings belonged and where they didn't. The thieves were single-minded, I gave them that. The paintings had not been tampered with, none removed. Was there still honor among thieves? I'd like to think so, but according to Fox News, no.

"I will keep you safe." He set down his glass and the photo and held my hand. "I'll even stay if you want."

His eyes were the bright blue of faience.

"You'll stay because you have no place else to go because you are too cheap to spring for a real hotel."

Nic nodded. "There is that." He absently massaged the back of his neck.

"You wrenched it." I scooted closer. I swear, just concerned. Funny thing about love, passion, and history, it can supersede almost any other emotion or reasonable doubt.

He smiled. "Still flares up, you remembered."

He closed the space between us, his back and neck apparently and miraculously healed. "I missed you," his voice dropped to a low growl that made the hairs on the back of my own neck stand up. "I have missed you every day for twelve years. I've been living like a man buried alive. Why did you leave?"

"I was needed."

"I need you." He ran his hand up my arm triggering both tingles and alarm bells.

Living a lie can be wonderful. For one night, for one moment of soul freeing joy nothing else mattered. I fully anticipated on paying for it later.

CHAPTER ELEVEN

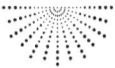

I opened my eyes and for just a second, a half heartbeat, I thought I was still dreaming. The light streamed in, calls from the canal. The apartment above us was silent, the owner still in bed. Miranda never heard the former owner, but I woke earlier every morning to the sound of the old boy slamming his cupboard and firing up his espresso machine. But this morning, there were no sounds from above. I could just make out the sound of canal water slapping against the side of the building.

I lay in Miranda's bed. I caught the shadow of the sculpture and edged out from under it. First, I was not in my single bed in Sacramento. Second, Miranda was not the person beside me. Nic was scrunched at the opposite side of the mattress, sheets clutched to his chest, body stiff.

Survivor sex is pretty damn good. Any sex is good, I admit that. Especially since I thought it was over, like forever. But an old lover helps, the patterns were still there, the expectations and techniques still recalled. It was like getting back on a bike, fun, furious, easy to crash.

I watched him sleep. How many days, how many weeks?

Funny when I felt Nic beside me again, he brought back memories of Max.

I was like a three-ring circus. In this ring, Miranda and her easy wealth and easy virtue. She was hell bent on a good time and was catholic in her tastes. In the next, Nic. Nic's ring was filled with sand and exoticism and, I stretched and touched the bottom of the black sculpture, pretty damn good sex. I even discovered that as much as I loved our antics, I also loved the man. In the third ring, Max Peters.

I believe I loved Max the hardest. Loved him the longest.

We met at the Milan Show. He was in his early sixties, top of his game. I was in my thirties and floundering. I had a few modeling gigs but couldn't sustain the look. My weight had ballooned, my skin was sallow, and I had just lost my apartment in Manhattan. Max took me home to Venice.

I regret thinking Max was terribly old because that attitude is certainly is biting me in the butt now.

Max Peters was like Pucci meets Gucci. He was wild during the seventies when so much fashion and ready-to-wear was little more than shades of beige. He created so many original fabrics he needed to keep the swatch books in the apartment just to keep track of what he had already done. He won so many accolades he was accorded his own center piece in Elle Magazine posthumously honoring his seventieth birthday. From Max I learned about wine, I learned about food. Best of all I learned what goes on behind the camera. Max introduced me to Deb, who introduced me to Miranda, who got me into parties, parties like the one where I met Nic. This then, was my circus, they were all my monkeys.

After my flings with Miranda, then Nic, then Miranda again, I heard that Max was ill. He would never admit it straight out, but I knew. I moved from Miranda's place to Max's to better care for him—continuing his designs, helping with the sale to LVM. When I say return to Max, it wasn't terribly difficult, he lived only blocks away from Miranda. But during that time Miranda and I drifted apart. She continued with her parties and her art, I was deep in the country of old age and death which no one visits on purpose. It was like I had moved to Siberia, or Bakersfield. Miranda and I didn't even meet at the market. I always arrived early. Miranda, late.

Max died the way he wanted. He had been happy, at least I hope he had been happy. His family had disowned him so long ago that they had lost complete touch. I served as his family. I immersed myself in his beautiful fabrics, the swatches; we made samples, he sewed first, eventually becoming so weak I sewed, and he directed from his bed.

The day Max passed; it was like a silent alarm sounded. It makes no sense, but it felt exactly like that, a dog-whistle-level alarm. Before I could gather my wits and grief, a representative from Holquist, Learnerd and Romano, a tall dour man dressed in a well preserved Yves Saint Laurent, appeared at the apartment mere hours after I closed Max's eyes.

The attorney held a list in his hand and proceeded to confiscate the fabrics and incomplete dresses and tunics and marched out, saying they would be in touch.

I was too stunned to protest even though I know that be in touch is code for never.

The next group, hot on the heels of the lawyer as if waiting on the street for their turn, were a contingent of former lovers. The young men pushed me aside as they barreled through the door.

In the crush I had forgotten the extra keys on my key ring. I owned a key to Max's apartment, the key to Miranda's apartment (which I returned) and the key to the storage center.

But my father had fallen the same night Max passed. In quick succession, Vincent, Vance, and Tina called to plead for my return to the states and care for my beloved parents. Parents I hadn't seen in twenty years.

You pay for your pleasure. While Vincent and Vance were working hard at their careers, raising second families, turning into pillars of the community, what was I doing? Running around Europe with people of questionable morals but excellent taste. They insisted it was my turn to be the responsible one.

I was the youngest, I was single. I was the girl. I had to return to the States. There wasn't much choice.

NIC STIRRED and turned to me.

"Good morning." He threw an arm over my chest. "Where is the hippo?"

I didn't even bother to open my eyes, relishing a picture of us younger, stronger and in love. We were not in love anymore, I was not even enthralled but it was a deep pleasure to lie beside him, appreciate the warmth, the male energy (at the usual all-time low), that soft look in his eyes.

"I don't know." I rolled out of bed and headed to the kitchen. I started up the espresso machine and checked my phone. Tiffany had landed in the states and sent along a detailed set of instructions to ship her paintings to her home. I thought she had taken care of that. Apparently, she had left the paintings at her hotel with instructions that I would be by to pick them up.

Her last sentence—make sure you show your passport—made me smile.

"You are fantastic, you know that don't you?" Nic watched me from the tangle of sheets as I dressed. I would say it was like a Taylor Swift video, but no, not really. Taylor doesn't need Spanx.

"You flatter me. And it's only because we just had sex."

He stretched and touched the bottom of the Nevelson.

"Maybe. But I do know I've missed you every day since you left."

"Nic, it wasn't working out. You took up with that assistant."

"Sarah. She was working on her PhD thesis on Hatshepsut and her architect Senenmut. Was he really in love with the queen or just using her?"

I narrowed my eyes. "Whatever."

"It was an interesting idea."

"Okay, did it work?"

"She couldn't find enough hieroglyphic evidence in the time she had." He shrugged and so much for Sarah. Since I knew Nic well, he was probably very supportive up until her committee rejected the dissertation draft. Then goodbye baby, which is a more unpleasant side of Nic.

The phone buzzed in the living room. I pulled on one of Miranda's sweaters. "Gotta get that. Family crisis."

"You always were responding to one crisis or another." He muttered.

I paused and looked back at him.

Then retrieved the phone.

I sighed wondering how long I could keep this, this silence, this moment.

I checked in with Chris.

Learning about poisons, He texted.

Any particular reason?

Mom saw a mouse.

I glanced at the missed calls. Tina had phoned three times. I did not bother playing back the voice mail, since I could hear her standing on a chair, demanding I do something about her rodent problem even though I was half-way around the world.

"What we need." Nic strolled into the kitchen. "Is more information."

"You think?"

"There is a party tonight." He waved his phone. "Given by the infamous Von Meiter."

I frowned. I knew the name. Which makes sense, I knew most of the infamous in Venice. Miranda insisted that the people on the edges of polite society made the best dinner guests.

"He is a collector as well." Nic quickly explained. "He would actually know about the hippo or anything else that has hit the market here in Venice. You need to talk to him."

"Why not you? If you know him?" Chris had stopped texting, his communication finished for the day.

"It's not that easy."

"There are lists of stolen items, right?"

He ran his fingers through his hair—he had enough to ruffle, mess, grab. My fingers itched to do it again. "The DLIR is down, they're digitizing the Library."

The Digital Library for International Research. I could put Chris on the trail, but not if it's off-line.

He read my expression. "They lost their funding."

"Shit."

"I know, that would have been easy. Look up hippos, compare, done."

"And then what?"

"If it's stolen, or even if it's just been accidentally found, we still need to know the provenance."

I nodded, here was the man I fell in love with, impossibly upright, as careful as a French savant but as covetous as an English lord in the wake of the battle of the Nile.

"Which is better?

He took a deep breath and did not meet my eyes. "Found can be a problem."

"You want to know where this hippo was found, and why it was so easy for Miranda to snap it up, likely for a bargain price?"

"It's priceless," he countered.

"Which means that any purchase price is, shall I say it again? A bargain."

"Von Meiter likes women."

"Young women." I countered realistically. My hair looked good, but not that good.

He smiled and reached out to touch my hair. "You always get what you want."

"That's not true." I protested. Good lord, that was not true; by all the busy, squabbling gods, it was not true.

"Yes, yes, it is." He leaned back, lighting tapping his coffee cup. "Besides, what else are you doing on a Saturday night?"

Michael Von Meiter was a collector, not of things most have heard about, but a collector nonetheless. He was popular in Venice, a man given to outrageous statements about the economy, about immigration, but, most popular, invectives against cruise ships. Even as far back as the 90s there were approving rumors that the protests blocking the cruise ships were being bankrolled by you know who. When I say protests, we are not talking about thousands of sincere people carrying heavy signs and marching all afternoon in inclement weather. The Von Meiter protests took the form of a hundred or so boats, gathered to block the larger ships and prevent them from disembarking, forcing the companies to rack up another expensive port fee and the ire of every passenger on board. Think the Lilliputians snaring Gulliver. The flotilla was basically a large floating party. All very lively and fun for the locals. Possibly annoying for companies managing more money that the Dodges ever imagined in their wildest fever dreams. If they pissed of thousands of tourists, all the better, more space for the locals, more room in the cafes.

Von Meiter was the unacknowledged hero of the effort, especially after it worked. The protests helped fuel the movement of overtourism. He was not only a local hero; he was generous with his Robert Parker-rated wine cellar.

How many years since I drank Von Meiter's wine? Too long.

"Just walk up to him and ask if there is a black-market outlet for stolen Egyptian antiquities in the shape of a hippo and if so, where are their offices?" I glared at Nic. I needed more coffee for this conversation.

He rubbed his neck. "Maybe not so direct."

I fired up the machine. "There is no other way to put it. Can't we just Google it?"

That at least, made Nic smile. But he was adamant, as the song goes—It had to be you.

I had five hours to slide into an exclusive, invitation-only, Venetian party.

IN THE OLDEN DAYS, back when it was less about your social media presence and all about who you personally knew, I could call, make arrangements and this model or that designer would suddenly become the It boy or girl of the evening and if all went well, that glow of fame would expand into weeks of fame and name recognition which in turn would be just enough time to book them into lucrative contracts. Once the furor died, the model or photographer or stylist would have the option to retire with a two-year Ralph Lauren contract and secure investments. It worked time and time again.

But I never employed my system for myself. I took a deep

breath and started to scroll through my contacts. Years, I had allowed at least three, if not more, years to pass without a word to my old friends, I believed the whole of the fashion world was lost to me. As familiar names appeared under my restless thumb, I smiled. Maybe it wasn't all lost.

I dressed in one of my newly created outfits, part from Simone's shop, part from Chez Miranda—flattering leggings, high heeled boots and a strategically draped sweater. My hair hadn't looked this good in years so to complement the hair I broke out some of Miranda's still-packaged makeup and touched up my eyes and lips. No reason to not look good for the embassy.

Nic had disappeared, I think he called out something like "later" while I wrestled into the leggings. He was the least of my problems. I was without a passport, I was twelve hours late for my return home and I was living in my dead friend's apartment; essentially, I was squatting. I hadn't returned Tiffany's paintings. There were many problems.

All, really, of the first world variety. I tucked the phone in my bra and shouldered one of Miranda's old Chanel bags.

The American Embassy was staffed by Italians all of whom gathered around to see what was essentially a before-and-after reveal.

"That is…you?" One young man grabbed my phone and enlarged the passport picture. He squinted at my phone, then looked me over as if he didn't believe me. For a moment I froze, what if they don't believe me? I shouldn't have colored my hair. My eyes must have widened. He grinned. "For your new passport, a new photo signora?"

Five young people assured me my passport would be ready in less than twenty-four hours. Or forty-eight hours. Okay, three business days at the most. Since it was Wednesday, I was grateful for Simone's insistence on a more expansive wardrobe.

I came across a pleasant little trattoria on my way back to the apartment. The pasta primavera was magnificent and loaded with fresh vegetables, so I was eating healthy. I dredged pieces of thick aromatic bread through bright green acidic olive oil and drank a carafe of the house wine all by myself.

I felt more alive than I had in years. Nic was right in a manner of speaking. I am very good at getting what other people need. I was so good at managing Dad and Mom that Vince and Vance were able to waltz in and take over, take credit, and quickly divide the estate into equal thirds. Play my cards right and I would be able to live frugally on my inheritance for the rest of my solitary, unexciting, uninspiring, back-of-the-family-home life.

Vanilla and chocolate espresso gelato helped ease my mood. I licked my spoon and watched the tourists wander through the square, then suddenly rush for cover as a flock of pigeons swooped down. I just covered my gelato and continued eating.

The local pigeons fear me. You don't want to know.

Paula and her husband dashed out to the center of the square, snapped a couple photos of the church, then ducked back under the covered walk to avoid the flapping pigeons. Weren't they scheduled to board a cruise ship? If Von Meiter's people were finished blocking the docks. I glanced up at the sun overhead. It was a nice day for a boat party.

The wine was good. The gelato was excellent. My credit card was scheduled to arrive this afternoon. All in all, a perfect get away. Except for the nagging feeling that my friend had not died of natural causes. But what then, was the cause? Killed for an artifact? That made no sense at all.

Death, at our age, was natural. Death because of Miranda's (and mine for a while) lifestyle was wholly anticipated as if early death was the only possible outcome for a life of enjoyment and fun.

I paid my bill with cash. The lock smith was scheduled for this afternoon, and I would need to sign for my credit card delivery. I would pick up around the apartment. I would say I would wait for Nic, but I learned a long time ago not to EVER wait for Nic. If did my own thing, he would show up when he was ready.

I walked by a suitcase storage store front, Keep Calm and Don't Carry On. Storage was a premium feature on an island. Miranda just crammed everything into the space she had, Max outsourced. It was odd thing to do, why not just get rid of your stuff? Max was great at jettisoning people and items he no longer loved, but perversely, he held onto the oddest things, people as well. Max could name every fabric he worked with. He could reminisce on the Pantone Colors in every swatch. He remembered the color of the year, by year, in order. He collected and saved the remnants of his career and insisted they all be boxed and labeled. He kept all his swatch books, hundreds of them, crowding the shelves in his work room. He gloated over colors and patterns, comparing them to the files in his computer, then one morning, he asked me to move them all.

"Throw them out?"

Max put a hand on his heart. "Oh never, never discard them, they are history. Someday someone will want to re-create a fabric or a moment. These are the only reference."

I pointed to the computer, but he shook his head. "You should know better."

I did. There was still no substitute for the real thing.

The fabric swatch books were large, almost ten by twelve inches and thick, thicker than a dictionary if a dictionary was made of fabric. I hefted one of them and eyed Max.

He considered me and my expression. He was sick, sicker

than he admitted. Pale under what used to be a perpetual Southern tan. Thinner than was fashionable. His skin was bruised and sallow. I could hear him at night, catching his breath.

"They don't need to be in the apartment. But they are important. Put them somewhere safe, don't even tell me."

I shook my head. He was increasingly paranoid, I attributed it to both old age and his illness. But my job was to accommodate him. I spent a great deal of time searching for a space, but finally had a breakthrough—Rachael, who was just opening her gallery. She suggested a company off the island. Use my name, she told me.

Enabled, I loaded up the Mini and drove to Porto Marghera. Most of the business and shipping and industry, blah, blah, blah, is off the island. Like so many tourist towns, the practical is built far away from the charming. As promised, the proprietor at the storage facility knew Rachael and was happy to accommodate me, offering a tiny storage area at a steep discount. It would not last; by the time I was finished moving all Max's stuff, furniture, paintings, an extra chandelier, I had graduated to the largest space the company had. I had the password and the only key. Max insisted I keep the key always, just in case he needed the samples again for reference.

But his designing days were over, he simply didn't have the strength. It was so sad. I felt like I was burying his dream, placing his work in a closed tomb, projects for his after- life. I managed to hold it together dropping off the dozens of books—I made three trips—but I sobbed all the way back to the island.

With a start, I realized I still had the key on my key ring. I had forgotten about it. I paid the bills for the facility, but Max didn't keep the receipts. I supposed he had a point, why would he need them? I made a note on my phone to return to find out who all that stuff now belonged to. Maybe contact Max's lawyers. I hadn't thought about them in, well, three years.

I shook my head. The likely suspects, pretty boys, former models, former lovers, would find the storage unit eventually.

After Dad passed, I dragooned Chris and Matt into helping clear out the garage. They were great workers, especially when I let Matt practice backing up the moving truck (my version of dangerous living). We unearthed lamps with frayed chords, an enormous air compressor with no cord at all. A flip of a sheet revealed boxes packed with yellow National Geographic issues from 1960 forward. Not even Friends of the Library accepts National Geographic collections. We unpacked wedding gifts saved for so long that the china patterns were back in style.

I thought of that garage as I worked through Miranda's extra bedroom/storage room She saved the most remarkable things: sparklers (for a US party), a collection of Spanish fans (I'm sure it was for a flamenco party), candles, extra dishes, a dozen mis-matched wine glasses.

If she hadn't been grateful for each item that brought her joy, I could be grateful on her behalf. Clutching a red fan decorated with black dots, I stood in Miranda's living room. "Thank you for all your help just when I needed it." I said out loud.

"Just when I thought it would kill me to leave Nic, you were there."

"Just when it tore my heart out when Max fell ill and could no longer travel, you supported my move into Max's apartment."

"Just when you needed me, I failed."

Finally, I cried.

CHAPTER TWELVE

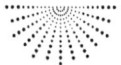

*T*he phone jumped and vibrated as if the caller was already angry. I reached to automatically shut it off, except it could be the embassy announcing a record breaking two hours turn around. I answered it without looking. I should always look.

"You must come home right now!" Tina was past glass shattering and moving in hysteria. I hadn't heard that tone since Chris stuffed three Jelly Bellies up his nose. All licorice, by the way. He had later explained he didn't like licorice and didn't know where else to put them.

"Why do I need to come home right now?" I sniffed and wiped my eyes.

"Matt's been arrested!" I had to pull my phone from my ear.

I sat down on the couch very carefully and glanced at my watch and did the math. First thing in the morning for Tina. Had Matt been hauled off in the early dawn? What on earth does a teen do at dawn to get arrested? Anything. Everything.

"Did he say why he was calling from jail?"

"Something about the whole car being picked up and everyone flung in jail, I can't believe these people."

A text rose to the top of the phone. I hit speaker to listen to Tina's rant on the Sacramento police and their obvious animal proclivities and read the text.

It was Chris, of course it was Chris, he was probably in his room, hiding from his mother, furiously texting his aunt.

Matt riding with friends. Open Containers. I found Nile, need more facts.

Will you be okay? I texted, meaning living for twelve hours without his brother.

I'm a big boy, He texted back.

"And that's why you need come home, I have to go to work this morning, I don't have time for this kind of nonsense. And the cruise is next week. You promised to be back in two days Vic, it's been much longer than that."

"Matthew is sixteen, he can drive Chris to school." I said.

"He will never drive again." Tina's voice was grim. But I've heard it before. She'd recover by this afternoon. Older parents don't have the energy for sustained follow-through, no matter how righteous.

"He will be fine, he's a minor, it won't go on his permanent record."

"Chris is beside himself." She used the cheapest shot she knew. And before today, it always worked. I took a breath and re-read the text from Chris. I'm a big boy.

"I am confident Chris will be fine as well. Do you want to leave Matt in jail for a while? You know, teach him a lesson?"

"Those are terrible places." Tina started in. "Who knows what will happen to my baby in there! Do you know what happens in those jails?"

"Just the Turkish ones." But she was no longer listening.

"Do you have your passport yet?"

"No." What a relief that I did not.

119

"I'll just have to bail him out myself." Tina huffed but with considerably less rancor.

"You are the mother." I pointed out, somewhat unnecessarily.

She hung up.

I texted Chris, Thanks for the intel.

Am working. And that was that. A focused Chris is a happy Chris. I returned a host of calls to get ready for this evening. My entrance to the most exclusive party in town was either going to be magnificent or a complete embarrassing bust. Go big or go home. And since I couldn't go home, I had to go big.

Nic dropped by as I was preparing for the evening. He called before walking through the unlocked door.

"Make yourself at home, No, I have not found the hippo."

"Love you too."

Ideally, I'd have a team—the makeup artist, the stylist, wardrobe. But I had called in enough favors all ready. I did not need to shoot my whole wad of influence on one evening. I could manage on my own.

"The last party I attended alone was Vince's retirement party."

"He's old enough to retire?" Nic called through the bedroom door which was locked since he didn't need to witness how the sausage was made.

I struggled into a couple of Spanx and wiggled into the dress—off shoulder, the décolletage revealing my considerable breasts. It was fabulous, I only hoped I would do it and the designer justice. I slid on low-heeled shoes, the better to avoid pitching into the canal with and emerged just as Nic set down an open bottle of Dolcetto.

"Oh, sweet Aten. You are worthy of the sun god himself." He paused and swallowed.

I tugged at the back strap of the shoe.

He finally found his voice. "Just ask, you'll be fabulous. Who had ever said no to you?"

That gave me pause. Had that been true? "It seems so long ago."

He threw out his hand. "Are you kidding? You used to sweet talk thieves into giving you their stolen statutes and papyrus. You were magnificent!"

"Max said no."

"He was sick, and he loved you." Nic softened his voice and beckoned. I took one step; I was about to be very busy. My phone buzzed vibrating against my breast. I ignored it.

"All we need to do is ask. Where did Miranda buy her statue, what else is out there, and what else does he know?"

"That's more than one question."

"Get him drunk."

I smiled, the answer for every problem. I accepted a glass of wine.

LINING up the photographers was fun. I quickly scoured Instagram to find who was currently in the neighborhood and found five old friends—delighted to hear from you—yes, I'll watch for you. They were a lovely bunch, I loved working as a photographer's assistant, the bright lights, big city, cheap hotels, chased by cops—get off the grass. An indisputably glamorous job.

I needed a good dress, a designer dress. Again, I flipped through my contact list. The old Rolodex that belonged to Max was still in my possession. There wasn't much to do the last few years stuck at home after a 6:00 dinner with the news blaring my parents to sleep. I copied all of Max's contacts into my database. It was a way to connect with my past, to remember what I used to be.

I never thought I would need his list. I never thought I'd use it. I shook my head, scrolling.

"What are you doing?" Nic asked before he showered, changed and disappeared for the rest of the day.

"I need a dress."

"You have a dress." Nic nodded to the bedroom behind me.

I looked up at him. Rumpled, bed hair that revealed how his hair had thinned at the very top of his head. No one over thirty looks good in the morning.

"I need THE dress." I corrected patiently. "You put me in charge of this assignment, let me do my job." Just saying it out loud was a bit of a thrill.

By the time Nic had showered and dressed, I was deep into my phone.

"Text me when you get back from the party."

I nodded, not looking up from my search—what was her name, ah, there she is, and hopefully in.

Nic kissed my cheek and sauntered out.

I watched him leave, knowing that he knew I'd let him back in tonight. No matter the hour. I could get anyone to say yes. My problem was I also couldn't say no.

But, but, but. Where had Miranda picked up stolen blue statures? Did we need to know where? Couldn't I just dump them into a bag, leave it at the Cairo Museum door, ring the bell and run?

It was an appealing idea. Of course, without a passport I couldn't go to Cairo just yet.

Mina Stanos was once great as everyone in the business was once great. Sustainability is the real art behind the artifice. Nothing protects you, not fame, not even fortune. Kate's suicide rocked the industry for at least ten minutes; people wondered if Kate Spade, fabulous, successful, beautiful didn't believe she had it all, what were they all doing? The questioning didn't last. To linger on existential questions of life, matter and meaning in a business that thrived on competition and constant change was to invite crisis.

I shook my head at my own cynicism. I flicked through the Google posts. Mina had fallen on hard times. She had been reduced to churning out facsimiles of designer originals for the ready to wear world. According to one fashion blog, Mina was one runway step away from designing for H &M.

She was here in town, that was the most important detail. I carefully locked the apartment door behind me, as if that stopped anyone, but it might annoy Nic. It would be nice if he had to wait on the chilly damp stairs for me to arrive home.

A valparetto ride and a short walk brought me into the center of a section of town well off the tourist maps. I walked past faded posters announcing the last month's blockage (read, party) to stop the cruise ships from sailing. Rave parties, roof parties, local happenings.

Mina greeted me at the door of an inauspicious warehouse. "As I live and breathe, Victoria Gardner. How is your former boss?"

We kissed three times. "Deb is as famous and fabulous as ever."

"And you, you are going to the Von Meiter party, you are doing well?" She regarded the clothes, the hair, and the makeup with professional interest.

"Just this once, so I want to make it count."

Mina was a tall, gaunt woman in her mid-fifties. Too many Sicilian summers had ravaged her looks. There is a saying – you can't be too thin. She was too thin.

Her atelier was a former warehouse, turned home, gutted again for use as a warehouse. White lines on the brick walls were all that was left of the rooms. The ceiling faded into the shadows. It was cold, the same temperature as outside. This must be brutal in the winters. But maybe she decamped to the south.

Mina leaned against her desk and watched me flip thorough a rack of long gowns. All different, all exquisite. "Whose are these?"

She dismissed the rack. "Mine, but who cares? I haven't been attached to a real label in a thousand years."

I nodded and pulled out a black number, long, with an elegant back kick pleat of sheer organza. I held it against my substantial curves. "Can you let this out?"

She glanced at the dress. "Of course."

"And if you were your own label, what would you call it?"

"Mina. I would have one of those one-word names. Mina. 'Who are you wearing?'" she said with a high mocking voice. "Oh, tonight for the Oscars I'm wearing Mina." She slumped against her worktable and flicked her ash in the general direction of an enormous glass Murano dish in the shape of a clown face.

"It will never happen. Did you say there was an opening at H & M?"

"I was mocking you, don't jump from the window just yet."

We measured. She asked me what the hell had I been doing. Did I know Miranda passed away from a heart attack?

"All that coke, all that booze, all those men." She listed Miranda's transgressions in admiration.

"All that life." I lifted my arms, she pinned and pulled until it all fit my, ahem, substantial form.

"You need jewels, black isn't your color."

"For no one older than thirty." I agreed. "Is George still at Bulgari?"

"Is he?" She rolled her eyes and lit up another cigarette. "Remember that boy he was with? Beautiful, irresponsible, almost got arrested one too many times, with poor George in tow." She blew out a puff of smoke. "That was you, wasn't it?"

"I just posted bail."

She nodded. "The party starts at 10:00. Pick this up at 8:00."

I placed a hand on her shoulder. "It's not the Oscars, but I'll do my best."

She smiled wanly. "Your best was always pretty good."

George did indeed still work at Bulgari. What Mina didn't know was that with some of Max's money, I was able to clear George's record, so he was eligible to work in one of the most iconic shops in the city. George wanted to design as well, but he was so good at sales.

"Oh my, my, Victoria Gardner—you look fabulous!" An older, I hoped wiser, George scooted around a glass counter and pulled me close.

"I thought I'd never see you, after Max." He blinked and trailed off.

There was Max and after Max. Another set of initials. AM.

"I need a favor." I explained the mission and my dress by Mina.

"She just needs a break." I finished my story.

"Don't we all." He was dressed in a beautiful suit, pointed Italian shoes, but his face was still young, boyish and charming. For a moment I couldn't remember if he still preferred boys. Didn't matter

"Can you spare a couple of things for tonight?"

He pulled out the Bulgari iconic serpent necklace. The overlapping snake scales created a sinuous and sexy line around my neck, the brilliant emerald eyes winked, the head almost nestled into my cleavage.

"Maybe a little much?"

He studied the effect. "Maybe not enough."

125

He returned it to the black velvet display form and from under the counter, pulled out a stunning circle of purple, green and red gems.

"The Tradizione. Semi-precious, rubellite, amethyst, and peridot, but it shows well. The cameras love it."

"Instagram will love it."

He clasped it around my neck, and I felt like I had been lit up from inside.

"Yes, yes." I glanced into the mirror and patted it carefully. "This will be perfect."

"You'll need a bracelet for your right hand, so it glitters when you wave to the paparazzi. You have organized the photographers?"

I nodded.

"Try this." He wound a white gold signature serpent loaded with twenty-six carats of pavé diamonds. "Don't remove it until you are back here," he instructed.

"Sleep in it."

"Yes, or don't sleep." He grinned. "Especially with handsome strangers. Where is the event?"

I told him.

"They have their own security. You should be fine. He glanced up at a case. "You have a bag?"

"I'll bring my old Lieber. The watermelon." I had just found it in the back of the closet, with two of Miranda's favorite Chanel clutches. I still love the designer's joke of turning food into art—burgers, popsicles, and the watermelon slice picked out in bright red and green crystals. We did a shoot for one of her rare features in Neiman Marcus's catalogue and I fell in love, which makes sense; the bags are worth as much as a bottle of Screaming Eagle wine. Which is to say, far too much. It was perfect. And my phone just fit.

He nodded. "That should work. You were always good at the unexpected."

The unexpected. I patted the necklace and glanced at my watch. I had an hour to eat and head back to Mina's to pick up the dress.

"I'll have these back Sunday afternoon. As soon as you open."

He pushed a paper across the counter. "Just sign here."

THE PARTY WASN'T the Met bash, but it looked pretty damn impressive. The night was black, the stars picked out like crystals, the waxing moon was just rising, not yet competing with Von Meiter's villa, lit up like a fairy tale castle. I grabbed the hem of my dress and carefully stepped over the sliver of canal to gain the red carpet. Even in low heels, cobblestones are slippery, I was happy for the security of the carpet.

I joined the line of guests clutching their invitations. I was conspicuous by my lack of same, but I took a deep breath and launched my plan.

I eyed the two large security guards flanking the villa entrance sporting doors carved by Bernini. The Von Meiters were an old family.

I fell back so there was no one behind me. I searched for my team. Ah, I paused, smiled and waved, making sure the snake bracelet caught the light. There was Don, his huge white Cannon lens stood out among the more reasonable 80mm lens. He waved and began shooting. He nudged the person next to him who, as soon as he saw me, quickly raised his camera. This wasn't Sports Illustrated, I wasn't a polar bear sinking into the warming sea, but bless his heart, Don was helping me make a scene.

I waved. Alison, another favorite photographer called out, "Vic, Vic! Over here!"

Mark, who mainly shot for *NatGeo*, pretended to compete, "Vic, over here!"

As soon as the other five or six (disappointing, there weren't many more) photographers heard Alison call out, they all focused—literally—on me. I walked slowly and posed every thirty seconds, showing the dress to best advantage, touching the necklace with my right hand so the bracelet would be caught in the limited square format of an Instagram post.

There was a dearth of rings in Miranda's jewelry box, Tiffany had made a through sweep, so I had compensated by wearing a pair of black elbow length gloves. The diamond-encrusted snake stood out like a lighthouse beacon.

I put a hand to my ear. "What? Oh, I'm wearing Mina—an original! MINA. Thank you for asking!"

Alison grinned, and burst off seventeen more shots. Mark kept his camera aimed at me and Don followed me like a compass stuck on North.

The particulars were all embedded in a text I'd sent them an hour ago. Mina's phone and website. The Bulgari store location. We were good on that score. Now the next part.

The guards eyed me as I slowly strolled up to the invitation check. I sucked in my stomach, held my breath and turned once more to wave at the photographers. Another group of guests arrived; their thick white invitations caught the light of the rising moon. This was my first time on the invitee side of the ropes. I longed to be back in the crowd, taking notes, shouting at the talent or the famous, camera lens banging against my legs, jostling for the best spot for Deb. I took a deep breath. The necklace flashed; the snake flashed. I had auburn hair; I wore red lipstick. I could do this.

I smiled at the larger of the two guards. I lifted the watermelon slice as if to produce my invitation. He eyed the snake and pulled back the velvet rope.

I nodded graciously, turned once more, waved and sauntered through.

I was in.

Nic's plan:

A. Find the host

B. Get an update on the black market for stolen artifacts.

C. Escape.

I did not disabuse Nic's helpful itinerary, but a party is not really the time for deep interrogation or deep activities of any kind. Parties are about light chat, compliments, catty comments, who is there and who is conspicuous by their absence. It's all about being seen.

That said, in all fairness, Nic was not a party guy. Drag him to any social occasion and he behaves like the stereotypical professor. He eats far too many hors d'oeuvres and traps hapless guests in lengthy monologues about his work. When we met, I thought it was charming and refreshing. But like most party tricks, it only works once.

I took a glass of champagne from an offered tray and stepped down the stairs into the swirl of people on the ballroom floor. If the redoubtable Beth Ellen could only see me now.

Von Meiter, my host, pushed through the crowd to meet me on the ballroom stairs. I knew of Von Meiter, but since he wasn't a close friend of Max Peters, I did not know the man well. He was in his seventies and still elegant in a classic tuxedo that almost hid his growing belly, which I assume was a product of too much gourmet food and 500-euro bottles of wine. Not a bad way to go. I wished my weight could be attributed to the same level of elegant living rather than one too many nights with my boys Ben & Jerry.

"Ah, you must be the lovely lady who is making such a scene."

I raised an eyebrow and held out my hand. He regarded the bracelet, kissed my glove and gestured for me to take his arm.

There are three kinds of parties: Polite, exciting and dangerous. Vince's retirement party was polite, Miranda's parties were dangerous, this one was exciting. My fingers tingled; my breath shortened. Depending on muscle memory, I leaned into my host and greeted the other guests as if we were old friends, because that's what you do. If you are here, you are an old friend of someone, right?

I hugged and air kissed. I even recognized some of the guests I hugged and kissed. Most were strangers, but at a party like this, we were all close friends, rivals, enemies, all converging for a good time.

After enough champagne and wine, the hugs evolved into kisses. I kissed strange men and women on the lips. I held out my snake-wrapped hand for more kisses and gracious gestures. I was warm, happy moving through the crowd, being part of the action, part of the scene. I had forgotten why I was there.

"Let's sit." After a couple hours, Von Meiter found me again and led me to a table tucked into an alcove that was built to showcase a large statue. A waiter dutifully followed and Von Meiter ordered more champagne.

"So, mystery woman."

"Victoria."

He regarded me under hooded eyes. He reached into his jacket and pulled out a cigarette case. Just the act of smoking inside a building was exotic. I felt terribly bad, very un PC.

He tapped the cigarette on the closed case then pointed it at me.

"Max Peters!"

I nodded. He leaned back, pleased he had solved the mystery.

"He was magnificent. Bold to the last." Von Meiter smiled and lit his cigarette. "I hear you were good to him."

"I tried to be."

"The estate is still tied up. Can't find the right heirs, not that the boys aren't ready to volunteer."

"That doesn't surprise me."

"Nor I. You are not here for Max, so what can I do for you?"

I sipped my champagne and regarded him. The room was packed, the noise level high enough to thwart conversation. I could see people resorting to simple gestures, many of them lewd.

I fished out the photo of our hippo from the crystal-studded watermelon and slid it onto the tiny table.

He recoiled as if it was a real snake.

"I don't know anything about that."

Really? I lifted my eyebrows.

He shook his head and took a deep drag of his cigarette. A waiter appeared carrying an amber-colored ashtray.

"Mafia?" I guessed. What else could make him pale, in his own house, where he could smoke without repercussions?

"Maybe worse." He knocked a tiny bit of ash into the tray.

I leaned back in the chair and tried to look comfortable and immovable. I crossed my legs. He took two more drags and studied me.

"I wouldn't talk to anyone about this."

I bounced my foot. "I'm not talking, I'm just asking."

He glanced at the photo. The noise of the party seemed to recede. Smoke from his cigarette obscured his face. I waited.

"Only because of Max." He ground the half-smoked cigarette into the dish.

"Of course."

He reached inside his suit pocket for a pen. "There is a shop. Ask to see their recent stuff."

He scrawled an address on a monogramed cocktail napkin. "Don't use my name."

I slipped both the photo and the napkin back into the watermelon. "If it's not Mafia, then who?"

He downed his glass and gestured for more. Three women spotted him and started to approach.

"Don't know. They aren't particularly organized. And not in a disorganized, organized way, if you know what I mean. The stuff comes in, one of the Stans, but it's all sold before the notification of stolen artifacts, photos, descriptions come out. Some people are caught, many don't even know what they have. Much of the recovery is dismissed as just another tourist duped. But recently."

The girls came close and pulled around him like a grand flowing cape. I smiled. A perk of power, the girls, the champagne, the friends for sale.

The blonde, and yes, one blonde, one brunette and one red head (I too used to curate crowd scenes) whispered in his ear. But his gaze was trained on me.

"Recently?" I caught the blonde's eye and smiled, a gesture she was unprepared for. I longed to tell her, enjoy! The window of beauty and opportunity is a narrow one; in three years, four if you take care of yourself, it will slam shut, leaving you out in the cold. It took a lot of will power to resist speaking the truth.

The girls never believe me anyway.

He fiddled with his champagne and shrugged the girl away. She stepped back a few inches.

"People have died."

"Which people?"

He leaned back. "People, accidents in Albania, accidents in Greece, accidents in Luxor."

I nodded. Accidents in Venice, but I didn't say it out loud. Was he involved?

"How?"

"No pattern. Victoria." He learned forward and stroked

the coiled scales of the bracelet. "Be careful. If this was a concerted effort, we would know the players, we'd know who to avoid, but since Arab Spring, it's hard to figure out the bad from the merely awkwardly opportunistic."

I finished my champagne and stood, the girls moved in, he followed me with his eyes.

Mission accomplished, for what it was worth, nothing like vague threats of danger to finish off a girl's evening. I made my way through the crowd heading to the exit, the same doors I entered.

I did not get very far.

A gentleman caught my hand and insisted on a dance. From him I was passed along to another man who, I admit, danced divinely. From there, I swooped into another man's arms. Like a Jane Austen novel, I moved through the party one dance partner after the next. The men held me firmly, they moved me around the crowded floor, it was almost like a Cinderella dream—the dress on loan, the jewels waiting to be returned. I allowed the gaiety, the lights, the flashes of jewelry to transport me as only a real ball can.

I didn't make it out of the building until the small hours of the morning.

Just as a good Venetian should.

CHAPTER THIRTEEN

*R*ather than take a bus, which were far and few between at this hour, I strolled along the empty streets in a happy daze cutting through St.. Mark's Square that tonight was clear, dry, and empty. The glow of the Basilica reflected off the treacherously smooth and uneven cobblestones.

Like magic.

I had lived so carefully for so many years. I didn't realize how much I missed the fun of wild improvident behavior. Was there an age limit on adventure? I took in the square, the silence and felt, at home. I also glanced around for unwelcome company. No movement, but I didn't linger for long.

I didn't want to be careful. But I did keep an eye out.

The watermelon vibrated. Since I had nothing to steal, I paused under the archway lining the square and glanced at my phone, hoping it was Nic, cold, uncomfortable Nic.

It was Vince, warm, comfortable Vince. Remember they had tickets for Florida and then they were due to catch a ship in a week. When are you coming back?

I dropped the phone into the bag without responding. Soon.

Cinderella had magic, I had footwork. All my finery needed to be returned.

I woke up and like teens all over the world, reached for my phone. I scrolled through my Instagram account. Me, me, me. Mina's dress was a hit. Excellent.

When I showed up at Mina's shop an hour later, she barely acknowledged me. Earbuds in place, she spoke in rapid Italian to the unseen woman on the other end. All I understood was yes, yes, and of course we can.

She waved to me and rewarded me with a broad smile, the expression lighting her eyes and erasing seven years from her face.

"Yes, yes, I still design. For Mardi Gras? Of course, we can create something original."

I carefully placed the dress on the counter. She mouthed, "thank you." I mouthed, "ciao." The exchange was finished. I hoped she'd be on the phone all day scheduling new clients.

Ironically, as I strolled through the pre-cruise streets, empty at 11:00 A.M., I was not accosted. Sunday morning quiet. This would have been the time. No one around, easy to run. However, I am a quick learner. I kept my bright green bag close and tried not to look like a woman draped in tens of thousands of euros. Funny, I didn't feel so cautious last night. I blame the champagne.

As promised, I had removed neither the necklace nor the bracelet. My naked body draped with little more than jeweled serpent and a loaded necklace looked fairly incongruous during my shower this morning, but I was taking no chances. I had wrapped a scarf over the necklace and tucked the bracelet under my sweater sleeve. If someone wanted the bag, they could take the bag.

No one took the bag.

After a stop for a shot of espresso, I wandered towards the jewelry shop, scheduled to open at noon. I planned to wait; I did not want the necklace longer than necessary. Plus, Von Meiter's warning had unnerved me. And to make it more unnerving, Nic had not returned last night.

I sipped my coffee and recalled that not showing up was one of Nic's things. He had a healthy disregard for time, his and anyone else's. He particularly disregarded my time, which I interpreted as complete disregard for me. The caffeine zinged through me and gave me courage. I remembered that I no longer needed to care.

As I walked into Bulgari, my phone buzzed. George nodded and we met at the counter displaying Bulgari's iconic snake designs. George whispered that his manager had had a bad night with his mistress and, to make sure no one else was happy, showed up at the store bright and early.

"Turn, turn," he said through a smile. "Look at that lovely necklace in the case."

In a stronger voice. "Madam, yes, we have the Zero rings right over here."

I obediently bent my head as if to admire the pretty rose-gold stacked rings while George deftly reached under the scarf and released the necklace. I felt naked without its weight. He rounded the same glass case and stood opposite me. He held up the necklace as if he had just removed it from the case. "It is amazing, no?"

"And can I show you the bracelets?" He followed up.

I touched the necklace one more time and he slid it back under the counter, turning the drawer lock with a decisive click.

"I would love to see the bracelets." I raised my voice, hoping I sounded like a matron of means.

We moved to that case. Serpents, diamond-lined chains, blue, gold, red, diamonds glittered under the strategically placed lights. He opened and closed the case keeping his eyes on me, as well as over my shoulder at his boss.

I lifted my arm and the snake emerged from under my sweater sleeve. "This is divine."

"It looks fabulous on you," he remarked.

"Oh, sure, brings out my eyes." I smiled, he smiled.

"Ah, but not today I'm afraid, I have lunch plans and I'm already late." I slipped off the bracelet and with a flourish handed it back to George. "You always have such beautiful things. You make a woman feel like a princess." He nodded. I could only hope the shop purportedly selling stolen artifacts would be this accommodating.

I suspected not.

I left, studying the napkin Von Meiter gave me and comparing it to the map on the phone. A message—Passport ready Monday.

Another message from Tina, well, at least she texted instead of calling. When are you coming home?

Passport delayed. I texted back. Wednesday at the earliest.

Cruise is Friday—with a frowny face.

Sorry. I hesitated, then added my own frowny face.

The little shop was only a block off the square. Nothing like hiding in plain sight. If you were a tourist, carrying your Odyssey, Holland America, Princess Cruise complimentary shopping bag, and you loaded it up with bargains that included stolen artifacts, how difficult would it be to track you once you landed in Croatia or Greece or what had Von Meiter said? Albania? Or one of the Stans.

Difficult. Those cruise ships were the size of a medieval city, how would even a well-organized group steal the artifacts back out of a random state room? Either they wouldn't or I do not possess a very adept criminal mind.

I entered the store, unlike the shops turned fast food outlets, this one looked like it was once a McDonalds now turned into a yard sale with shelves. A woman in her late twenties greeted me from behind the bulk of an old-fashioned cash register.

I smiled and approached the counter. To the right of the huge cash register was a woven basket filled with blue faience pieces; they could be plastic, they could be the real deal. How obvious would it be if I snatched them all up and poured them into my purse?

Obvious.

There was something familiar about the woman. Her hair looked hand cut and was streaked with faded pink highlights. Poor thing, her skin was pocked and rough, well covered in foundation a shade too light. She slouched against the counter as if exhausted. Too many wild nights. Like I could criticize.

I reluctantly left the basket alone, nodded to her and purposefully wandered through the shelves. I didn't want to seem to anxious or focused on that basket of possibly stolen goods. The shelves were dusty and crowded with junk. This was exactly the kind of store Miranda loved best. You could pay pennies for something precious; you could overpay for something worthless. It was gambling, thrilling. The chase and the hunt all in one.

I touched a dusty Murano glass vase. To even find the right kind of bargain you'd need an eye, education and connections, an interesting collection of disparate skills. I had perused the UNESCO Cultural Objects at Risk before I left the apartment. The range of items was remarkable and depressing. So many beautiful culturally important objects were sifted out of the sand and spirited out of the country. Faience, small ceramic jars, gold coins, gold necklaces impossibly elaborate, like what Schliemann discovered in what he decided was Troy and subsequently loaded onto his wife. This is how good it was in the nineteenth century—Schliemann actually took a photograph of his wife, wearing irre-placeable, ancient jewelry before she walked out of Turkey wearing it all. And no one stopped her. The necklace and headpiece were never recovered. Now there's an interesting plot. I ran my fingers, still perfectly tipped in those bright red gels, through a dish of beads and chains. No Trojan treasure here.

I sucked in a breath and examined a small chunk of plaster. But what if I did find something amazing?

I knew quality. I knew originals from copies. I didn't realize how much I missed my old life, a life that I had curated as carefully as Von Meiter curated his beautiful girls.

I earned my degree at FIDM in San Francisco because, in my parents' eyes, San Francisco was not as dangerous as New York City. And in the late '70s, they had a point. But to their consternation I fell in love with Manhattan anyway. And there is where I plied my trade, briefly as a model, longer as an assistant and stylist. Was the pay good? That was always the Vince/Vance question. What are you paid? Where is your 401K? Retirement? Life Insurance?

Where indeed. At the time the pay was secondary to the adventure.

I touched the glass objects—the cheap ashtrays shaped into awkward gondolas, bowls of grimy Murano glass-candy.

I trailed past plaster casts of Anubis, Isis, and Tut. A whole shelf of Tut. Popular guy. I tried to linger long enough to make returning to the basket a final, last compromise. Trying to look disappointed, I returned to the basket. I needed them all, but what would that look like?

I didn't care what it looked like.

"I love these!" Using my index finger, I stirred the blue statues, some were a bit heavier than others, were the plastic ones more solid? They looked newer and, of course, in better shape. The real ushabtis were faded, cracked and lighter.

"I love that these look used." I commented.

"Yes," The girl stared at my bag, then stared at me. "We just received this collection. The legend is that the Egyptians buried these little figures in their tombs to work for them in the afterlife."

I shifted under her gaze. Finally, after a few awkward seconds passed, she spoke.

"You're not Miranda."

"No." I met her eyes and started. "Cindy!"

For the first time since I entered the store, she offered a genuine smile. "Vic." The last time we spoke, she was dressed in full Goth—black lipstick, black hair and nowhere to go— and I mean that literally. Miranda had kicked her out in favor of her returned lover. Me.

I felt bad of course, Cindy wasn't so bad, profligate, and spendthrift with Miranda's money, I didn't feel bad about ending all that. But out of guilt I had bought her a ticket out of Venice so she could start over somewhere else. Like Poland, I'm not stupid.

And now here she was, looking a little worse for the wear. Gone was the thick black eye liner, the pale powder, the thick platform boots all the better to stomp you with. She was dressed in a flattering sheath printed with giraffes, a thing two spring seasons ago. On her, the tiny print looked fresh and appropriate. If it wasn't for her skin and the haunted look in her eyes, I would have said the transformation was a miracle.

She in turn stared at me. Obviously, my confinement with my parents had not improved my looks.

I held out my hand, the purse dangled from my arm. "I'm surprised to see you still in Venice."

"I left, just as you told me."

I nodded. "I thought you were in Warsaw."

"I was, it was amazing, and I met all sorts of interesting

people! They gave me a chance to work back here, and here I am back!" She opened her arms to indicate the store.

"How long have you been working here?"

"Just six months." She nodded. "Pays pretty good for retail. You like those?"

I continued to stir the tiny blue statues. I pulled out the dozen or so that looked more or less authentic.

"Miranda took the whole basket." Cindy commented as I laid out my little workers for the next life. Miranda always took the whole basket.

"It must have been strange to see her." I ventured.

She bit her lip. "Oh, not so much. She picked up a couple things, they weren't valuable or anything. We talked about old times. She has a great place here."

"She did." Had Miranda improvidently invited Cindy for a re-acquainting drink? Had Cindy been invited to the Walk Like an Egyptian party? I was about to comment about Miranda's death, but changed my mind.

"You've been away." Cindy took her time and wrapped each little statue in tissue paper. I wanted to grab them and just stuff them into my purse, but I kept still.

"She looked good." She dipped her head. "You too."

I grinned. "That was the most insincere compliment I've ever received." Except for my sister-in-law telling me I was good at caring for people. That still stood as most self-serving compliment on record.

"I hear you took care of Max."

"You heard right."

She took a breath. "I'm sorry he's gone."

"He was a good man and took care of a lot of people."

She frowned, but I distracted her with a twenty-euro note.

She nodded and took the cash while I managed to stuff the little guys into the Max Peters, wrapping and all.

I touched her hand. "It's good to see you doing so well." Again, instead of saying I'm so sorry about Miranda, I held my tongue.

"Bunch of great connections and the money is pretty great. I'm saving for my own shop." Her litany had a rote quality, but I was too much in a hurry to pay much attention.

"That's wonderful." I bade her goodbye, happy that one of Miranda's rejected girls ended up at least better than she began, no matter what must have happened in the interim. When Cindy landed with Miranda, she had practically been run out of New York, with those "you'll never work in this town again" kind of threats. I was glad she found something because even as I loaded her up on a train headed to the airport, I was not confident Cindy would thrive in the wild.

Once in my possession, I really didn't know what do with my find. Return them? Add them to the collection in the hotel hold?

Three young men sped across the plaza and brushed by me, almost knocking the purse from my arm. I turned, but they disappeared around the corner.

Or show them to Nic and watch the expression on his face. Yes, that sounded more interesting.

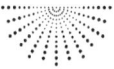

CHAPTER FOURTEEN

*N*ic sat on the steps leading to Miranda's apartment. He looked a little damp, as well as appropriately pale and dejected. I smiled and stood in the door savoring the moment.

"You changed the locks." He accused, but there was no bite in his voice. "Again."

"This morning. There is still art in there, and my stuff, sometimes me. I changed the locks."

He nodded.

"And where were you last night?' Okay, I couldn't resist, and it was a very, very old conversation. He will say, I was out. I will ask where and he won't tell me because I should trust him.

"Out."

"Out where?" I swept by him, key in hand.

"Out, jeez, don't tell me you still haven't learned to trust."

When I first met Nic, I was dazzled. My very own Indiana Jones. But unlike Jones, Nic didn't often have a whole group of close compatriots to help him. He worked alone, hiring the locals when he needed more digging, laying them off when the work slowed. He spent most of his grant money on permits and bribes. Mostly bribes. As I said, he was the poster child for hope over experience.

And me? I had no more hope. I had crappy experiences. I poured Nic more espresso.

"I'm working on a new project." He hunched over his cup and stirred in too much sugar, it gritted on the bottom of the cup like sand.

I shuddered at the sound.

He took a breath as if anticipating my cynical response. I wasn't cynical, but after about six months in the field, and numerous conversations with his peers, I realized that as romantic and handsome and convincing as Nic was, he wasn't very astute at picking the right digs or the right time. He was tenacious, he was determined and in his own fashion, he was loyal. But not necessarily successful. Took me a while to figure it out, and then another year to realize I needed to cut my losses. Hope is most certainly the thing with feathers. I glanced at my watch, 1:00 P.M., just in time for wine. I poured a glass and joined him at the miniature café table.

He slid his coffee saucer back and forth on the table surface. "Okay, you dragged it out of me. I'm working with a corporation, can't tell you who. They are building a discovery park, like those dinosaur digs in Wyoming where you can unearth your own dinosaur."

"And you are building one with an archeology theme." I sipped my wine, I had nowhere to go, no place to be. The realtor, Maria, may or may not stop by with clients. I glanced around the apartment with relief, it was undisturbed. Gotta love locked doors.

He leaned in, he had aged, we both had. But those eyes, I couldn't look away. "This will be a boon to the area. Egypt needs more tourists, especially in Luxor, a lot more. I can help create a park, a draw, get people excited and passionate about archeology again."

He was warming up, just as he did about ten minutes into a university lecture.

As he explained, I just listened. I had no doubt that people would pay good money for the privilege to sift sand under the hot Egyptian sun, it would be authentic, it would be an experience. And lucrative. The gift store, likely featuring tees printed with sayings like "I dig the Nile" and other erudite sentiments would bring in hard cash. The possibility for exploitation would be endless. I needed to support him and this new dream.

"A little off mission don't you think?"

"My contract with the university wasn't renewed." He knocked back the coffee and set it down, hard. The cup rattled in the saucer.

"I'm sorry." I put my hand on his. Both of ours were rough from work.

"Just trying to keep body and soul together."

I smiled, he loved that phrase, it called to mind canopic jars where body parts were divided and stored, ready for reunification. I thought of the heart weighed and judged, the whole of the spirit traveling over the Nile by boat, and if all went well, reuniting with the body in the afterlife: body and soul. But this was maudlin, he was maudlin. To cheer him up, I retrieved my purse and upended it so the wrapped ushabtis tumbled onto the table.

He blinked. "You found the pick-up point?"

"Of course." I appreciated seeing Cindy looking so good and so confident. Yet there was something that nagged.

"Bought the lot for twenty euros."

"I'd say you got a hell of a bargain." He held up a tiny statue to the window and squinted. "Some of these are the real thing."

"I thought so." And selling the real thing for only twenty euros was not good business. Unless you knew where they went. Transporting them safely out of one country to a country with more cooperative officials would be worth the twenty euros.

He picked up a tiny statue and studied it then set it aside. "Why didn't you wait for me?"

I studied the real statue. What was lucrative? Priceless? Dangerous?

"Tired of waiting." As I said it, I realized it was true. I was tired of waiting.

"You," Sirens interrupted him.

I rose to the window. Speed boats roared down the canal spraying high plums in their wake. Black smoke billowed from a spot just off the square. There were of course, many shops, many apartments, many buildings surrounding the square. It wasn't necessarily that specific shop. I glanced down at my collection, illegal certainly, but worth killing for? Worth destroying for?

I picked up my purse and tossed my phone into its now commodious interior. "We have to go."

I grew up with wildfires. Roaring fires consuming enormous, unfathomable swaths of forest and fields, snaking down hills in bright uneven lines that glowed in the night. Smoke pouring over unaffected counties delivering heavy particulate matter. I was used to a vengeful Mother Nature who shared the pain across as many counties as she could.

Contained in a tiny stone medieval town, fire is something else. The key is to keep the rest of the town from crumbling under the flames or collapsing into the canal. By time we arrived on the scene, firefighters had abandoned the tiny store to its fate and were busy spraying and choking the fire around it. Quick containment is everything.

The street was packed with shop keepers and residents all

anxiously watching the progress. The store itself was already a charred shell, the only things left were the black struts of the second and third floor. Most of the stone facade streaked with smoke and dripping with canal water.

"I can't believe it!" The voice was hysterical, loud, attention grabbing, and familiar.

I turned and watched Cindy push her way to the front of the crowd.

"No!" She cried and fell into a heap on the cobblestones. Ah, that's right. I remembered now. Here is what will happen next: a sympathetic passerby, or better, someone Cindy had met last night at a rave, appears. Cindy marvels at the total coincidence and they in turn make sympathetic noises, pick her up and take her home by way of a nice restaurant and the Gucci outlet.

I'd witnessed her system more than once. It worked well during shows when there were plenty of young men at loose ends, happy to save a troubled and very pretty girl. I was disappointed that by now, she hadn't come up with a better scheme.

No one picked her up.

My phone buzzed. Tiffany demanded to know where her paintings were. I had to get to her hotel and ship them. Right now!

turned the phone off. One drama queen at a time.

Cindy glanced up from under her eyelashes. But the members of the crowd simply gave her a few more feet of space. No takers. After a minute or two she stood, brushed herself off and ran her hands through her hair. She was still wild-eyed. That much appeared authentic. I moved towards her.

"It's all my fault, it's all my fault." She looked around, but apparently did not see who she expected to see.

"Stop saying that." I hissed. The owner of the shop, a stout man with an impressive mustache waved his arms and rolled his eyes. I couldn't make out what he was telling the police, but the journalists just behind the yellow caution tape were taking copious notes.

I dragged Cindy into a nearby café while she hiccupped and tried to catch her breath.

"I didn't talk, I said nothing, right? You were there, did you hear me say anything about anything?"

"Who did you not talk to?" Von Meiter ruled out the Mob, which was comforting. I eyed the charred remains of the shop. Not comforting enough.

I positioned her with her back to the wide café window so I could keep an eye on the street. Nic had jumped into the fray and was speaking very loud, very bad Italian drowning out the owner as well as the police.

"No, no, just..." She wiped her eyes with the back of her hand. I pulled out a tissue and handed it over.

"You always had all the right things." She blew her nose and wadded the tissue into the palm of her hand.

"What is your fault?" I kept one eye on Cindy and the other on the store owner. Nic threw up his hands and turned away from the scene as if abandoning the whole issue.

"Just a minute." I waved to a waiter and ordered three glasses of house red. I exited the café to retrieve the third member of our jolly party. Something else Californians know, when surrounded by devastation: share your wine.

The store owner stroked his mustache and gestured broadly for the benefit of the journalists. Journalist. There was only one left at this point, a young woman who, I'm sure, was hoping for an exclusive. She'd have to wait a little longer.

I swooped in and took the man by the arm. "It's all right, let's have a drink."

He brightened at the invitation and willingly followed me

into the café. After seeing Cindy, he fell on her with loud cries and kisses.

"But you should not be here. You were picking up!" He finished, anger replacing his initial relief.

"I missed the boat, I couldn't make it through the turnstiles, they were checking boarding passes."

I regarded her for a minute, but she revealed no more. I pushed a glass of red wine to the owner. "Your whole shop," I said sympathetically.

He nodded miserably and drained his glass. I gestured to the waiter for another.

I cupped my hand in my chin. "Why do you think this happened?"

Cindy stiffened. He muttered in Italian. Something about dealing with the devil. I did not let on I knew his native language. Partially because I didn't want to try to sort out what happened under a barrage of accented Italian, and partially because it's handy to not let on you understand even half the words a man mutters under his breath.

"I don't know." He said in English. "You," he turned to Cindy. "You know them, why aren't you on the boat?"

"I told you, I couldn't get on!" The two squared off against each other like a couple arguing minutes before their fiftieth wedding anniversary party.

As precious as that was, I needed to move it along.

"You had such an interesting and eclectic inventory. How will you replace it?" I leaned in and tried to catch his eye, but he wouldn't meet my gaze. He instead stared into his wine glass, then deliberately picked it up and drained it again. I raised my hand for another glass.

The wine was quickly delivered.

He picked up the full glass and finally looked at me. "Why?"

"I'm interested. I'm looking for a hippo like this." I pushed the photo of William the Met hippo across the table. He glanced at it but shook his head. Cindy turned away. She nervously fingered the stem of her glass.

"Aren't we all?" Cindy said under her breath, in English by the way.

The owner leaned back in his chair, wine glass in hand. He watched the action outside the window. The young journalist scouring for quotes encountered Nic who held her enthralled as he happily lectured to a new audience.

"Is this something you can get for me?" I tapped the photo.

He shrugged and squinted at the wine as if it was the most interesting item at the table. He muttered something in Italian.

"You have a guy?" That was the loose translation.

He nodded unsurprised thatI understood.

"You have a guy where?" I pressed.

"Albania. Butrint." Cindy admitted. She set her own empty glass on the table and looked expectantly at me, but I wasn't interested in plying her with wine.

I nodded and pulled the photograph back. I had never been to Albania; it wasn't exactly a fashion shoot destination. Although I supposed you can find anything interesting to photograph in any country. The ruins of Butrint were, as far as I knew, the one single tourist attraction on the Albanian coast.

Didn't have a boarding pass. I studied Cindy who, with no more wine coming, was now holding the store owner's hand. I cocked my head. Did she pose as a tourist to shuffle the merchandise though by boat or small cruise ship? I was pretty sure there were no customs at every port, that wouldn't be sustainable. Did she actually catch a ride on one of the ships? That took quite a bit of nerve. I was impressed despite myself.

I planned on quizzing her later, but there was no need, she was suddenly willing to talk. I don't think it was because she wanted to help me. But she seemed fond enough of the little owner.

"It's my fault. I said it would be a great way to make money. Just pick up some bags of merchandise from Albania, the ships just do the one stop and take the bus back to Venice.

She meant she took the bus, not the ships. "That's a long bus ride."

She grimaced but said nothing more.

"How can I find your contact?" I just plunged ahead. The police were clearing out, the fire had been battered into an ashy mess. The young journalist's attention was flagging even though Nic's enthusiasm was clearly not. He gestured broadly as if to encompass the whole of the Adriatic history lecture. I glanced at my watch; the poor thing had twenty minutes to go before Nic would be willing to wrap up, ending with a summary and quiz.

Cindy shook her head, tight lipped. But the man who just lost everything was suddenly not so circumspect.

"Odyssey Cruise bag, this week only."

"I don't speak Albanian."

He sighed and in English, "No one does."

I left them with a band new bottle of wine. I approached the waiter to pay the bill, but before he could pull out the credit card machine, the manager stopped us. He ceremoniously returned my card. "No, no pay. We pay for his wine."

I touched his shoulder. "Thank you."

The journalist had made her escape, not waiting around for the pop quiz. Nic was finally glancing around, hopefully wondering where I was, but I wouldn't bet on it. I quickly looked at my phone: all quiet on the Northern California

Front. I scrolled through my contacts, there was the shop name and map. I deleted the contact and smiled at Nic.

Cindy emerged with the owner who held the bottle of wine close to his chest. She kissed his cheek before approaching Nic and me.

"You don't need to get all involved. It's no big deal. They were just mad that we shortchanged them, we didn't have any more hippos."

"None were found." Nic commented.

She looked at him, surprised. "Found?"

CHAPTER FIFTEEN

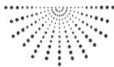

*T*iffany texted, let the realtor in.

In a couple minutes, I texted back.

Passport is early, open from 2:00 to 3:00 PM

She's at the door, let her in now, Tiffany texted.

Nic had pulled ahead of me striding past crowds, swinging his arms to give him more space in the crowd. I followed clutching my pinging phone.

There is a reason why middle-aged people are always looking at their phone, and it's not because we are playing Candy Crush, although that is a good guess. The demands from every generation are funneled into a single device. Older parents need immediate answers, younger children need immediate reactions. Situations that require management and wisdom, arguments that require a referee, all jamming into the phone nagging and cajoling and not taking turns. If Steve Jobs weren't already dead, he should be shot.

Just one more minute, tell her to wait, I texted. I'm on my way. Nic was too far for me to call out. I gave up and veered to the embassy. A woman without a man may be like a fish without a bicycle but a woman without a passport is a beached whale not even Greenpeace can save.

The embassy men were delighted to see me and handed over the passport with a flourish and a number of comments on my improved photograph. I nodded and thanked them, saying no, it's not necessary to show everyone in the office my photo, thank you.

It took me five minutes to get the passport into my hands. My phone pinged and buzzed in my purse like one of Miranda's toys. Set on high.

Passport in hand I hurried to the apartment.

Nic was not waiting on the lower steps, he was up on the landing chatting away with, I assumed, the realtor in question. I hesitated. Should I let the woman in or text Tiffany that I was here and about to let the realtor in?

I just climbed the stairs, key in hand.

A petite bird-like woman stood comfortably on the narrow landing. Nic hovered over her. Unlike the tone of Tiffany's text, the realtor smiled calmly and greeted me.

"I'm Maria. You must be Vic. I already met Nic here." She wore a bright pink knitted Chanel, eschewing the long pearls for a chain made of inch-thick gold links. She wore enough pink and gold to illuminate the top of the dark dank stairs.

"A pleasure to meet you." I reached around the woman and fitted my key in the door and swung it in.

Maria stepped right after me, Nic following.

Maria glanced around, hands on her hips. "I just can't believe she is gone."

"Did the girls contact you directly?"

"Yes, I was in Miranda's address book. Thank God." She wasted no time. She marched around the tiny place making notes on her phone. As I looked at the apartment through her eyes, I reluctantly compared it to Max's place, something I avoided doing while I lived with Miranda because I never thought it was fair. Max lived on the ground or rather canal level. It was a godsend when he was finally reduced to a wheelchair. I could still take him out, rolling him straight onto a waiting boat. Boat rides were his favorite outing. Bouncing over cobblestones in a wheelchair was not comfortable, Max insisted that just the one street trip loosened every tooth filling he had. During the last few months, I hired a speed boat to take Max around the lagoon at full speed.

"This will work." Maria glanced out at the canal view beyond the somewhat dirty windows. Max hired a cleaning service to come armed every month to keep his floor-to-ceiling windows facing the patio perfectly clear.

"How did you know Miranda?" I pulled myself out of the Max memories and tried to be at least a little more responsive.

She stopped taking notes and waved her arm in the general direction of the eat-in kitchen that doubled as the dining room. "Everyone knew Miranda."

I glanced at the bare space. It seemed lonely. It needed the dining table pulled out to its maximum size and set in the middle of the room. It needed a bright tablecloth, colorful centerpieces, ignited sparklers and a crush of too many interesting people waving full wine glasses, competing to be clever, yelling to be heard.

"She was good at parties," I offered.

"Ah, yes. I was at the last one, you know?" The woman regarded the scene of the crime with regret. "It was Egyptian, she played that old song, you know the one?" She made a motion like the flat hieroglyphs everyone misinterprets.

"Walk Like an Egyptian?"

"That is the one!"

"So much good wine, did the Egyptians drink wine?"

I nodded.

"We all got those little plastic statues as favors. It was quite fun."

I stared at her as if she was a winning bingo card. Fun plastic statues. Miranda probably knew something of Egyptian artifacts; she couldn't live with me post-Nicholas and not pick up something. Apparently, all she learned from me was that small blue statues made clever party favors. All the nice-looking statues made it to the table; the older ones, the ones that didn't look quite as nice or as blue, those were dumped into Miranda's drawer. Party favors.

Parties were not supposed to kill you. Well, maybe a really good party.

"I'm living here for now," I said.

She sighed. "That's all right, living here is probably the best thing. You can let clients in, right? But no more parties, okay? We want to keep the place clean. I have a couple already interested."

She made a couple more notes. "You moved some of the paintings."

"I took them to the King Tide Gallery."

"Good." She hesitated. "Maybe move out a few more? Keep that larger one, keep that set of four. And the bedroom…" She walked into the bedroom and regarded the enormous Nevelson hovering over the bed like the Borg cube.

"It's a little intimidating," I admitted.

"It wasn't here when you lived here."

I was taken aback. "No, how did you know that?"

"Miranda never stopped talking about you." Maria smiled and waved goodbye as she left the apartment.

I looked at the intimidating art, black, spiky.

"I never stopped thinking of her either."

· · ·

"WATER, WATER EVERYWHERE," Nic mumbled. He had lined up the statues I had just purchased on the tiny café table. The sun slanted through the windows highlighting dust motes. Each statue was about three inches high, three were intricately carved with the symbols of the servant's job—wheat thresher, builder, scribe. The other two were little more than an outline of a figure, made in haste or mass produced. The fakes looked better, plastic injection molding. Brighter colors.

Nic rejected those and lined up the five authentic statutes.

"Where did they originate?" I asked.

"That is the question." He stroked his chin. "I would ask the question, the Cairo Museum will ask the questions, even the Getty will ask the question." He smiled, "Maybe especially the Getty."

In their early years as a flush new museum, the Getty acquisition team had made, as Nic put it, a couple of errors in provenance. The team spent obscene amounts of money acquiring anything and everything Hellenic, sure of their own expertise, not asking many questions. Some of the curators were legitimately fooled, some curators were fooled because they so badly wanted the beautiful Greek statues to be genuine. One curator walked away with a fortune and one was indicted for fraud. It had been rather ugly, but fortunately in LA, memories were short.

"My nice shop owner mentioned he had a contact in Albania."

"They aren't from Albania."

"You think?" I needed more wine.

Ancient Egyptians didn't bury their dead anywhere but Egypt. Egyptians conquered but did not colonize, which is why we all don't walk like Egyptians. If you aren't buried in Egypt, you won't be able to enter the afterlife; you need the

Nile, you need the West Bank. Egyptian artifacts came exclusively from Egypt.

I had a new passport with many, many blank pages.

"We could follow the trail to Albania."

"Or just return to the source," he finished. He was clearly unhappy about it.

"Don't you want to know who is stealing artifacts and smuggling them out of the country?"

"They are just a few statues." He gestured to the figures. Just statues. Just workers to be buried with their masters.

"Which means there's more," I quoted him.

He closed his eyes. "I'll take care of it. You stay here and deal with." He waved at the paintings. "All of this."

Egypt is larger than it looks on a map. I hadn't spent two years with Nic out in that desert not to understand that. I needed more information than just It came from Egypt. Where? What dig? Someone had found a burial site, one that likely produced more than just these tiny statues. The more ushabtis you had, the wealthier you were. That's a pretty easy equation. I wanted to know. I wanted to know why Miranda had been sacrificed, why Sig. Esposito had to lose his tiny shop filled with junk and antiquities. I wanted to know.

My phone buzzed. Rachael had some questions about the paintings. I texted her I'd be right over.

"Good idea," I said to Nic. "You go back to Luxor. I'm going to Albania."

CHAPTER SIXTEEN

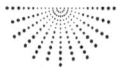

*A*s I left the apartment, I passed a handsome young man. He tipped his hat, I nodded in response. I love this hipster-hat-wearing generation. The young men wear their ties and rolled sleeves and heavy beards with such panache. At the tender age of sixteen, Matt rocks the look and I accommodate him with gifts as trendy as I can manage. This young guy was at least ten years older than my nephew, but I was, in turn, old enough to lump the boys together. Distracted by thoughts of Matt, I texted him as I walked to Rachael's gallery.

Afternoon cruise crowds thickened as I neared the square. I clutched my purse close to me. I will always be paranoid about my purse, worried, cautious. I glanced behind me but only saw a group of gondoliers, resplendent in their striped shirts, strolling out of a trattoria to the docks. I considered, for a minute, buying one of those hidden waist packs for my cash and new passport. Then, no, the last thing I want is more bulk around my already bulky middle. I held the purse to my side and walked.

I did not bring my now precious passport to Rachael's

gallery. Before I left the apartment, I stuffed it under the bed behind the first drawer. It could converse with all the vibrators, like a perverted Toy Story XX.

"I have good news and bad news," Rachael started as soon as I walked through the door.

"Give me the bad news."

"Some of the paintings are copies."

I nodded, that made sense. I had no real skin in this game, I wasn't depending on the collection to garner much more than a few memorable Italian meals. But I did need to retrieve the paintings for Tiffany. I hadn't paid attention to where her paintings ended up. At the hotel? That seemed an unnecessary step. Ah well, that was for later. I had other concerns.

"Are they all fakes?"

"No, those two," she gestured to the Chagall and the smaller Picasso. "Those two are the real thing. How Miranda managed to buy them at all is astonishing."

I studied them. "Unless the person who sold them to Miranda thought they were fakes." In an abundance of plastic statues, the real ones could be overlooked.

"What's the good news?"

Rachael handed me a wad of euros. "Even copies can be sold for cash."

After a brief negotiation, Rachael found two hardy men to follow me back to the apartment and very, very carefully detach the Nevelson from the bedroom wall. It was a tricky business. I adverted my gaze and tried to ignore the bumps and exclamations of the two workers.

Matt got back to me. He was fine, forbidden to see those bad friends again.

I'm sure he was.

The installation was carried downstairs in five pieces. The men carefully stacked the art into a hand cart and rattled it down the street. Real or not, I was happy to replace the black boxes decorated with wood cut out squares and symbols for a mellow Turner replica of the Grand Canal. I would sleep much better without that black stuff hovering over me. It was an overpowering keep out sign. What had Miranda been thinking?

Nic had disappeared, but it wasn't my job to keep tabs on him. Had we owned phones back in the day, our whole relationship would have been easier. Like with Matt and Chris, I could follow Nic as a friend and know exactly where he was at all times. But did that help? Tina followed the boys, well, mostly Matt, and called him regularly. Where are you? Take a picture and show me.

The only thing that low-atmosphere hovering accomplished was that Matt was a master of disguise and subterfuge, which aren't necessarily bad skills, just not necessarily what Tina and Vince had in mind. If Matt wanted to visit with his bad friends, he would.

Nic would have created the same kind of fakery my own darling nephew was so clever at doing. So never mind. No matter how advanced the technology, there will always be a young hacker one step ahead.

On the way down the stairs I removed the extra key from under the cherub.

I planned to take myself out to dinner, courtesy of Miranda's fake paintings. I passed the young man again. He could have been in one of Max's ads: tall, dark hair, good bones. I nodded hello and he nodded back and returned to staring into his phone. Waiting for a girl. I was pretty sure he liked girls. It wasn't my concern.

I found photos of Nic, Chris texted me. He is with a group of men.

Thanks, you're the best.

The best what?

When Trish delivered her late-in-life boys, back to back, I was summoned from Milan where I was on the verge of something interesting, to help with the new baby and old toddler. I love the boys but I'm not really the maternal type, I tried to stay for as short a time as I could and dashed back to Milan barely six months later, but the opportunity was lost. Some people can shuck off obligations as easily as a cheap dress. I can't.

The best nephew ever.

Matt is back, Mom grounded him.

He'll be out in 24 hours, I promised.

He always is. Chris signed off.

How does Matt stay in school if he is so busy making ill-advised choices? Chris. When fifth-grade Matt couldn't for the life of him learn his multiplication tables, third-grade Chris showed him how. It escalated from there, with Chris taking over Matt's homework, turning in flawlessly executed math pages and, later, English papers. By high school Matt had figured out that he didn't quite look or even sound like a straight-A student and so would dumb down Chris's papers before turning them in. Solid Bs. Matt would attend a strong college like Sacramento or Humboldt State. Chris wasn't sure where he wanted to go. I am voting for Stanford. Chris may be antisocial, but he is brilliant. There would be a place for him in a university, even if there wasn't for me.

When I was digging in Egypt with Nic, Chris developed quite an obsession with the field. I admit I used his expertise and brilliant research ability to my advantage, so I'm in no position to judge Matt, and all three of us know it. To this day Nic is unaware of my secret research weapon. My best nephew.

We don't need to review the dinner—how I relished this wonderful refined civilization run by people who knew what they were doing. How I missed obsequious waiters, pompous sommeliers, overpriced wine that after the first sip, is pronounced worth it. I missed the absolute indulgence of a good meal. It was heaven itself and soothed my nerves sufficiently enough that I was only a little surprised to see Cindy perched on an enormous pink Samsonite case blocking the apartment stairs.

I allowed an eye roll, then nodded for her to follow. I did not offer to carry her suitcase. The case crashed and banged behind me like a wrecking ball.

Just inside the door, Cindy dropped the heavy case with a crash and headed to the tiny kitchen.

"I think I'm in trouble." She rooted around for a bottle of wine. "Salvatore, that's the owner, you brought him wine." She held up a bottle of same and brought it into the sitting area. "He wants to know if you're married by the way."

I love the Italians.

"I'm not married, by the way, and yes, if you're dealing with people happy to burn down a whole business to make a point, you are in trouble." I set down two glasses and retrieved the wine opener.

"Where is Miranda?"

It was hard to say the words out loud; in fact, I had been able to avoid it since I arrived. We all just acknowledged the loss, didn't need to dwell, didn't need to get all crazy.

I looked at Cindy, it was about to get crazy.

"She died, a week ago."

Cindy's eyes widened in shock. Her knees buckled and she dropped on the couch. She looked like how I felt.

"What?"

"Heart attack," I explained.

"But she was."

"Heathy, social, in good shape."

Cindy dropped her head in her hands and began to sob.

I watched her for a moment. I had forgotten about that

163

particular superpower of hers. She used to freak out Miranda with her tears because they just wouldn't stop. Miranda, who was not a crier, was always at a loss and always ended up promising Cindy anything if she would just stop crying.

I opened the wine. She sobbed. I poured two glasses, she cried. With mine firmly in hand, I nudged her off her off her enormous purple suitcase and dragged it into the tiny bedroom/luggage closet.

"Don't cry." It was a useless admonishment. Once she started up, her tears were as difficult to stop as a King Tide. "You can stay here. Until we figure this out."

Just this morning I had insisted that the extra room could be billed as a study nook. Maria had wrinkled her nose at even this generous definition. A one-bedroom apartment is not an easy sell. People have children, relatives, sleep overs, sudden friends who appear at your door as soon as you have a place in Venice. Maria relented and we listed it as a child's bedroom.

"But..." Cindy's eyes were soaking wet and ringed with so much smeared eyeliner she looked like her old Goth self.

I retrieved a dishcloth and held it out. "Don't worry, the apartment has already been robbed. I don't think they'll return. Besides, they already have my purse."

"I'm so sorry." She began to cry again.

I sipped my wine and watched the lights appear in the hotel across the canal.

After another five minutes of sobbing, she slowed to a hiccup and drank her wine.

She wiped her face, smearing the white towel black.

"So," I was purposely cheerful. "What have you been doing with yourself?"

"After Miranda, I tried to get back into modeling."

I sipped the wine and waited.

"I toured around. I met a nice girl and we went to Greece."

I nodded. What I remember of Cindy, she was good at meeting people who then helped her in many and all ways. She moved from relationship to relationship until she wore out her welcome either because she stole something important or because she stole something trivial and was caught. Or because she slipped back into drugs, or just because she had little to contribute to the conversation. She still looked good, so depending on the kindness of strangers was still relatively easy to do. She was canny, she was clever, and she was a hopeless addict. And I had just handed her a glass of wine. Who is the enabler here?

She drank the wine and glanced around as if I had an array of paraphernalia and cocaine (at least that's what I remembered she liked best, doing lines in our tiny bathroom, explaining that she was always this energetic and cheerful first thing in the morning) on display. No drugs, honey, just alcohol and caffeine.

"You went to Greece." I prompted. And their entire economy collapsed. Coincidence? Where had she toured next, Syria?

"She was nice, but you know, it didn't work out." She sniffed. I didn't want to hear the details, the screaming, the epic crying jags, the last-minute cash grab even as she was firmly escorted out the door.

I am an idiot for helping her. But I can't help helping.

I picked up my phone and texted Nic.

I poured more wine for her. I poured more wine for me. "You returned to Venice?" I prompted.

She sniffed. "I like it here. I met a nice man and he said Salvatore needed help in his store, all I had to do was pick up some of the products and bring them back to Italy."

With Amazon Prime available all over the world, that didn't seem plausible. I waited.

Nic texted back he was on his way.

"How long have you been here?" A more neutral question rather than How long have you been smuggling stolen artifacts? How long have you been selling stolen goods? How long have you been avoiding the authorities? See? I have learned to ask better, more casual questions. Learned that from my long-time association with my too clever nephews.

"A year." She sniffed.

Nic rang and I let him in.

"Hello." He offered his hand to Cindy who gave him a limp-wrist shake.

"What happened?"

He scooted me to the end of the couch and sat close to Cindy. He took her hand and patted it, the avuncular uncle, the soothing professor. I could have been jealous, but this was his way to drag out information. I let him do his work.

"You are upset, who did this to you?"

"I don't have a job anymore." She wailed. "What will I do? And Miranda is gone! I can't believe this!" A new audience, she started the tears again. I quickly poured myself more wine.

"Get another job?" He hazarded. He glanced at my glass and I retrieved one for him and poured a generous amount.

"No, they said I couldn't work for anyone else."

"They?" He ducked his head and tried to look into her eyes, but she wasn't having it.

She sniffed and drained the wine glass. I topped off both. Nic eyed me and I shrugged. He started it.

She sniffed again, Nic patted her hand and the story haltingly came out. Rather than drag it out word after word, I'll summarize. Two men approached Cindy and set her up as a clerk in the Venetian souvenir shop. All she had to do was show up every day, which took more concerted effort than you may think. Every week she would to take a short trip out to Greece, or one of the Stans, pick up a package and return it to the store. The items in the packages went into the inventory.

"Who purchased them?" Nic patiently pulled out the rest of the story.

She shrugged. "I don't know, I never saw what was in the packages. It was easy until a couple months ago, some new guys came to the store and changed everything. I had to take the cruise ships and I had to go to Albania. Do you know what's in Albania?

"Not hot Greek beaches?" I guessed.

She ignored me. "I liked the cruise part. I charged my drinks to a random room, ate a good dinner and the people were really nice."

Nic was now interested. "How did you board?"

"The logo bag. That gets you in. Most of the time. Enough of the time." She amended.

Getting in was actually the easy part. She would claim she lost her boarding pass and gesture with the logo bag. If she couldn't make it onto the cruise ship, she'd have to take the long bus ride to Butrint and back. And there were no free drinks on the bus, so she hadn't liked those two trips very much.

"They said it would be fine, I didn't need to do it anymore and I'd still get my money." She started in to wail but Nic must have squeezed her hand so hard it startled her, and she stopped crying.

"They? Who is they? Who are these people?" His tone was sharp.

"Two guys. Not American, they have a different accent. Like I said, they are new. They stopped at the shop once.

Mostly they just text. And I, you know, just do it." She shrugged, a little more composed.

"You must be exhausted," Nic suggested.

She nodded. Taking his cue, I hustled her off to the bathroom for a proper shower. I pulled out the black towels in case there was still mascara left.

When I returned, Nic was busy on his phone.

"Stolen goods. They must have picked them up from somewhere in Egypt and are routing them through various countries."

I watched him carefully. Were these the same men who stole my purse and ransacked my (Miranda's) apartment? Maybe, maybe not. Nic seemed genuinely perplexed, like this was new information, information he was not particularly happy about.

"She's not flying," I pointed out. That was all I needed to say. It was too easy for customs to take things. Too easy for TSA employees to rifle through checked luggage, steal anything they want with only a little orange note with the excuse that breakage and theft was in the name of security. Everyone is a terrorist. If Cindy were to fly, the gig would be up before she could board the plane.

He looked at me. "Stolen antiques are big business."

"A big deal." I knew that.

"Worth destroying a business."

"Worth burning the evidence."

"Worth killing for," he said quietly.

I knew that too.

CHAPTER SEVENTEEN

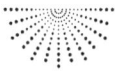

*T*here is no easy way to reach Saranda, Albania. Which is why stowing away on a handy cruise ship made so much sense.

"There is no airport?" Nic was incredulous.

Cindy, fresh and cherubic from her shower, just shrugged. She reached for more wine, allowing her robe to gap. Nic ignored her effort. Wine in hand, Cindy wiggled close to him. He talked over her head at me, the organized matron. Now why isn't a competent, organized woman as erotic as a damsel in distress?

Suppressing a sigh, I scrolled on my phone. "Shares are sold, invest now, but no flights, no building, no." I glanced up at him as if this were a surprise.

"Infrastructure."

"Roads?"

"Unfortunately, yes. The best way to reach Butrint is to fly to Tirana and take a bus to Saranda."

"And we are doing this why?"

"That's why we always tried to take the cruise ships." Cindy was being helpful.

"Stow away?"

She frowned. "Just a ride. No one got hurt."

"Until today," I pointed out.

She slumped in the seat and crossed her arms. Ah, now that gesture I remembered.

I put my hands on my hips. "My best friend just died, and I want to know why." And a store had been burned to the ground and a young woman was in trouble.

"You made a great researcher. That university job," Nic began.

"Was rescinded. I know."

He nodded, it was a sore point, not his fault. Back when we were a thing, he had been sympathetic, now, not so much. Or Cindy had sucked out all his sympathy, it lay like a desiccated mummy between us.

"A weekend in Albania," he repeated with a grand display of displeasure.

"It's an up and coming thing, the Rivera of the Adriatic."

"Lesser, minor Adriatic," he corrected.

Cindy hunched lower, all attitude with perky breasts. The Fates were unkind. I wasn't unkind per se, but I did want my pound of flesh.

"You can stay here. Just let Maria, she's the real estate agent, in tomorrow." "When?"

"In the morning."

"Early?"

"Yes, early." I waited. No good deed goes unpunished. Maybe that should be my mantra instead of Can I help you? I should listen to that line from The Producers "Stop helping!"

"You don't need to stay here." I offered.

"I'll get up."

"Ah, thank you. The agent will text me with her report. I appreciate your help with this."

Not comfortable with the living arrangements at all, we

reluctantly left the tearful Cindy with instructions to stay put over the weekend and only venture out for important errands, like gelato. I'm not heartless.

We flew Ryan Air from Venice to Tirana; it was only a little less frightening than driving.

Nic and I went around and round—take the bus, take the train (no overnight train, I'm officially too old for that nonsense.) We could fly easily enough into the capital, but it was eight hours by bus to Saranda and another forty-five minutes by bus from there.

Nic tried to slouch in his airline seat but it didn't have much give. Or recline. "I can't believe I'm doing this."

I patted his hand and forestalled mentioning the long bus ride ahead. "You'll be fine."

I am unfamiliar with the ins and outs of commerce between former fascist states and communist regimes. I imagined it would not be simple to smuggle things from one through to another. All the guards would need to be in on the action, all the right people consistently paid.

The Albanians are not good at commerce, but they are giving it their best, awkward shot. There were for instance, hotels. I booked us into the most anonymous hotel available at the last minute, the Tirana International Hotel. It is adjacent to Skanderbeg Square and offers spectacular views over the square and the city. A popular hotel would give us cover. I assumed there would be plenty of action, many exits and entrances, not only of guests but curious tourists. The website even pointed out that the hotel was a popular meeting place for spies against communism. Perfect.

There is nothing so disturbing as brutalist architecture backing up against renovated tradition. Like Zagreb, Tirana has created a face of culture and beauty, but the beauty is literally only a block deep. Move far enough into the center of town and you'll be lost in mammoth uncompromising gray structures giving no clue to or indication of their purpose. I was determined to stay in the improved section of town. To distract Nic during the plane flight, I read "After years of being closed to the world during the communist regime of Enver Hoxha, Tirana seems to have become the glittering beacon of a brand-new Albania." All well and good, but we had to get to Saranda from here and to play the average Odyssey Cruise guests. And I look nothing like the slender winsome Cindy. I figured I'd deal with that discrepancy when or if I was challenged.

"Not close at all." I continued to read, studying, and reading between the lines. Cruise ships routinely dock at Saranda. And they would need buses to take them to Butrint. If Cindy could hitchhike on a cruise ship, Nic and I could certainly sneak aboard a tour bus.

The taxi to the hotel was typical in that we experienced a half dozen near accidents on the way. I wondered if that car Matt had been passenger in had a near miss; was that why the police pulled them over? I couldn't believe that even at the tender age of sixteen, Matt didn't understand about open containers. I needed more time with that boy.

The hotel was appropriately solid and comforting. I had booked one room for the two of us, it would look odd if I hadn't. Not that we took advantage. We were both too distracted by all the recent events and fell into bed like a married couple: we stared into our phones until we fell asleep.

I planned to take one of the first buses leaving for Saranda. Nic could barely get out of bed, but he did it. "Why are you punishing me?" He groaned and staggered to the bathroom.

"Why not?"

I was confident that a mere eight-hour bus ride would be a piece of cake. Not really. By the time we reached

Saranda I was not confident that my poor numb butt would ever recover. Nic could barely disembark. We were in no shape to do much of anything except to find a place to stay in Saranda before, we hoped, hooking up with a tour group.

Saranda is a resort on the Albanian Riviera; in fact, you can ride a ferry from Corfu to Saranda, they are that close. Back in the bad old communist days, government officials convinced the good people of Saranda that the bad people of Corfu were on the verge of invading. Possibly this weekend. Better be prepared. If you've visited Corfu, then visited Albania, you'd know how ridiculous that claim is.

In a fit of romance and self-preservation I looked up Trip Advisor and, based on little more than a glamour shot of the beach, chose the Hotel Piccolino.

We checked into a decidedly less glamorous room than the night before. The bed looked just adequate. I missed those days when beds, rooms, hot water didn't matter. When reclining seats and leg room did not matter. When a bus was a fine and reasonable way to travel. Not anymore.

I changed into one of Betsy Johnson's more sedate summer dresses, the jagged hem both revealing and concealing, which I thought a good idea, at my age a flash of leg was quite enough. "Let's go to the beach."

I didn't give Nic time to argue that he'd had his fill of sand and going to the beach was a busman's holiday. A group of tourists clustered at the reception desk as we exited the elevator. Two men, taller than the rest, gazed over the crowd and eyed us. I batted my eyes and leaned into Nic.

"Kiss me," I whispered.

He turned away from the men and kissed me lightly on the lips. I returned the kiss, moving Nic off to one side, behind a cabinet.

"Two men at the reception desk." I whispered.

He glanced over his shoulder and nodded. "Think those are your purse snatchers?"

I automatically felt for my purse, but I had left it in the room.

"I never saw them. I don't know."

He glanced again and I felt his body tighten. "Let's go to the beach."

We walked down and out of the hotel to enjoy an almost deserted arch of sand.

It was lovey. Not like the Riviera. But that was okay.

"Why are we here again?" Nic complained.

"Because why else travel to this lovely place?" I waved my hand at the sea and sky. "It has a charm, admit it."

He grunted. I squeezed his hand. Hard. Clearly it was up to me to keep up the appearance that we were geriatric romantics.

Cindy, even after a lot more wine, had not been much help. She was just a part in the system, her own individual cell. Like any staff working for a corporation she had little concept of the whole of the business. She did not know the mission statement. She just showed up and did her job.

"I made so much money!" She had cried, wiping her eyes on a blackened towel. "I was almost out of debt."

"Out of debt?"

She nodded. "I owed some people money."

That was never a good statement to make in Italy.

"And you were almost done?"

"I just had to take one more empty bag to Butrint and bring it back full."

"To here?"

"To the shop and then I would get my payment."

That was simple. What had Miranda admitted after the closing scene with Cindy? That she wasn't the brightest candle in the Murano chandelier?

The question was why.

I asked that out loud as we strolled along the sand. No one could hear us and no one, as far as I could tell, followed. There wouldn't be any reason to, they knew where we were staying.

But who were they?

"I don't think it's a big deal, that's why."

"What's not a big deal? Isn't trafficking in stolen goods, any stolen goods a big deal?"

He squeezed my hand. "You've been out of it for a while."

"Only five years." I was defensive, but he was right. I had been out of it, for what felt like a lifetime both in terms of relationships as well as technology. The whole of the Mideast had fallen into chaos since I had lived there. I myself had complained that I had lost more than just those five years between Max and my parents, but I didn't like it pointed out.

"This is really nothing, a few items, taken from some-where in Egypt, maybe even someone's warehouse or attic and brought through poor Albania and sold through a busier port, like Venice. It's not as if the Venetians don't know how to do this kind of thing."

"True." But that wasn't all. Miranda didn't die for a handful of insignificant items. At least I didn't want to believe she did.

"Then why did you agree to come with me?"

"I didn't want to lose you."

I blinked but let it stand, I didn't want to ruin the moment by asking for more explanations.

We dined in the hotel and finally began sharing some of our past, some of ourselves.

When Nic described the past, some of his more successful finds, success that grew as the years passed, his blue eyes lit up, he gestured with his hands and distractedly drew his long fingers through his hair. I just gave in. I gave in to his

175

conversations, our history, and to sharing a bed with him for one more night. We had aged, there was no denying that parts that were once firm were much softer and processes that once were fast and furious had fallen into categories charitably described as slow and languorous. We made love to what we were then, and for just a small moment, what we were today.

I sent Nic down early to fetch coffee. When he returned, he didn't recognize me, for which I was grateful.

"You look old."

"Exactly the idea." I adjusted the wig. The polyester blouse felt odd against my skin. I had so quickly adapted to silk and linen. Fabric makes a difference, the weight of it, the drape of it. I remember trying on a blouse in Target. It was perfect for my new job as caregiver. But the polyester made my skin crawl, the mirror image cried. In the end I just couldn't buy it. But the same outfit is quite effective as an invisibility cloak.

Nic was dressed as himself. But that too was the idea. He was the lead, the target, I was the courier, if I could pull it off. We did not know if our contact would be looking for Cindy specifically or just for a lone woman carrying a canvas bag featuring the Odyssey Cruise logo which is just the name Odyssey in serf type. Easy.

I picked up same and draped it over my shoulder along with a large handbag that had forlornly sat in Francisca's shop for two years.

"You look like one of the horde." Nic hiked up his jeans and eyed me.

"I'm supposed to. Now, come on, the buses leave at 8:00."

No matter how much we argued, or how many times Nic searched Google, the only way for us to reach the ruins was by tour bus. We rejected hiring a cab because it would draw too much attention and we'd may be remembered. It was bus or nothing. I was not about to allow Nic to choose nothing.

We paused at the hotel entrance. There were five hotels clustered together. The Odyssey would need to dock out in the deeper water and tender guests into town.

"What are we doing?" Nic whispered.

"Wait for it." I nudged him towards the entrance to the Hotel Brilliant, (how could it be not?) The hotel, large and commodious also featured western toilets for the ladies.

Sure enough, a bus marked Odyssey pulled up to the hotel, minutes later a stream of ladies exited and rushed into the lobby.

"Now?" Nic asked.

We walked slowly towards the bus, I motioned him to enter; I would wait and board with the first group of ladies, fresh from their comfort stop. At this point no one would count us. Cindy explained that guests were counted as they exited the ship and as they entered the ship, the middle was not as important.

The ladies swooped back, chattering about the hotel, the buffets, the entertainment, I swung in behind them and found an empty seat in the back.

We had one moment when a young woman wearing a name tag marched up and down the bus. She looked straight at me, but her gaze didn't linger. I smiled, but she had already moved on.

We were off. I turned to my new seatmate. She was roughly my age, but dressed much older.

"You all have the same bag," I said unnecessarily.

"Oh yes, the cruise director said it would help identify us and get us the cruise bargain."

It probably alerted the locals that this was a tourist ready for increased prices and decreased courtesy. No harm, no foul, the tourists would be gone in less than three hours, replaced tomorrow by a whole new batch. Customer service is wasted on the transient.

Fortunately for my sore butt, this bus ride was not as long as the first. We bumped through villages packed with three story buildings that had been abandoned at the second story. Every few minutes we were rewarded with a glimpse of the blue sea. Flowers dotted the rolling hills and the air, once we left the edge of the coast, was mild.

We pulled up to the official comfort stop. From there we would walk as a group through the ruins.

Nic disembarked before me. I watched out the window as a half dozen thin boys accosted him waving beads and trinkets. They had picked the wrong man. Nic held up one hand and barked at them. They fell away as if he were Tut come to life. He strode into the rest stop alone. The boys recovered and descended onto a group of ladies. I didn't know the word Nic used, but I shook my head and strode forward, not looking directly at the children. Some of the ladies were caught in negotiations.

"Six, six US dollars."

"That is highway robbery, young man."

"Five fifty, great bargain, you get best price. No one else but me."

"Shouldn't you be in school?"

The early stages of commerce are often not smooth.

I had read ahead and offered to lecture Nic, but he resisted my suggestion with a grunt and a hand. "I got it. Ruins. Busman's holiday."

Butrint was interesting. The town had been first established as a Greek colony, improved into a Roman city, and finally built out as a Byzantine administration center. It was abandoned in the late Middle Ages. Like Ephesus, the bay, the heart of commerce, had silted up and left the city, high, dry, and irrelevant. It's easy to make out the layers of building material that represent each epoch. It's cool

I followed the line of tourists shuffling up and down the slick stone steps of the ruins, griping about the lack of railings. Cake layers of Greek, Roman and medieval buildings greeted us at every turn. I had read that because no one cared for the area for years (and years), much beautiful Roman mosaic flooring was perfect, intact.

Except we couldn't see them. Every newly discovered floor was quickly hidden again under a thick layer of dirt. A placard with a photo of the floor explained the workmanship and unique patterns of what you were unable to see. The floors were covered in soil so thieves couldn't chip away at the tiles and spirit them away.

Nic joined me at one of the covered floors. He pulled up and opened his mouth, but I stopped him. "No lectures. I get it."

He deflated like an illegal hot air balloon over the Valley of the Kings. "Just a few notes?"

I shook my head and adjusted the empty Odyssey bag on my shoulder. We headed into the heart of the ruins to find the park guard.

There were two guards, both dressed in the uniforms of all National Parks all over the world: dull green. A little Max Peters orange would have livened up their ensemble considerably. One guard, an enormous man, completely bald and fierce was busy discouraging people from buying anything in the tiny gift area (little more than a shelf with a few books and five postcards) by refusing to make change. The second guard, just as large as the first, leaned back in a rickety office chair, eyeing the tourists as they paraded through. The chair creaked in pre-splinter anguish.

Was he waiting for Cindy? I kept an eye out for the two

men from last night, but did not see them, which meant nothing.

The lounging guard caught my eye and nodded. That was the signal. I stepped around the guard who had been talked into making change after all, and held out (subtly), my empty bag. He in turn held up his enormous hand and shook his head.

"Pink bunker."

I nodded and walked past him, shuffling through the partially uncovered buildings, the surviving arches of a medieval church, and finally out to the parking lot to once again pass the gauntlet of enterprising urchins.

Nic joined me as we boarded the bus, pretending to introduce himself. He followed me and we sat together in the back.

"I'm your new friend?" I plopped down, empty bag on my lap.

He closed his eyes and leaned his head against the seat. "The women sitting in the front all wanted to talk."

"Yes, that's what we do."

"I couldn't handle it, the quizzing, searching information. What do I do? Am I retired, am I married? What deck am I on? Is this my first cruise? Why do your people do this?"

"Because since your people don't offer it up first, we have to pry it out of you. Like you're a mysterious dig in the thick rain forests of Peru." Peru reminded me of Chris, who reminded me that my time was severely limited, Tina and Vince needed to leave on Friday, and it was Tuesday. I pulled out my phone, but there was no service. When we returned to Venice, I would book a flight for that night, so Wednesday, tomorrow, I would be gone.

"It's exhausting." He glanced at my bag as our guide walked the aisle counting heads. "Did you get it?"

I shook my head. "He said to check the pink bunker."

Nic frowned. I shrugged. Our guide, gripping the back of the driver's seat, announced we would next see something from the communist era.

"Back in the communist regime all Albanians built bunkers on their day off, Sunday. There are about 150,000 bunkers all over our country to protect us against invasion."

"It must have worked." Nic said under his breath.

"Shhh."

"We will stop by the coast to see a good representation. These bunkers were built between 1960 and 1985."

"Bunkers," I repeated. I didn't say more. And no, I did not raise my hand and ask if some of the bunkers were painted in festive colors (like Lilly Pulitzer pink).

The bus ride to the coast was short. After only about fifteen minutes we again slowly disembarked the bus and were encouraged to explore the coastal bunkers on our own.

"Ten minutes." The guide called out. "Back on the bus in ten minutes."

Like a reality game show, ten minutes to spot the pink bunker.

Some bunkers, all round domes, were practical. Many were large cement buildings able to protect a dictator against nuclear attacks if it came to that. These tiny versions scattered all over the rocky beach were only large enough for one, maybe two people if they stayed horizontal. Across the water Corfu glittered invitingly.

I crawled down the slope to the water level and started to wander between the cement domes. The bunkers may have been built in deadly earnest in the 1980s, but the following generation expressed a much different attitude. The bunkers were no longer gray and formidable but covered in neon bright spray paint—here was a Max Peters, Peter Max, Gucci, Pucci extravaganza, exposing the whole thing for what it was —ridiculous.

A few domes were tagged with images that made clear the new purpose of the structures. Many were pink. I glanced at my watch. We only had five more minutes. Nic took the high road and examined each bunker as if he was a professor of archeology. I glanced up from one bunker and noticed that a clutch of three ladies were stalking Nic. I should warn him.

The guide called out—four minutes.

A glowing pink bunker a bit taller than its neighbors loomed up. The top of the dome reached my hip. I glanced around. The ladies were closing in on Nic. The guide was calling out, clearly now, one minute, back on the bus.

I crouched and used my phone to look around, leery of thrusting my hand into a dark damp hole.

The bunker floor was covered in sand, and smooth. I shined the flashlight around.

"Vic!" Nic called out. "We have to go!"

To the left, tucked up against the sloping wall was another canvas bag. I dropped my bag and picked up the new one. It was empty.

Damn, damn, damn.

I exchanged the bags anyway and quickly hiked back to the idling bus.

Nic was already in his seat, looking as innocent as he could, which is to say, not that innocent.

I sat and held onto the empty bag, not wanting to say anything until we could talk under the cover of the bus engine noise.

"That's it?" He whispered. I nodded.

"Son of a bitch."

As we barreled back down to our hotel, I felt around inside the bag and pulled out a business card of—yes, our own hotel. I held it up.

"What would I do without you?" He took the card and

turned it back and forth, as if it would reveal more information, maybe something written in invisible ink.

"They aren't making it easy." In fact, the whole day was wasted. We could have stayed in the hotel, made the exchange there and we were done. This seemed too convoluted.

Nic tucked the card into one of his pants pockets. "May as well see it through."

He settled back and closed his eyes. This was why he wanted to sit next to me. He didn't have to talk.

"What would I do without you?"

That phrase sent a shiver down my spine and made my stomach grow cold and heavy. It was what Tina said after that first month I rushed home to stay with the new baby. It was what Vince said after I had lived with Mom and Dad for a year. It was what Tina texted. It's what Max whispered. It was what Miranda breathed before she fell asleep.

What would they do without me? I had two days to figure out who killed Miranda. And I wasn't even close.

MADONNA'S "INTO THE GROOVE" drifted though the PA system as we entered the Hotel Piccolino, ratty business card in hand. I glanced at Nic, but he was intent on finding the hotel bar.

New, unfamiliar music is a lovely, pleasant background. Old music, the music of a specific time, is distracting. You either know all the words and are compelled by some lizard part of your brain, to sing along. Or the song makes you cry. There isn't a single Madonna hit that doesn't transport me back to my ill-spent youth. Well, ill-spent according to my parents, according to my brothers. No house, no husband, no children. But I told my mother, I'll always have Paris. Paris a number of times. Over and over. I love Paris. Cairo, Milan,

Venice. There is nothing more satisfying than reflecting on an ill-spent youth.

But if I want to relax, give me hip-hop with its decided lack of nostalgia.

Madonna did eventually find her groove. Nic and I separated, and I entered the bar first like the start of a bad joke—a former photo assistant walks into a bar...and orders an iced tea.

I was already dressed for invisibility and stealth. The casual slacks in tan, a short sleeve blouse in light peach, the sensible tan walking shoes. I pulled back my hair, my beautiful auburn hair, and tucked it under a scarf and topped it all with a yellow visor.

During the bouncy ride back, Nic announced that he would be the lead. He would meet whomever at the bar and get the goods. He announced it assuming I would agree and because what would he do without me? I would back him up.

I would have preferred to dress differently, bat my eyes and over drinks encourage our contact to overexplain his position, the hippo, the find, the dig, I was confident I would get it all and it would only require two gin and tonics to do it. When they aren't paying attention, men often underestimate our reasons for listening to them so intensely and for too long.

But no, this was to be Nic's thing.

I hesitated at the door to the bar, glancing in to see if I would be welcome, more to see if there was a table adjacent to the bar. There was. I sat down and pulled out a guidebook to the ruins. It was so badly translated it was painful to read.

Eventually a waiter approached me, just as Nic walked in.

"Iced tea. And make sure there is enough ice." I whispered.

The man lifted an eyebrow and I struggled to look as sincere and naive as possible. How dangerous is iced tea in a foreign country? As dangerous as crossing the street in Rome or sky diving in unregulated Bulgaria. Seriously. Order the local drink: vodka in Saint Petersburg, gin in London, wine in France. Or beer. Beer is always a good choice, preferably in the bottle. And wipe off the neck.

But iced tea? Deadly.

While I waited for my dangerous drink, I kept my head down and studied the brochure. Nic hiked up to the bar and ordered a bourbon, no ice. His job was to look dejected. I scooted my chair a half foot closer. He did not look up.

Our mark waltzed in and correctly singled out Nic. My drink was served with a pitying look. I avoided the waiter's eyes.

The men greeted each other as men do, with one-word, single syllable utterances and a quick head bob.

The new guy hitched up on the bar stool next to Nic. He was not, interestingly, one of the men from last night. He was blond with long curls much like an aging member of Queen. Half the size of the guards, he still carried himself like a man armed with a concealed weapon.

My first impression was right. All the countries in question were in the middle of regime changes (always rough on the general population). Another group muscled in on the first, like a hostile takeover. They must have intercepted today's drop and were now ready to negotiate for a piece of whatever pie Nic was holding.

"You are missing something?" His voice was low, but I caught the words. I cupped my hand around my ear to filter out Queen's back beating "We Will Rock You."

Nic nodded and kept his eyes on the shelf behind the bar. Even with the back mirrors doubling the offerings, the bar inventory maxed out at a dozen bottles.

Nic offered the card to the man who took it like it was ice in a drink.

He pocketed the card. "We can make you a deal."

Nic nodded.

"1,000 euros. Cash."

I wanted to ask about the store and almost hissed it out from under my breath but Nic, fortunately, read my mind, or probably my agitated vibrations.

"And the store?"

"We took care of that. You deal with us now." He added. "Direct."

The man slid off the seat and walked away. Nic downed his Jim Beam and left the bar. I waited, eyeing the tea, longing for a shot of bourbon. But that would not be in keeping with my persona. I sighed, left bills on the table and followed Nic out.

There is a reason the most memorable Greek tragedies are based on human hubris. Since I believed I was invisible, I was careless. Who pays attention to a gray-haired older woman?

Two thugs.

The men who I had noticed at the hotel in Saranda abruptly reappeared in the hall. I ducked my head to avoid eye contact and hunched my shoulders to look exactly what I looked like: an older woman. Nothing to see here.

They marched past me, and just as I took a deep breath of relief, one of the men grabbed my arm and swung me around. The deep breath caught halfway, and I gasped out loud.

"Don't scream or we kill you." The taller blonde, our refugee from Queen, jabbed something very hard into my very soft waist. I struggled, but that only inspired him to shove the gun more deeply into my side and squeeze my arm harder. His partner grabbed my other arm. I searched the empty hallway but Nic was nowhere to be seen. In fact, there wasn't a soul around. Damn the off season.

The shorter bald man pulled me forward, but the taller man didn't move. This was not going to end well. Two more steps, and my arm socket would give from the pull. The blonde barked at his partner who jumped and the two finally coordinated their hustle. They propelled me down the hall and through the emergency exit doors, which, despite the alarm warnings listed in three languages, made no sound. The landing was narrow, devolving down crumbling cement stairs. There was no place to go but down. I stumbled twice, trying to find footing between the treacherous debris, rocks and dirt. The man behind me stumbled and cursed.

"Quiet!"

It took a second to figure out how to protest. I went with the little old lady who was silly enough to order iced tea in a bar.

"What are you doing? Who are you! Where are we going? You can't treat me like this I'm an American Citizen!"

"You, quiet or I shoot."

A little old lady from Duluth, Minnesota, would have believed him. I stopped talking. The stairs curved to the right. There were no signs and no exit doors as far as I could see, but I couldn't see much. The light was dim. Forty-watt bulbs swung on single wires over the stairs. I did my best not to stumble, because every time I listed to one side or the other, the gun jammed deeper into my side. Finally, we reached the end of the stairs. The bulbs flickered, then blacked out.

Both men cursed. But the man behind me had the fore-sight to bring a flashlight. The weak light illuminated an ordinary interior door, no alarm, no exit. The first man jerked it open and pushed me. The basement was grim, clearly used only for storage. Taking me to the top of the hotel would have be kinder: a view, fresh air. But no less dangerous. Like most of the buildings we passed, the top of the hotel was an unfinished mess of rebar and cement. I learned that as soon as a building is finished, it is taxed. Thus, if a building remains unfinished—no tax. The towns we passed through this morning all took advantage of this tax loophole and as a result, looked like they had just survived a major bombing. Or maybe a bombing would improve them. It was still up for debate. Solid cement walls, dank. Ridiculous.

They threw me onto a rickety chair that pitched to the left, I righted it, trying to keep my balance. The blonde thug (seemed an appropriate categorization, they didn't strike me as part of a more organized system, maybe it was their suits, old, rough, like they had to dig up something they last wore to their sister's wedding twenty-five years ago) roughly tied my hands behind my back, snaking the rope through the slats of the chair. The other faced me shining a flashlight into my eyes.

The gray wig itched. I hoped it was staying firmly in place, I couldn't tell. I was used to plopping them onto models, not wearing them myself.

"What do you know?" He demanded in English.

"I don't know anything!" I raised my voice to that old-lady pitch, channeling my mother and every other elderly woman I encountered at the doctors and senior discount day at the Safeway. Sorry, ladies.

"I was just having tea, you have terrible tea here, what kind of country is this?"

"A free one, an emerging economy. We will never..."

"Shut up."

The other man shut up, I couldn't see him, but sensed he was no longer behind me.

My essential problem was that I was terribly excited. I have never, ever been viewed as a threat, never worried about getting abruptly shoved into the back of a windowless kidnap van, I'm not even cut off in traffic. Me, Victoria Gardner a kidnap-worthy threat. I was feeling pretty important until they started hitting me.

Flashlight man hit me across the face, almost knocking me from the unstable chair. Pain shot through my head, my arms jerked to brace my body and protect me from the fall. One of the slats gave. My head snapped back, and I sucked in a breath of choking dust and mold.

"We don't ask again. Tell us what you know!" He held up the flashlight like a bat. The light illuminated the room like a searchlight operated by a drunk. I followed the light. The storage room walls curved. There were no windows, so this could be one of the re-purposed bunkers I learned so much about this afternoon. Free-standing cupboards lined one wall. Thick bowls and plates, the kind favored by university commissaries, spilled from sagging damp cardboard banker boxes. Wide spatulas and large forks for industrial-size cooking were jumbled together in makeshift crates. The utilitarian equipment spoke of years of heavy, tasteless meals.

My phone buzzed. Of course, it did. I was trapped in a third-world cement underground ground bunker and for once AT&T comes through. Marvelous.

"What is this? Are you spying?" The man tucked the flashlight under his arm. The light pointed behind him, illuminating the door and plunging him into darkness. He realized his error just in time.

"Find the phone!" He flipped the flashlight around and illuminated my purse, now furiously vibrating. The partner gingerly unzipped the bag and pulled out my phone.

"Recording?" Flashlight man thrust the phone into my face so close I couldn't read it.

"Hold it away, please." I said calmly.

He pulled it away. It was a text, disappearing as soon as I

could read it. It was Tiffany, something about the realtor and Cindy and an offer on the apartment.

"Text her back, tell her I'm tied up at the moment."

"She knows nothing." The blonde man, we will call him Oslo, barked.

Flashlight man, we will call him Oscar, threw the phone and it bounced off my chest and landed at my feet. I struggled against the ropes, burning my wrists, stretching the rope at the cost of tightening the knots. But nothing gave. Of all the cheap-ass materials used in this country, they had to make good rope. Perhaps it was an import.

"Then what is she doing with him?"

Oh, dear lord Horus. I stopped struggling. "We are old friends." I enunciated the words.

The men smirked.

"I'm just here for a romantic getaway. You know, he is quite irresistible." I tried to conjure up some tears but was unsuccessful. Cindy had a black belt in tears, I was clearly not as gifted. "He said it would be romantic." I at least produced a catch in my voice.

Both men puffed up on behalf of all males in every country, emerging economy or not, all of whom believe with every fiber of their being that they are the final word in intellect, cunning, and sexuality, contrary to any woman's reactions or even careful explanation.

"I told you, asgje." Nothing. I could tell from his tone.

"What do you want?" I asked again.

"Where is Dr. Ratzenberg going next?"

"Why would I know that?" God's truth, when did I ever know what Nic would do next? Shit. Talk about sleeping with the enemy.

"She knows nothing." The other man repeated. Well, yes, I did know nothing, until you two came along.

The flashlight suddenly went off, the man uttered an oath

that sounded pointed and strong. I wasn't sure if we were done or if the flashlight batteries just gave out. A phone buzzed, not mine this time.

"We go." And just as abruptly as I was taken, I was abandoned.

"Hey, you can't leave me here." I yelled. My phone buzzed again and illuminated the low ceiling. It did give me a second of light. The door, dim across the room, was firmly shut probably locked from the outside. Oh damn, damn, damn.

I waited until their footsteps faded. I pushed at the chair. The slat finally gave, and I could pull my hands out. But they were still tied behind me. You know those actors who quickly jump through their hands so their hands are in front and they can do all sorts of escape—based activities? Think Jackie Chan or James Bond.

Yeah. About that. I couldn't lean over because my hands wouldn't ever clear my butt. I awkwardly lowered to the gritty floor and after what felt like five excruciating hours and almost dislocating both arms in the process, I managed to pull my tied hands under my butt and wiggle them out from under my legs (easier). It was not a sanctioned move from Senior Stretch, but it did the job. I hit the flashlight app on my phone, which had a fifty percent battery life and spent a number of precious minutes picking apart the knots to free one hand. This all took far longer to do than to explain.

I rattled the door. Since what was stored here wasn't all that valuable, there was no deadbolt, just a lock like on a domestic bedroom door. I knew from experience that a determined brother could smash a big hole through the typical suburban hollow core door (and pay for it with his own allowance, I'm not naming names. Vance.). And a pair of intrepid brothers could jimmy a lock with, what was it? A spatula. They had used Dad's best metal barbecue spatula.

With the phone in one hand, I rifled through the rejected

utensils until I found the heaviest spatula. With the phone on the floor for light, I worked the tip of the spatula between the doorknob and door frame. Two strong leveraged pulls and the door frame gave. It had taken Vance and Vince longer but that was because I was yelling at them from inside my bedroom and throwing all my stuffed animals at the door to distract them. My bedroom was ostensibly my own sanctuary and off-limits to boys. But they never did respect my boundaries.

Free at last. I turned off the phone and dropped it back into my purse. My left hand was still bound in rope. It looked like I forgot my safe word.

I closed the door behind me, jamming the spatula under the door to keep it from falling open and revealing my escape.

There wasn't anywhere to go but up. Our storage room was essentially a dead end. How long would it have taken for someone to find me? Had Nic even noticed my absence? How is it possible to get building permits for a hotel that doesn't offer adequate fire escapes?

I climbed to the first landing very cautiously, pausing to listen to any echoes or sounds. Fortunately, my shoes were silent. The first door grimly warned me about fire alarms. I took a pass and climbed to the second landing and second door, the one Oscar and Oslo used. It too warned about fire alarms, but I had had enough. I pushed open the door and emerged next to the restrooms on the ground floor of the hotel. No alarms. False advertising.

I righted myself as best I could in the ladies' room, happy to pee and to thoroughly wash my hands and abrasions. The rope dragged in the sink. I glanced around. The paper towel dispenser was empty but fortunately it was one of those older models equipped with sharp teeth to tear off sections of towels. I shoved my hand under it and sawed at the rope around my wrist as best I could. After a minute, the rope gave.

In a more sophisticated scenario, I'd keep the rope and submit it as evidence, looking for strands of hair, DNA, all those CSI kinds of things. My parents were certain that any trace you left in a restroom or public space could be traced directly back at you, so they were very careful in public spaces. Mother had watched a special report on the FBI and was frightened enough by the re-enactments of dozens of FBI agents invading the homes of innocent citizens that she vowed to never take a chance. I chucked the rope into the trash and headed out, pushing open the door with my bare hand just for good measure.

Nic, bless his increasingly black little heart, was pacing in the lobby. His hair was standing on end as if he had pressed his finger into a light socket. "Where have you been?" He cried when he saw me. "What happened to your face?"

"I ran into the door frame."

He looked at me in astonishment. "Jesus. We need to get out of here."

I raised my eyebrows. Ouch, it hurt to move my face. "Need?"

"We can leave tonight." He moved to the front desk, but I stopped him.

"We can't leave tonight, there are no buses running. We have to wait until morning."

His eyes traveled around the lobby, he reached out and pulled me close. "Okay, okay. You're right, you're always right." He looked into my eyes. I swallowed but resisted saying anything more. "Did you know that?"

"I did not know that, but I'm right this time."

CHAPTER EIGHTEEN

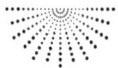

 $\mathcal{W}$ e walked in lockstep to the elevator, Nic seemed reluctant to let me go. I snuggled closer on the elevator ride. My shoulder ached, my arms hurt, my torn skin needed to be covered in Neosporin. But at least I was safe. Nic locked the door, secured the chain and I shoved the only chair in the room under the doorknob.

"Who did this to you?" He sat on the edge of the bed and watched me as I bustled around inflicting my version of security.

"Oscar and Oslo."

"They gave you their names?"

I put my hands on my hips and glared at him with my one good eye.

He held his hands up in supplication. "Sorry. What did they want?"

"You."

"Ah."

"I appreciate you coming with me on this incredibly unproductive goose chase. Apparently, I could have stayed home and tortured you for information."

To his credit he didn't bother to prevaricate. "At the bar, what did you call him?"

"Oslo. The one with the blond hair."

Nic nodded. He followed me to the bathroom where I washed my scraped arms again for good measure. "They know me from the archeology project, they think I know where the source of the hippo is."

"And do you?"

He shook his head. "They aren't our guys; I don't know where they came from or what they want."

I straightened from the sink, wincing as my back tweaked. I needed to stretch, but it always looks so awkward, and I did not need to look any more vulnerable in front of Nic.

"Where did they come from?"

He shook his head. "I don't even know. This was such a bust." He reached out and lightly touched my sore arm. "I shouldn't have gotten you into this. I'm sorry."

I met his eyes. "We need to go to Egypt."

He shook his head, which was astonishing. I thought he'd jump at the chance to return. But even if he didn't want to keep going, I did. I wanted, I needed to discover the end of the story even if he did not. I was the victim of violence; I was the victim of theft and I had lost my best friend. I was all in. At least for forty-eight more hours.

"Don't you want to find out who is stealing precious artifacts?"

"Not so precious," he replied.

I needed a shower and started removing my dirty clothes. I regarded the blouse. It was impressively ugly. No one in my past would have ever approved. And no one in my present would approve either. I shoved it into the small bathroom trash can.

"Precious enough. Valuable enough." I eyed the can;

195

would it hold the slacks as well? I tried. "I want Miranda to rest." I balled up the slacks. "I want to understand why she died."

The slacks barely fit into the tiny waste can. "Is that too much to ask?"

The ball resisted my initial stuffing. "We all need a reason, a good ending to our story." I lifted my bare foot and stomped down on the wad of indestructible beige. Those clothes would never pop out again. Triumphant, I faced him in my bra and panties.

"You've thought a lot about this." He regarded me with at least a modicum of appreciation.

I pulled off the wig and dropped it on top of the garbage can. Now the can looked like a badly dressed robot.

"I've been around death for quite a while now. I'm practically a professional."

About sleeping with the enemy. Life is shorter than we think. I had insisted on following the lead to Albania, dragging Nic along, not realizing that Nic was part of the problem. Cindy could be part of the problem; the thugs Oslo and Oscar were part of the problem. So out of a whole menu of bad choices, Nic at night was an easy yes. That's what happens when you get older. You take the easy yes because the odds are good and you've already experienced the worst of the nos.

I woke later the same night, my phone lit up and furiously vibrating. I pulled it to me and held it at arm's length to see better. Cindy. I could take her call or wait for her text. I chose text.

Men at the door. What should do?

Lock, go to bed.

When back?

Two more days. I thought of telling her we were headed to Luxor, but then changed my mind.

I woke stiff and sore, facing an abundance of missives from needy strangers and loving family.

Maria, the real estate agent texted me and demanded that Cindy open the door; she had more prospects. This did not look good for us.

Matt texted me, he was out with friends, other was mad, what should he do?

Chris had sent a photo of the proposed Luxor Deep Bay project. The photo was clear, pulled from a website. Twelve men stood in a line on the sand, no identifying monuments on the horizon, so they could have been anywhere. The tall man in the center held a shovel decorated with a red bow. No one smiled. To the far left of the group was Nic.

He groaned and rolled on his back. "On the phone already? Are you ever off that thing?"

I held up the phone to him.

"I can explain." He made to grab the phone, but I held it out of reach. "I told you, I'm consulting on the project."

I studied the phone. "It says here you are the resident archeology expert."

He nodded, but he was clearly not proud of the title.

I read more. "Dredge the Nile? Is that even possible?"

"They want to dredge the Nile for bigger boats, create a longer dock." I continued to look at him, making him focus on my bruised face.

"They want to make it so deep the Suez will look like a drainage ditch." He was sulky, like Matt the afternoon we caught him emptying the fireplace ash all over baby Chris.

"That doesn't sound sustainable."

"Since the dam, it's easy. There is no more flooding and the silt doesn't back up like it used to. Besides," he muttered. "Anything is possible."

I gave him a disgusted look. "I'm sure anything is." I

turned away and texted Matt with possible excuses that Tina hadn't already heard.

What was really depressing? I was not surprised. These are the people who allowed a circus strong man to haul a full-size obelisk to London and probably helped him load it onto the barge. This is a government that doesn't arrest men who use dynamite to blow up inconvenient monuments standing in the way of more remunerative tombs. They are too overloaded to worry about a little more digging along a river that had survived Libyans, Nubians, Hyksos, Napoleon and a dam.

"They need the tourism," Nic said, reading my mind. "It's their only export."

"That and black-market artifacts."

"That has a place as well," he admitted.

"Tomb robbing."

"Done before the mummy was even fully stiffened," he countered.

"I know that."

"It's been a long time."

I rubbed my face, avoiding the sore bruised sections. I had to go home. I could go now, be there early and ease Tina's mind, and reassure the boys that their aunt, at least, could be counted on.

Nic sat up and stroked my bare back. "What if a whole ship load comes? Double, triple the fees, the food, the guides. Egypt could be popular. It could take the boats that other countries are currently rejecting. If your people are starving, why wouldn't you do anything to make it better?"

I remained silent.

"Hungry people riot." I said. "Hungry people demand change."

He gave me a look. While Nic was busy with coeds and lectures at UCSB, I audited a class by Dr. Fagan at the height of his popularity. I remembered a great deal about Egyptian history and myth. A surprising lot of it was returning.

In the end I kept my enemy closer. I had a feeling so much of our trouble would circle around and land back on Nic, so for answers, I might as well stick with the evil I knew. The good news was we could fly directly from Tirana to Cairo.

The Cairo airport had been remodeled. The arched girders and sandstone floors and ceilings reflected the tombs and temples most tourists hustling through the corridors were scheduled to tour, like a taste of delights to come.

I took a deep breath; the air was bone dry a term that well could have been invented by the nineteenth-century explorers as they dug for Egypt's treasures. The air conditioning was turned on frigid. I shivered but did not complain. I was back, wasn't I? When I left Nic, striding purposefully through this very terminal, I carried not only heavy luggage, but also a heavy stone in my stomach, convinced that I would never see the pyramids again.

I paused, relishing my return.

Nic studied the departure board searching for our Egypt Air flight to Luxor.

I automatically clocked off airplane mode on my phone.

The texts pinged like a wild party. I glanced up and located our flight—on time, out of Gate E14. I dropped my gaze and studied my phone. Tiffany and Lucy texted together to both me and Maria. What did we think? Who were these buyers? Did I have their names? Where were they from? Where are you?

I did not say where I was since I was supposed to be grounded in Venice with no passport.

Those Italians are so inefficient! Tiffany texted.

Yet Maria, with I assumed Cindy's help, was showing the apartment to three prospective buyers today. The girls couldn't complain.

But complain they did.

Nic turned away from the board. "We're at Gate E14."

I smiled at him like he was Ramses II and followed. Fortunately, Nic headed in the right direction.

We passed crowds of passengers heading towards the exits. I glanced at a few young men as they passed by. Attractive, but not dangerous.

Tiffany wanted to know the offer price.

I felt like I was boarding the final boat with Anubis and heading down to the underworld, hoping all my goods, shipped ahead so to speak, would be there and intact when I needed them for my next life-round. And here I was, on a next round. I never thought I'd be back. I never thought I'd do anything like this; despite years of cautionary news stories, I certainly never thought I'd get beat up.

I took a lungful of the chilled artificial air and plunged back into the adventure.

Be careful what you wish for.

I pressed my head against the plane window trying to catch a glimpse of the pyramids. The privacy of the flight was a perfect time for Nic to confess everything: why he could support dredging the Nile of all things, why he knew about the stolen artifacts, and, frankly, what did he know about Miranda's death? Maybe I needed to tie him to a chair and beat him with a rubber hose.

We disembarked quickly since we didn't even have carry-on luggage and headed past the stylized papyrus columns decorating the Luxor airport to the paint scratched cabs parked in the brutal sun.

"Winter Palace." I slid into the back seat.

"Too expensive." Nic slid in next to me and slammed the door.

"Not it's not, it's perfect."

I gave him a look and he actually shrank back. Good. "I've

camped with you on the perimeters of more digs that I care to remember. I've been a good sport all my life. The beds in Albania were tragically uncomfortable. And I would like a modicum of security and working fire escapes." Forget hunger, a couple of sleepless nights was enough to trigger a revolution. I certainly was ready.

"Because I say so," I added, a phrase I picked up from my sister-in-law.

A text from Chris—Did I know that green wallpaper was made with arsenic?

I did not know that, I texted back.

Three more texts from Tiffany, mostly about her need to quickly sell Miranda's apartment and what was Maria doing anyway?

I reminded her that Maria was showing the house.

Tiffany texted that Maria couldn't get into the apartment. Cindy should be there.

Cindy, Tiffany informed me, was not there.

Shit. I glanced at Nic who was lost in thought or just didn't want to engage in more conversation.

I texted Cindy. I texted Maria and described where the additional key was hidden. Well, not so hidden now.

At least Maria responded in an internationally understood smiley face. Using all the emojis in my texts called to mind hieroglyphics.

The cab pulled up to the covered portico of the Winter Palace. Not looking like qualified guests, we climbed the left curving stairs to the second-floor lobby.

I love this hotel. Just being here allows me to be Agatha Christie scribbling notes for Death on the Nile or Amelia Edwards and Barbara Mertz recording their adventures both real and marvelously fictional. I was again an archeologist. Even if just for the night. I had one night.

The lobby was spacious and cool flanked by (ironically)

Corinthian topped columns. Well-dressed men and women lingered in the lobby. It was mid-day, a few tourists braved the blistering sun by the pool but, most guests stayed under protective umbrellas and awnings, retreating to their cool hotel rooms.

We walked past the curved stairs to the upper, and older rooms. The wide gardens in the back were welcoming green. Out the front doors ran the Nile and across was the West Bank. The Valley of the Kings shimmering in the heat. Later I would visit the best souvenir shop in town situated on the street level just below the gently curved walkway.

Adventure, sex, and danger. This was it then, I had to figure it all out right now, no time to waste.

While Nic paid for our room, I checked in with the family.

Chris texted that Matt was finally out of prison (likely just repeating what Matt called it. I would hardly call Matt's room a prison. In fact, for about five years, it was hard to pry the boy OUT of his room. He obviously didn't remember that phase, nor did his mother). Chris was now looking into related finds close to the Luxor Bay dig. I texted him that Venice was lovely this time of year confident he'd pass that along to Tina. As much as I wanted to, I did not post any photo of the hotel or the East Nile Bank on Instagram or Facebook.

The hotel where Tiffany had left her paintings texted and asked what to do with them and when was I coming to get them?

I called, regretting the cost but it was necessary. After a protracted argument and assurances, they were willing, once I offered a decent amount for their trouble, to ship the paintings themselves.

Fed Ex, I suggested.

"That is more expensive."

"Worth it at this point." My phone buzzed again.

Matt was actually on probation and would not be able to drive for another year. Tina treated me to an alarming number of exclamation points.

Tomorrow, I texted. Just have a few things to wrap up.

We accepted an offer for the house, Vince texted.

I was officially homeless.

Nic over-tipped the bellman because the poor man couldn't understand that we really did not have any luggage. We followed the bellman in single file, Nic in the lead as I scrolled through more family texts: the offer for Mom's house; the offer for the apartment; ominously, nothing from Cindy; and one from Chris, a minute ago—check this out and a link.

I followed the link while Nic waved the key card over the door lock.

Chris had found an article posted last month. The dredging project, the Deep Nile Port would be an enormous port, purpose-built for larger ships. Safe and secure, the promoters anticipated that the dock would increase local prosperity, raise up the economy, and offer unprecedented value to their visitors. No longer would guests need to suffer strangers trooping thorough their small river boats to reach the dock (river boats dock four deep requiring the passengers in boat four to reach the shore by walking through the lobbies of boats 1–3). No longer will tourists languish on the deck of a small Nile boat with nothing but a drink and the stars. With a deep-water dock, full luxury cruise ships could bring tourists from Cairo to Luxor in the style in which they all pay to become accustomed to. Okay, that last bit was mine.

I scrolled down. A picture emerged, a group of men in hard hats, the organizers and investors, and (I enlarged the photo) their own personal lackey, Archeologist Dr. Nicholas

Ratzenberg who was quoted that no legitimate archeology sites were in danger from the project. There were no settlements or work villages, let alone tombs or even late-Greek burial sites. The project could go forward with residents having confidence that nothing of value would be disturbed.

Our hotel room was decorated in late excessive imperial; it looked like one of Napoleon's savants had just stepped out. A wide bed was framed by a half canopy. Tall windows swaged in green velvet overlooked the West Bank. Three inlaid end tables were scattered around, and an empire marble topped coffee table designated the sitting area.

This was more like it. I wandered to the window while Nic washed up. To the far left three enormous orange cranes punctured the sky. I texted Chris: Excellent job, what else can you learn about illegal trafficking in artifacts?

Still on poison, he texted back.

Anything interesting?

Some poisons look like something else.

I puzzled over that, but Chris was finished for the evening.

"Want to see it?" Nic absently rubbed the back of his neck.

"The deep port?"

He nodded. "It's just down the road, we can walk."

"Close to Karnak?"

"Not even that far."

That was depressing news, I worry about any project close to Luxor. Even though Nic was on the record claiming there was nothing important buried at the dredge site, who really knew what was buried in the Egyptian sand? Who knew what important artifact, mummy, palace, could be destroyed? We strolled under the heat of the mid-day sun. Nic's hand was stiff in mine. I tipped my face into the brutal sun that even as it ruined my skin and faded my auburn highlights, I loved.

That the proposed port was even this close to the hotel as well as the most famous temple complex, Karnak, was appalling. All I could envision was a huge twenty-five deck ship between us and the glories of the West Bank. The high decks blotting out Aten, the sun, and throwing shade on all the residents and workers.

It was a longer walk than Nic promised. Almost an hour away. The sun, welcome during the first half of the walk, now pierced through my scalp hotter than a laser peel. My feet hurt. I wasn't wearing walking shoes; I was wearing sandals I picked up from the Albania gift store. They were not up to the hike. I could feel a strap start to give.

Working digs are little more than huge, carefully marked holes populated by interns and students excited by small things half covered in heavy dirt and sand. This was much worse.

The three cranes I saw from the hotel window marked out the project. Like the worst nightmares of Sobek the crocodile god, the jaws of the back hoes had bit chunks out the riverbank. River water slowly circled in the declivities swirling flotsam and plastics in the blocked eddies.

"See? Bigger boats." Nic gestured with obvious pride.

"Bigger boats." I repeated, my eyes on the dirt, then to the Valley of the Queens shimmering across the calm river.

"People want action and excitement," he continued to explain, then elaborated as if he had memorized a brochure.

"Gambling, dancing, entertainment. You can't offer that on our tiny river boats. There is nothing to do at night here, and to attract more tourists, we need to change with the times."

We.

I let it pass. All that change world stuff? I was too tired, too demoralized. Only a handful of really dedicated people still change the world and when they do, FOX News cuts them down. It's no wonder that so many retirees feel they earned long afternoons doing nothing but dreaming on ships that plied the ocean, the rivers, the Nile. But when you do retire, what about dreams? With thoughts like this, I should just get embalmed today.

I glanced at Nic, frowning at the sand as if more tiny artifacts would sprout like zucchini in a home garden. He hadn't published a quite a while; if he had, Chris would have found the article and forwarded it to me.

My treacherous heart surged with pity, was Nic unable to afford his own ethics?

"Is this where the digging park will be?" I asked gently. Maybe the plastic along with the real artifacts were part of the park, seeding it so there is always digging success, like the shells on the Disney island, like the authentic gold panning experiences in Alaska. Look, how easy it is to find things, all you need is a ticket and fifteen minutes.

"What?" He looked up at me and frowned, as if he forgot I was there.

"The park?" I nudged gently.

"Oh, it will be around here, you know, once the dock is built the park will be filled in after that. But first."

"First you need to authenticate or disprove that there is any historical significance." I put in.

There must be a great deal of pressure to not discover any artifacts.

He was lost in thought. It was the last quiet moment we would share.

He shoved his hands in his pocket. "You don't understand. You've been living with other people for so long you don't know what it's like to be on your own."

That drew me up short and I automatically raised up like a bear. And you don't poke the bear.

"Excuse me? Since when was being responsible for everything in my household as well as invalids, not being on my own? Do you know how utterly claustrophobic yet devastatingly lonely that life is? Do you have any idea what it is like to not go where you want or do what you want with no end in sight? You try it. If I recall, you can't even keep a cactus alive."

"Ouch, sorry." He held up his hands in supplication. "I hit a nerve, sorry."

CHAPTER NINETEEN

*W*e walked more slowly back to the Winter Palace. The texting had calmed, for which I was grateful. Chris texted that the site in question could have been a burial site, but it was still unconfirmed. Only one archeologist had discovered anything, and he had retired long ago.

From what university?

UCSB.

Can you contact him?

Of course.

I pocketed my phone and flashed Nic an insincere smile.

Much restored after a drink at the hotel bar, Nic continued his justification for a project that seemed, on the surface, rather obscene, but clearly representing a big investment. Big enough to kill for?

"It's a great idea." But Nic wasn't looking at the site, his eyes were fixed on the valleys across the Nile.

"The current regime needs an economic win."

"At the cost of their own history." I sipped my white wine and followed his gaze. The West Bank was the land of the dead because that's where the sun went to die every day, before Nut gives birth to it in the morning. My favorite god is Nut. She swallows the sun every night and gives birth to the sun every dawn. Many tombs feature Nut. Her long body arches over the ceiling, protecting the sarcophagus and representing the everyday miracle of death and birth.

She was swallowing the sun now. It hung low and orange over the valley hills.

"It's not like they don't do this kind of thing every thousand years or so. The Ptolemies weren't exactly preservationists, neither were the Muslims."

"Napoleon."

"Didn't last and the only way to save artifacts was to ship them out of the country."

"You are not convincing me."

"I don't need to convince you, I need to tell you that these are not rulers, they are thugs, extortionists and have only their own reputations to solidify, they need a nice big dock that hosts four or five large cruise ships."

"Built by?"

He shrugged. "Partners with money. The idea is to bring over all the parts up the Suez then assemble the ships in Alexandria and sail them up and down the Nile. It will make for a lot of press, lots of positive attention, tourism will increase. Look how great Egypt is again."

"It's always been great," I put in.

"You say. They need rather more than academic promotion."

"It takes time." I considered the raw ground, the crumbling edges. The Nile no longer flooded, which was, in a way, a pity. Controlling the river engendered its own problems and unintended consequences. I lived on Max's first floor apartment long enough to understand the downsides of river living. I didn't blame the locals for getting fed up with losing their river side homes every year. Yet I always thought the dam and lake were little more than a giant vanity project for Nasser, not much different from Ramses II who built the enormous Hypostyle Hall in Karnak. Or the pyramids. The country was riddled with vanity projects.

And here we are again.

"It should be finished by January." Nic seemed be reassuring himself more than me.

"Not at the rate they are going." Even if the builders were coincidently the same people issuing the permits and approving EPA studies.

Dr. Anderson. Chris was up late. He sent along another article. The research confirmed the area was little more than a village and burial site for workers. Of no consequence. Made of mud, the village had been destroyed year after year until the turn of the century when families just gave up and moved to higher ground.

So Nic was right, the area really wasn't of historical value.

Unless someone, an intern, a worker, a digger, found a charming, adorable hippo. It wasn't difficult to imagine what revealing the provenance of my hippo, especially with the reputation of The Met's William, would do. Finding the hippo, linking him to the current project, which does not photograph well, would be like strangling a kitten on YouTube. There would be protests, there would be damaging press. Questions. Even if Nic stood on the sandbanks waving his arms and declaring there was nothing to see here. The regime, the men in charge, would not hold up well under any kind of scrutiny.

The term is overtourism, but right now, that's not a problem for Egypt. If you shoot tourists on a regular basis, like those shoot tourists who died at the Temple of Hatshepsut, you end up with a pretty low visitor count. Egypt and tourism did bounce back the following year. But if limiting cruises is a thing in Venice, it seemed Egypt was ready to welcome them with open arms. Unless the hippo was from that site. The news would slow, or even stop while the hippo debate raged on. All the resort money would rush across the Red Sea to Sharm El Sheikh.

Nic broke the silence first. "Where is it, Vic? You aren't safe as long as you are the only one who knows."

"Nice try." I wiped my forehead, but it was so hot, my perspiration just evaporated. "I told you, I don't have it."

"They don't know that."

I opened my arms. "Yes, they do. They stole my purse and searched my apartment, and I did not bring it with me to Egypt. I. Don't. Have. It."

He frowned. "Then why are they still following us?"

"If I don't have it, maybe they think you do."

"They are just middle-men, I don't know them. Why would I put you at risk?" He trailed me into our room. I stopped so quickly he bumped into me.

"Is that a serious question? You never hesitated to put me at risk. Remember lowering me into the underground tomb?"

"You were the slenderest person there."

"I have never been the slenderest person anywhere."

"I could trust you," I amended.

The tomb had been dark, smelly and stifling hot. I could make out a few painted figures, harvest offerings, a cartouche. And a whole floor littered with sharp debris. It wouldn't have been so bad except someone, and I'm not making accusations these many years later, dropped me.

"And you can't now?" It was an unfair question. He had to trust me. We were now dealing with two competing companies, both run by members of middle management so well-siloed that no one knew what anyone else was doing, what the other team knew. On the one hand, the original group, a man who was feared, worked outside the Mafia and used lovely girls like Cindy as their mules. On the other we had our emerging-economy men, Oslo and Oscar, who were busy with their own version of a hostile takeover.

Hostile.

"I'm taking a shower."

When I emerged, fluffing my hair, Nic was on the edge of the bed staring at his phone.

"Need to contact the construction people? Give them the all clear?"

"They said they would call in an hour." He glanced at his watch even though the time was displayed on his phone.

"Why the wait?"

He shrugged. "Why not the wait?"

He was not the guy in charge, that's why the wait. I knew that game. By making him wait, the men in charge were asserting their power. Poor Nic.

It was like waiting for Godot. With little else on our schedule, we left the room to explore Luxor Temple. It was close to the hotel, an honestly easy walk, and better than staring at each other in the bar. We both felt better when we could move around.

"He seems odd." I passed by a formally dressed young man, the conservative suit a marked contrast with his youthful face. It was like passing Magritte's The Age of Man: discreet, business-like and out of place.

Nic glanced at him and shrugged. "They still do business here."

"I didn't mean that."

"I know what you meant, don't worry about him, keep an eye out for our tall Eastern Europeans."

"With long rock star hair and guns."

"Yes, possibly with guns."

"And they aren't your people."

He touched my bruised face, fading to a gross green (the British description is bilious, but it was fading so it wasn't necessary to get the terminology exact).

"They aren't my people. They are just opportunists. Dangerous because now they are desperate." Thank you for that confirmation Dr. Ratzenberg.

"Aren't we all?"

"Dangerous?"

"Desperate."

I did not care why we needed to travel to Egypt. I did not care that Nic couldn't just call and assure his people that all was under control. I indulged in the moment, conscious that my moments were ticking away.

I threw Tina a bone and texted that I now had my passport and would return at the end of the day tomorrow. I did not wait for her response.

By the time Matt and Chris graduated from high school, it would probably be time to care for Vince and Tina, or Vance would want to have a turn at having a full-time, live-in maid. Or someone will break a hip. I shook my head and tried to focus on the moment.

We strolled down the renovated Avenue of Sphinxes. The sphinxes were always here, lining the path between Luxor Temple and the great Karnak complex, but for years (thousands of years) the statues had served as climbing structures, planters and glorified ash trays. No more. Tourists loved the Avenue, Egyptians loved tourists; the temple path was beautiful and well cared for.

The temple pylons, two towering walls, loomed over us as we entered the temple. There is no question you are entering the house of the gods, many gods, and like any good temple or mosque or church, it was built so you really felt the glory and the awe.

At the entrance, just on the other side of the pylons, were the remains of a mosque, built on top of the temple when the temple was so thoroughly buried the top of the pylons were ground level.

The phone pinged—Tina.

I pulled away from contemplating the mosque and making an inane comment about life, sand and preservation and moved to the shadows of the first hypostyle hall—lined with thirty-two columns, all sanded clean, but back in the day, would have been brightly painted.

We've been really patient, but you owe it to us to return home immediately and help the family. We let you live in mom and dad's house rent free and now you need to come back and help with the boys. They are out of control. Need I remind you that I'm still working? And Vince is busy with Rotary and can't be watching the boys every afternoon. I …

She must have hit send before finishing the rant.

I read the text again. Owe them? The hairs on the back of my neck stood up.

Nic stopped and turned. "What's wrong? Bad news from home?"

I looked up from the phone. "Do you think I am codependent?"

"With Max?"

My eyes widened. He shrugged. "It was always Max this, or Max said that. You never detached from him, even when you were with Miranda."

I must have looked as stunned as I felt.

He took my hands. "It's okay. We had a great run, I loved you. I still love you. I had excitement and sex on my side. I was willing to take that for as long as I could. Miranda too. But Max was like your father."

I tipped my head.

"Your Victorian, controlling, overbearing father."

"I loved Max." I said.

"And he loved you." Nic confirmed.

"Shouldn't I love my real family the same way?"

He fixed me with a look I couldn't read.

"Haven't you already loved them enough? Come on, see how they restored some of the friezes. I don't agree with the restoration technique, but you can't argue these are fabulous." He led me away, chattering so I could compose myself.

I had a tiny hope that left on their own, Vince and Tina would find a way back to their own children, that they would actually parent. But I'm not Mary Poppins. I am me, an aging fashionista, but maybe with a little *ista* sill left.

Nic spied the friezes first. "And here we are."

I followed him, still holding the phone in my palm, anticipating Tina's follow up text. But the phone remained silent. I was just slipping it into my pocket when a movement caught my eye.

The temples are usually crowded, I don't know what Nic's people are concerned about, but there seems to be plenty of tourists brought in daily to admire Luxor Temple and Karnak before loading into buses to sweat through the tomb tour of both Valley of the Kings and the Valley of the Queens. And of course, the obligatory stop in a factory featuring hand-carved artifacts, anything you want as long as you want poor-quality marble.

A large tour group from Japan flowed into the hall and wedged between me and Nic. To a one, the young ladies were dressed head-to-heel in Prada, as if they had all raided the Prada flagship store in Milan, which they very well may have. Wearing bright flowered dresses and high-heeled Mary Janes, the girls moved slowly because of the heat and their finery. I enjoyed the contrast of light bright fabric against the harsh earth-toned columns. Their guide held a yellow umbrella and spoke rapidly, gesturing with a handful of brochures. The group paused and nodded as their guide walked them through the temple calling out—this many—this tall—this old.

I always admired the shear audacity of the pharaohs. They had the manpower, they had more food than they needed, let's build a pyramid, let's build a grand hall. Let's build an incredible rock-cut temple just to show the Nubians who is King. Commissioning large buildings and tall phallic obelisks in honor of yourself is apparently a human impulse that never went out of style.

I strolled towards the recently (to me) revealed friezes, complete with more hieroglyphs. Chris has a hieroglyphic typewriter app and for about two years texted me in hieroglyphs. Not necessarily exact, the Rosetta Stone aside, trading an ancient image for a western symbol, like A is for Vulture, will reasonably lose much in the simplification, but close enough for a good time. Champollion would be proud.

Long blond hair glowed in the direct sun. My first thought was—he needs a hat. My second thought was, holy shit, Oslo, my Albanian kidnapper.

He held a guidebook, Fodor's or Frommer's, Rick Steves doesn't do Egypt. Oslo's partner, the man who met with Nic in the bar, caught a glimpse of me and gestured to his pal. Who, in turn, gestured to the next hall grander than the first, with a frown of disappointment. His partner was not having it and moved quickly towards me. But the Princesses of Prada cut them off, ooh and aahing at the tall (it was this tall, the guide was probably explaining), and I was suddenly gifted with precious seconds to disappear. But where the hell was Nic?

I stepped over a Do Not Enter barrier, red and imposing, and struggled along a rubble-strewn alley that snaked behind the main temple walls. Oslo and Oscar of course could meet me on the other side, but the rubble was easier to navigate than the Russian and French groups from Viking Cruise. I ducked out and brushed my legs. Nic, oblivious to the crowds pushing and photographing around him, was deep in thought as he stared at a section of preserved wall.

"We have to go," I whispered.

"What?"

I glanced over at the entrance to this hall, the blonde had just negotiated the entrance waving his guidebook and arguing with his partner.

"Now."

He followed my head nod and his eyes grew large. I glanced around, how much had the temple changed? Ah, not by much, fortunately.

I led Nic through the Christianized temple, easily converted by hacking out the faces of Isis and her child Horus, replacing them with Mary and baby Jesus. The temple looked like a dead end. But I remembered a slight opening at the back, easy to negotiate when I was thinner and younger, a bit challenging this afternoon. I winced as my new shirt and slacks grated like cheese through the opening, but I pushed through, both because I did not want to be stuck and because I needed to show off. I sucked in my breath, held it and pushed through worried I'd crack the wall, but it held.

Nic came through a little easier, I helped get his head clear of the stones and pulled him through by the arm. This was a younger person's escape route.

There isn't a back way out of the temple complex and, by the way, we were located in the center of town, so I figured we'd hide behind a food truck selling falafels rather than make a mad dash across the barren open desert. We had a head start, but no plan. We ducked over the untrodden debris, pushed behind the more beautiful walls. We dodged around the back ignoring the admonishing signs—Don't Touch, Do Not Enter, Don't. We dashed past the No Exit sign and tumbled out onto the sidewalk. Nic glanced back and gestured for me to crouch behind the parked cars.

Nic coughed, trying to catch his breath. We had kicked up quite a bit of sand, ancient stone and modern dust. Plus, the squeeze was a little extreme. I placed my hand on the scarred car for balance. There isn't a car in Luxor, or even Cairo that escaped the paint searing sandstorms common this time of year.

"How did you know that back way?" He gasped.

I patted the side of the car and raised up enough to see if we did indeed escape.

"Old escape route. I used to dash out to shop, then slide back in."

"I never noticed."

"No, you did not."

That was before the handy hieroglyphic app. I had picked up the ability to read some hieroglyphics and demotic but not enough spend hours in study. Nic took another breath and hacked unpleasantly. I turned my head and pretended to examine the car.

We rose again, urban prairie dogs. A tour group, this time made up of beet-red Germans dressed in flimsy tank tops and tee shirts and (to me) uncomfortably tiny shorts, clustered around the falafel stand. A trickle of tourists exited the temple at a sedate pace, no one was in a hurry. No one looked like they were searching for someone.

"They can just return to the hotel," I pointed out.

Nic slowly stood. He extended his hand to help me up. "It's not about being found." He grunted and helped me get to my feet. "It's about safety. Relative safety," he amended.

I brushed off my shirt and slacks and I took his arm. Even in a strongly Coptic city, it was better—easier—to be literally attached to a man. I would never walk three steps behind him, but still. In the past I often enough pretended he was in charge, whispering behind him, telling him what to say.

I squeezed his arm every time I sensed he was about to glance backward. We headed toward the Winter Palace, the city on our left, the Nile running silently on our right. There is a saying in the Egyptian Tourism Bureau: Where the Perfect Climate Can Be Obtained." It was indeed perfect.

I breathed in the hot dry air and raised my face. The true god or not, the sun here was important, worthy of worship.

"Why don't they just wait outside the hotel, drag us into a car, and dump us in the desert?"

Which is exactly what they finally did.

CHAPTER TWENTY

*A*s soon as Nut swallowed the sun, we ventured from the hotel for dinner.

We had just gained the street when a battered car pulled up. We made to step around it, but before I could move, I was hit from behind. I remember falling forward. I don't remember catching myself since I was occupied with the flashing pain and trying to come back to consciousness.

When I came to (like the phrase, then everything changed, I really have always wanted to say that), I was prone on the back seat of a very poorly maintained sedan. Under me was a restless Nic, all lumps and elbows. A blanket that smelled like it had been stolen off a camel smothered us.

I poked an arm and was rewarded with a grunt. Do I claw back the blanket? Do I stay down? What was the protocol?

"Where?" Nic's voice was muffled. "Where are you getting the statues?"

Oh, like they would helpfully blurt that out while driving us out to the desert and certain death.

"Shut up."

A dull thud. Nic stiffened. I inched my hand up to touch his shoulder; it didn't calm him, but I felt better.

The roads leading straight out to the desert are often blocked or covered in drifting sand, I was confident that I would be able to tell when we hit what would be essentially the point of no return.

I did not relish being dumped out in the desert, not with Nic, not even with T.E. Lawrence, not even with Gertrude Bell. Not with anyone. I would prefer to be dumped any place else—the slums, the souk, the Nile itself since it's surprisingly clean. That supply closet in Albania filled with handy tools.

We bumped along for more time than it takes to reach the desert. Which way? West over one of the few bridges over the Nile? Or east, into nothing much beyond the suburbs of Luxor?

Please let it be east, at least we could quickly figure out where to head, we'd have a goal.

It was not east.

The car stopped. I was pulled out first, coughing and brushing the hair from my eyes. My feet met hard surface, not the open desert at all. As I caught my breath, my captor did not lose his grip on my arm, which was still recovering from the last encounter. But was it the same man? I tried to make out his features, but my eyes weren't focusing. At my age, it takes longer to recover from a direct assault.

The man behind me kept a grip on my arm as if there was some place to run. Nic stood on the other side of the car catching his breath. In the shadows our captors scanned the empty parking lot then pushed us forward.

We were at the foot of the Valley of the Kings, which judging by the empty lot, closed at 5:00. The scores of merchants selling everything from rugs to textiles to tees had all packed up for the night. No sign of a night guard, just the locked visitors center and a chain pulled across the only road into the center of the valley. Above us I could just make out a corner of Mena House, where Howard Carter lived for years while he dug everywhere, including the unpromising section that eventually revealed Tutankhamun's tomb. West of the Nile, the land of Anubis where the dead live.

"I don't have enough for admission." Nic commented.

One of men raised his hand as if to hit Nic again.

Were they wearing masks? Oh lord, Aten, Isis, and Horus. The two of them were masked, which meant, according to all the TV I had reluctantly been subjugated to, we might survive.

I was dismayed there wasn't more security. I opened my mouth to say so but Nic gave me a look, why guard the dead? Especially since all the tomb entrances were gated and locked. Why lock in the dead? Keep animals out, keep careless tourists out. Keep murderous kidnapers out.

Like a nightmare tour where the guide insists that you see everything during a one hour stop, the men pushed and dragged us through the center of the valley to the southwest end of the West Valley finally stopping at the entrance of a tomb about fourteen feet from the valley floor. In the fading light I could just discern the sign: KV 25. The metal gate hung open as if expecting us. Damn.

My keeper pulled me up the metal stairs, making impatient noises when I stumbled. I righted myself and tried to find my footing, but he kept jerking my arm, pulling me off balance.

Nic behind me was more vocal. "I'm coming, don't pull on me. I can't see very well, I'm old and where will I run?"

His captor was as unimpressed with the protest as mine. No respect for their elders.

We plunged into the tomb following the dark narrow corridor. When Nic and his captor entered, their bodies blocked all available light. My captor stubbed his toe and swore in Italian. He fumbled for his phone and flipped on the flashlight app.

We passed the best of the wall art, protected by plates of plexiglass, ostensibly to protect the wall paintings, but the barrier ended up effectively trapping even more moisture. The moisture and salt push the paint away from the walls, like frost pushes up back-yard dirt. Just our breath, just the water content of our bodies leaches the beautifully painted tomb walls. Tourists come to see the tombs; tourists destroy the tombs. Egypt needs tourism, but tourists may not be the best answer.

Our captors were not all that concerned with our comfort or curiosity. As we moved forward the paintings faded into smooth plaster walls, ready for decorations that will never appear. No Anubis, weighing the heart against a feather, no loaded barca heading to the afterlife. No women decked out in their stiff linen gowns and stiffer headdresses. We walked past the black square entrances of side tombs and were shuffled over a plywood board bridge and into the main chamber. KV 25 wasn't a grand tomb; in fact, it wasn't much of a tomb at all. Which was a very bad sign. Visitors to the Valley of the Kings were currently limited to entering three tombs, which means only the most beautiful, like any tomb for a Ramses, will do. But this out-of-way tomb with a broken gate? Not so much.

We hiked in the flickering flashlight—Nic, for the first time, keeping his mouth shut.

Familiar with the idea that the reason criminals rob banks is because that's where the money is? Forget tombs. Except for Carter's spectacular find, there is little left in the average tomb except for the remains of the pharaohs themselves and even their remains were often ravaged for the amulets and gold folded into their wrapping linens.

And who were the robbers? Not, as you would guess, men like Belzoni or even Nic. Tomb robbers were often the very fellows who built the tomb in the first place. Who else would know where all the booby traps were placed? Who knew best how to negotiate the maze of dead-end cuts and blocked corridors than the men who built them? When I was with Nic, we excavated at one of the worker villages situated only a few kilometers from the Valley of the Queens. There Nic and his fellows found gold, masks, vases, tiny replica barcas, whips, furniture, jade, gold, and corals. All carefully concealed in tunnels under the village, tunnels that clearly lead to the valley tombs next door.

The pharaohs really did just keep on giving.

The two men pushed us onto rough cut rocks and set the phone on the edge of the empty stone sarcophagus, so the light illuminated the bare ceiling. No sign of Nut, goddess of the day and night.

Nic's face was in shadows. We weren't yet tied up, that was a help. But the guns the men held flashed in the light.

"Just tell me where. Where did you find the statutes?" Nic pleaded. I stole a look at him. He did not know?

"We don't care about the statues." The kidnapper's voice was a bit muffled behind his mask.

I squinted in the dim light. What kind of mask was he wearing? It looked like the full head coverings favored by Mexican wrestling champions, but it was all black. With an open zipper slashed across the mouth.

Oh, good gods. All of them.

"What exactly do you want from us?"

"Be quiet, we are thinking."

I nudged him, Nic, not my S & M aficionado. "What are you thinking?"

"That it's amateur hour." His face was in shadow, but he couldn't disguise his tone.

"They may not let us go." I finished softly. Suddenly, and I did not want this, I missed my nephews; even if I left for California within the next hour, I might not get home in time for Tina and Vince to catch their flight. What would they do without me? I had resisted Tina's entreaties, but I loved those kids. After 9/11 they were my reason for living, and my excuse to escape the destitution of Manhattan. I wiped my eyes and for once hoped that Nic had some kind of plan.

He did not.

The other man, who also wore a fetching head covering, checked his phone. He nodded to his partner. He approached us to deliver one more fatal blow.

"This should hold you."

He raised his arm. I closed my eyes. Nic grabbed me and pulled me to him, either to comfort me or use me as a shield, I was no longer clear on his motives. I took a breath, ready for the pain, a final blow.

And nothing.

I did not expect nothing.

A muffled scraping and a call from just outside the tomb door. I opened my eyes, my would-be executioner was still holding the small gun, but his partner had stopped him.

"Listen." The other man spat out.

Nic released me and carefully moved to shift his feet under him. I pushed up as slowly as I could, my leg muscles screaming in protest, my back was tweaked from the awkward drive out. I flexed my toes to confirm there was still blood circulating. Would we run? Knock over the men, overpower them, wrestle the gun from their hands and in a hair flipping moment of triumph call out, Now we have you!

"They will hear you." Nic pointed out helpfully.

The acoustics in these tombs were marvelous, a guide can talk from one long end and the last person in the tour group at the other could hear every word. A gun shot would echo from one end of the tomb to the other and inspire the armed guards to join in. They don't need much encouragement. In my imagination, I downgraded from hair-flipping triumph to finding myself in the middle of a show down, one of those innocent victims of gun violence so popular in the US.

Nic was in full crouch now, I felt him tense, ready to jump.

I felt around for a weapon, okay, a stone; that was the dominant feature in a partially cleared tomb, rocks. I found one close. My fingers closed around it as I too started to rise.

The men looked at each other just as a shout came from the entrance. They conferred in grunts, a language I've heard Chris and Matt use as their own wordless communication. A guy thing, women always use words. Many, many words.

Nic almost reached full standing, but our friends were too fast. One shouted to the guards that they would be out in a minute. (At least that's what I thought he said, my Arabic was rusty, it's been a long time since I negotiated for oranges in the market). The other guy hit Nic so hard his head sounded like a watermelon against the rock tomb wall. He slid, unconscious to the floor, his head landing on my far softer lap.

The men yelled to the guards and turned back to me. I instinctively raised my arm to ward off the blow. Too late, the man pushed me hard, just as he had Nic. I tucked my head forward, so my shoulders took the blow against the wall. I groaned for good measure and slumped over the more authentically incapacitated would-be hero.

The two men scurried out of the tomb taking the light with them. As soon as the light disappeared, I opened my eyes and listened, rolling my shoulders. My hand hurt; I probably ruined my manicure. It would take weeks of PT to work out the damage to my back. But I was in one piece.

From the entrance there was a lot of noisy shouting and

yelling, but that could have just been conversation. I listened absently stroking Nic's poor head. The guns were not engaged, the shouts reduced to murmurs. There was likely an exchange of cash and unfortunately for us, an escort off the premises. I waited. Yes. The bang of the gate, the click of the lock.

I took a breath. We were trapped.

Only after counting to a million did I feel it was prudent to move towards the entrance. I nudged Nic, but he was still out. Should I stay or should I go? I didn't want to hang out in the recesses of the tomb, not when I could press against the entrance gate and scream for assistance, spooking the hell out of the guards. I pulled my phone from my jeans and turned on the flashlight. Nic's head was bleeding, but his eyes fluttered. I trained the light right in his face, resisting the urge to slap him awake. He groaned, a better rendition of pain than my groan and his eyes fluttered. He frowned against the bright light, I set down the phone and raised my hand to help him.

He blocked my hand. "I'm good. Stop helping me."

I touched his head. He winced.

"You're bleeding. But head wounds always bleed a lot." Copiously, actually. Matt once somersaulted off the bunk bed and smacked his head on the dresser. There was a lot of blood. Once we were through dragging him, and his hysterical brother to the emergency room, the bedroom looked like a kindergarten massacre, which used to be an exaggeration.

"Well, better you walk than me dragging you to the entrance."

He winced at the thought.

"Not that you don't deserve to be dragged a quarter mile over sharp rocks." I mused out loud.

He grimaced but wisely remained silent.

I helped him up. "Come on, we can see if my AT&T services reaches into famous wadis."

We slowly made our way to the entrance of the tomb. I kept the phone off, needing to preserve the battery. There was only one way out, we didn't need the light.

"I don't suppose there's an old, undiscovered until right now tunnel that leads to the workers' village?" I braced my sore shoulder against the walls, unhappy with the damage to the paintings, but there was little else I could do, my legs were not up to the task of keeping me completely upright and mobile. Nic wavered ahead of me.

"None found so far. That would be too easy. Once the tombs were completely stripped, the access tunnels were filled." He dragged his feet. I stepped up, wrapped my arm around his waist and between me and the hard wall, we moved painfully forward.

"They did not kill us after all."

"I didn't think they would."

I left that alone. Our captors seemed shorter than Oscar and Oslo, but I hadn't yet encountered the best of the bad, Nic's actual partners. Nic was heavy against me. I pulled him, bracing against the wall, feeling every small imperfection in the plaster. I'm sure, leaving marks. After what seemed like hours, we reached the entrance.

I dropped him and tried to poke my head through the bars of the gate. No luck. All I could do was to mash my face against the bars and looked up. I could just make out the moon, now clearing the tops of the cliffs.

"What do you know about KV 25?"

Nic slumped on the ground. He winced and pulled out a sharp rock and tossed it aside.

He sighed. "Unfinished, obviously. Belzoni opened it up but didn't find much worth taking. And if he had, he would have taken it."

I worked my hand through the bars. The lock was facing out, but if I angled my arm exactly right... The popular tombs, Nefertari's being one, Tut's being another, sported real doors, locks ,and climate controls to preserve the tomb integrity. Nefertari's tomb, restored to its initial glory, is actually closed to the public and only a few very well-heeled tourists are allowed in. I wouldn't even be surprised if they were asked to hold their breath. Which begs the question, do you keep it safe and locked? Or risk exposure to share the art with the world? There is a virtual tour of the tomb, maybe that's enough.

I stretched my fingers just touching the lock but didn't know quite how to smash it since my range of motion was limited. I pulled my arm back and slid down the wall across from Nic. The moon gradually cleared the peaks of the valley offering just enough light to see him.

"Not even an interesting tomb. We can't even while away the hours hunting for lost papyrus fragments, overlooked tunnels, a small canopic jar, bones."

"You read too much."

"I've been accused of worse." I squinted at him, he was awake, that was good. I remembered that the doctor told me to not let Matt nap after his head injury. Keep him awake was the unnecessary advice. The boys had never napped a day in their combined lives. Which is why Tina so desperately needed me during those early years—two wide awake toddlers. Not an easy gig.

What if I never saw them again? If I didn't answer Tina's texts, if I didn't return, would Tina keep me from my nephews? Boys I considered, in some ways, in convenient ways, my own? I sniffed with the back of my hand, the only clean part of me, wiped my nose

"Hey." Nic's voice derailed my pity train. "Hey, it's not that bad, we...," he trailed off reaching for the gate frame.

"It's not that. What if I never see Matt and Chris again?"

"I said it wasn't that bad. The worst…" He rose and looked more closely at the frame. "The worst is we spend the night here."

"I've been in more uncomfortable spots with you."

He didn't even take the bait. Why was I crying? I would see them again of course. I would text Tina. I would fly home tomorrow, it would be close, I might even arrive just as Tina and Vince boarded their own flight. But I could make it. Who am I if not the sum of my good deeds?"

"I know," he admitted. "At least this is not as bad as Edfu."

"Or Derr. Or Aswan. Or Aten" Not the tombs themselves, although we were free to wander through them after the tourists had dispersed. Nic sometimes wandered through during business hours to act the part of an informed expert and real archeologist. Our work was always about a mile away in the worker villages. We lived in tents, ate bread filled with sand (which is why even the pharaohs suffered from bad teeth) and canned tuna. Naming off the worst accommodations distracted me. I took a breath and tried to feel grateful I was not camping, that I would, eventually, find a shower and collapse on grit-free sheets.

Nic swore and sucked his thumb.

"Don't put your hand in your mouth, you'll get sick." I finally looked at what Nic was doing.

He was jiggling the gate frame. It rattled loudly, echoing off the stone-filled valley.

I was about to protest that someone would hear, but that would be the point wouldn't it?

"Light?"

I turned on my phone. A single bar, three new texts from Tina. I held up the phone flashlight to the hinge.

The hinge. Then I remembered Pirates of the Caribbean. Don't bother with the lock, just remove the jail door hinges.

In our case the gate hinges were logically located on the inside of the tomb entrance.

"Not as romantic as discovering a hidden tunnel." I pointed out unhelpfully.

"It's never romantic. And this option is easier on the knees, the preservation of which I am increasingly committed to. You don't happen to have a chisel or a screwdriver on you?"

"Would they have let me keep it?" I was grateful I still had the phone. Then again, what good is a phone with no service? I squinted at the project at hand. Maybe these kidnappers, thieves, weren't so stupid after all. Although I was still trying to figure out the motive.

"Pen? You could MacGyver it."

He pulled out a cheap Bic (he never spent money on things like pens) that I was certain wasn't up to the job of pushing out steel hinge pins. Then again, a nicer pen wouldn't be much more helpful. With the tip of the plastic blue cap, Nic applied a little pressure on the right, a bit of pressure to the left. I was cross-eyed with boredom by the time he had carefully worked out the first pin. It fell to the rocks with a satisfying clang. Nic crouched down to work the second hinge. I did admire his patience. He took satisfaction in the slow reveal, an effort that cried out for stop-action video. He loved the gradual unveiling of a beautiful piece, a perfect painting, a chunk of pottery. I did not have enough patience to make it as a field archeologist, but I did understand the process, the grit of the work. And I could discuss it, even lecture about it. I stifled that regret and held the phone steady.

It was natural to think of death while trapped in a tomb. Death on the walls, the afterlife imagined and recorded to keep it contained and knowable. We all die, now here is what happens afterwards.

Max would have stood before Anubis and handed over his heart to be weighed against a feather with a clear conscience. I saw to that. How you die wasn't important, Anubis cared if your deeds in life weighed heavily on your heart.

I imagined Max traveling to the next world on a well-appointed designer boat, rowed by all his previous pretty, pretty boys. I hoped he was able to take his laptop with him. It had been his whole focus those last three months when leaving the apartment was unthinkable, when we sat inside for hours, days, weeks. My only outing was to walk to the edge of the river side patio and take deliveries from gondolas and increasingly, speed boats. Oh, and trips to remove all those worthless sample books to the storage center off island.

Maybe Max took those sample books with him too. What was the hieroglyph for sample book?

"Is there a hieroglyph for a computer?"

"You are kidding right?" The center hinge pin dropped. He tested the gate. I helped pull, but we couldn't create an opening wide enough to slip through. He sighed and gestured for the light again on the lowest hinge.

What kind of barca would my parents have taken to the next world? A private, one of course, they most certainly wouldn't ride to the next world in a boat filled with strangers. My parents always had a thing about strangers. Sometimes Chris reverted to a stranger-danger mode, not talking even to people he had met before, the grocery clerk, the school crossing guard; they were all suddenly terrifying, ready to do him harm if he looked them in the eye. His grandparents harbored the same intrinsic mistrust. All three required me as their buffer against the perils of the outside world.

"Nic, who is building all those cruise ships?"

He lay on the sand and worked while I held the light overhead, I didn't want to blind him.

"A company in Albania."

How better to support an emerging economy?

The last pin hit the sand with a quiet thud. I stepped back to allow Nic the honors. He wrestled the heavy door off the hinges and pushed it out to the ground just outside the entrance.

"That will be interesting to explain." Nic's arm trembled even as helped me over the gate. I allowed him to lean on me again as we slowly made our way through the brilliant, moon illuminated valley. The valley is covered with limestone chips, all reflecting the moon light. It wasn't as bright as day, but it was bright enough for our shadows to follow us. Once we hit the main trail it was easier going.

"So now what? We can't return to the hotel. Our perpetrators will be there waiting for us."

"I know."

"I know you know."

He sighed. Some women are attracted to the strong, deep, silent type. I was increasingly not.

We stepped over the chain across the road to the parking lot. Finally, the phone displayed two bars, enough for a call.

"Here, I'll get us a car." He reached for the phone, belatedly taking over. Had he always done that? I couldn't remember.

"And deliver us right back to the bad guys?"

"No, so we can get back to town." I watched as he searched for the number and connect to our hotel.

Did the perps return to the scene of the crime or was it just the victims who returned, searching for closure? And why not kill us? You don't need a gun; a nice knife would be silent and deadly enough. Why didn't they think of that?

Maybe they just wanted to slow us down. Maybe they too

wanted their hearts to eventually weigh favorably against a feather. Hang out in enough tombs and it becomes important.

"Why kidnap us at all?"

Nic held up one finger as he connected with the hotel. He spoke, he listened, he spoke again, he raised his voice. He threatened. After fifteen minutes he clicked off the phone. "They don't send cars out at this hour," he announced.

"Yes, they will." I held out my hand and he reluctantly returned my phone. I glanced at the battery, twenty-eight percent. Not bad. I scrolled to recents and called back. I raised my voice to the helpless old lady tremor and launched into my lost, abandoned, dire situation. How was I to know there were no more buses leaving the Valley after 6:00? This kind of thing never happened in Pittsburgh, yes, I would like a ride right now. Yes, my phone battery is about to fail. I gave them my name and room number hoping they would not automatically connect me with Nic, but he hadn't gotten far enough in the conversation—rant—to give out his name.

"Yes, I'll be right at the entrance of this place, past the parking lot? Oh, thank you, young man, you are a credit to the Winter Palace." I clicked off and looked at Nic in triumph.

"How do you do that?"

"It's my only superpower."

"Not your only one."

It would take half an hour for the car to teach us. We walked to the parking entrance and sat on the ground in view of the road.

"The artifacts came from your future dock project."

He looked at me bleakly. "You are very smart."

"It explains why Oscar and Oslo know your name and your movements." They were all in the same game, just different divisions. And what team did our S & M kidnappers belong to? Were Oscar and Oslo branching out? Hiring new team members?

"We should just leave Luxor," he proposed.

We sat in silence. My stomach was the loudest sound in the valley. What did Nic gain from this? Hiding a find? Who else was on his team? What was the game?

"How are your parents?" I asked in the dark.

"Good shape."

"Who takes care of them?"

"My sister has it all handled."

I waited for more, but that was the end of it. Sister takes care of everything. Gotta go. I dropped my head on my knees. Were they all the same?

A headlight finally illuminated the road.

CHAPTER TWENTY-ONE

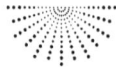

*W*e had been shoved, kicked, hit on the head and kidnapped. As we bounced back to Luxor, my assignment was to search for another hotel. Since you know, I was good at getting what we wanted. I glanced at Nic who was gazing out the car window. I slouched down, the two bars were holding, I was at nineteen percent.

I texted Chris first.

He announced that the family was falling apart.

Your words or mom's?

Mom. Says she can't alone. My heart flipped. I knew that. I've always known that. It takes a village to raise a child, right? I was that village. On call. Tina was probably amazed I had stayed away for so many days. I was amazed myself.

"Do you want to stay in town, or should we get the hell out?" Nic twisted to look behind us, as if we were pursued. We were not.

"Don't you need to stay for the project?"

He shook his head. "It's gotten out of hand. I say we get out."

I glanced at him, his hands scraped raw, his eyes blood

shot, a disturbing dark patch of blood on the back of his head. Huge dark circles under his eyes made him look every one of his earned sixty-five years.

Behaving yourself? I texted to Chris but really wanted to ask the same of my former lover.

"Some people retire at 65." Nic grumbled. "Did you check the Hilton? It's always crowded, that would work."

"Good idea."

Built a trebuchet in the living room, Chris texted.

"You're buying," I said.

He nodded. He instructed the driver to take us to the Hilton and sat back.

Working? I texted.

Tomato cans into the next street.

Oh boy. Excellent.

I glanced at Nic and texted Chris, What have you found out about poisons?

The Hilton is not as romantic as the Winter Palace, but I appreciated being greeted by a waiter in white offering me a tray of bright red hibiscus juice. I ducked in the gift shop minutes before it closed, waving Nic's credit card. I grabbed a sun dress that emphasized my cleavage and bared my arms because I had had it with sensible coverage, new sandals and a Hello Kitty purse, just large enough for a phone and passport. My jeans were ruined, so no pockets for me. There was some makeup in blister packs by the front counter, I took one of each not even examining them closely. I chose the largest bottle of Advil they had. Nic strolled in after checking us in and added a pair of shorts and a tee with I heart Egypt to the purchase pile. We escaped to our new room without further incident.

Tina's first text was a series of exclamation points. I couldn't tell if this was a response to the tomato-can-launching trebuchet (had Chris told Tina they had hit the dead center of a roof? An admirable shot. If it wasn't your car).

Or to Matt's need for a fire extinguisher.

Or Chris's sudden interest in deadly poisons.

I texted a smiley face back to Tina just before the phone went black. I waved the phone at Nic. "I need to find a charger."

I hiked back down to the gift store, but it was closed. How on earth could I survive a whole night with no cell phone? I glanced at the front desk. Ah.

Yes, they did have additional chargers, guests leave them in the rooms all the time. The young man at the desk was happy to find a charger that matched my phone. I promised to return it in the morning. He shrugged as if it did not matter, maybe he already knew that I too would abandon it in my room.

With no phone to distract, the elevator ride felt excessively long. I fingered the phone and eyed the elevator for an outlet. No luck. I made it all the way to the room before, quite abruptly, my legs no longer held me up.

I sank on the bed and eyed my new clothes, but I didn't have the strength. I fell back on the bed in a puff of dust. I held up the phone and the new charger in each hand, weighing them—feather and heart.

"Come on, you always feel better after you've cleaned off the sand." Nic took the phone and charger and plugged them in. He pulled me to my feet and let me to the shower. Which, twenty years ago, would have been just right for two. Tonight, the physics of it was too much. One misplaced leg and we'd tumble out in a crush of glass.

We took turns. He was right, I always felt better after a shower. Once we were showered, we stood draped in white towels. My body ached from the cramped car ride and chilly tomb. Nic needed a shave and the left side of his face was turning bright purple. But the blood was cleaned, and the wound wasn't as bad as it had looked while we were underground.

We were a mess.

He gestured to the clean white bed. He pulled off his towel. I pulled off mine.

We groaned with lust and groaned when a muscle spasmed. Like art, the sex was marvelous, creative and pointless. Exactly the sendoff I needed.

I lay on the cool clean sheets and pulled my phone to me. Nic snored beside me. I let him rest. I felt too nervous. While the sex helped, it did not completely mitigate my edginess.

I was no closer to learning why Miranda had suddenly died. Obviously, she had survived her thin years. During the height of her career, she was a devotee of extreme dieting combined with bulimia. Sustaining that kind of activity does not do your heart any good. Could her daughters be right? Did Miranda's heart, taxed from years of the finest drugs, best booze and fun friends simply give out? Her daughters could behave like a heart attack on a stick. And Cindy had delivered enough chaos to overwhelm a saint. But Miranda weathered all of it with good grace and an open heart, not a damaged one. She did not deserve to die. She did deserve an answer. Or more to the point, I did.

Miranda died alone. It made me catch my breath. I did not have much to go on, except Chris's focus on poison. Could Miranda have been poisoned? By drinking what? And what kind of poison manifests like a heart attack?

More to the point, who delivered it? Someone she knew and trusted. Someone who knew how to pour a drink strong enough to mask the taste of a drug. Someone she wouldn't be suspicious of and wouldn't think twice before accepting drink or food from their hand.

Someone who could quickly search the place while

Miranda passed out. I didn't want it to be Nic, but he wanted what Miranda had. And he probably searched the place and tidied it up behind him. But murder? I glanced at him; his face younger in repose. Nic was many things, but never a murderer.

Then again, we all change.

CHAPTER TWENTY-TWO

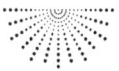

*T*hank you, Hilton, for the good mattress. But not even an excellent mattress can mitigate demoralization and depression. I had to leave, soon, really soon. As we ventured downstairs for breakfast, I searched for flights home.

The morning was blessedly breezy, not too hot. We sat under a patio umbrella and toasted our escape with freshly pulled espressos.

Nic suddenly set down his cup and focused on something unpleasant over my shoulder.

"Shit."

I twisted to get a look. Walking towards us was Cindy.

Cindy wasn't a Rachael beautiful or even a Miranda beautiful. Those women had that ineffable it, the ability, as they say, to make love to the camera. Every photographer I worked for lusted for models who could tell a story in the curve of her swan neck, in the roundness of his shoulder. Photographers search for that ability to tell a story and then ruthlessly exploit it because that is their job. And for a time, the model is a star, so it's a fair exchange. The models who can transfer all that story and attitude to the runway, and stay upright as well, those are the models who become super stars. I stuck to photography, it was more interesting and ever changing.

Cindy was naturally thin and blessed with long skinny legs. But she didn't project much personality, nor did she have much stamina. She had a breakdown during the New York show. Something about being tired, sticky and the shoes pinched her toes.

Unfortunately for Cindy that show ended up being all about Jimmy Choo. Oprah had publicly announced that his were the most comfortable of all shoes. Possibly in all the world, possibly of all time.

Complaining that the shoe of the decade pinched her toes was a strategic mistake. Cindy was fired that afternoon.

I lost track of her due to complete disinterest. She ran into Miranda at the Milan show, one of Miranda's last. They either clicked right away or got very drunk in a big hurry and then clicked. Cindy traveled back to Venice on Miranda's dime and quickly moved in. Her contributions included bringing home inappropriate friends and spending Miranda's money like a drunken sailor or a former model just off her diet. The girl could consume pounds of food without damaging her figure. One of her more annoying qualities.

I came into the picture a year later. Saving Miranda both emotionally and financially.

Cindy was out, I was in. And because of my well-honed sense of guilt I helped Cindy on and off. Here and there.

And now she was back. Cindy was well wedged between two men. One of the men held Cindy's arm, the other gripped her around the waist. The third followed closely behind. What was puzzling, they were not my overbearing thugs from a developing economy. But altogether, the group of them looked familiar.

I squinted. That was it, they looked like a DKNY ad from what, ten years ago? Cindy staggered in her impractical high-heeled pumps. The man beside her was forced to hitch back his stride to avoid knocking her into the pool.

The first man was blond, blue eyed and had a Russian vibe. The second was just as tall, American by his body type and his walk. The third was one of those impossibly beautiful Italian men with the fifty-fifty chance he still lived with his mom.

The Russian pushed Cindy into a chair, the rest remained standing, the better loom in a menacing manner. My first reaction was to call a waiter to order her drink. My second thought was no, I don't care if she's thirsty. I hoped she was thirsty.

Cindy glanced up at the three men. "Some friends." She muttered.

As compelling as the mystery group was, something else distracted me. I squinted across the Nile. The river was calm. The mountains and valleys of the West Bank glowed in the sun, until they didn't. Was that fog? Nic shifted and pushed away the remains coffee.

"We have been following you for days," the Russian started.

"You haven't even gone to the apartment," the American complained.

"All the way out here. And I had a job," the Italian growled. Ah, I recognized the voice.

And I recognized their faces. I had seen them on posters, on the backs of People Magazine. The Italian's skin was as ravaged as Cindy's, the other two were not, as they say, aging well. What was the saying about deserving your face at fifty? They were likely only in their early forties.

I looked at the boys, the pretty, formerly pretty boys. My eyes darted to the riverbank. There was no fog on the Nile.

This was a billowing brownish yellow. It had overtaken the valley and was rolling over the West Bank.

"Max," I guessed.

Cindy leaned forward. She clearly had had enough, which was impressive, she was able to handle quite a bit. But she, unlike us, obviously hadn't slept. Her makeup was hastily applied, the concealer was the wrong shade making the dark circles under her eyes more prominent. She had been crying.

She leaned across the table to Nic. "You just need to stay here, in Luxor. You know, just…" She glanced at her keepers then looked directly at Nic. "Stay."

As if he were a dog. Nic glanced up at the men and glanced at me.

The wind picked up. Cushions blew off the lounge chairs. The remains of my pink saccharine packs blew off the table.

I watched Nic and caught his eye. I gestured to the West Bank. He glanced over, his eyes grew wide, but he remained as silent as me.

The men did not step back. Cindy was immobile. Three of us, three of them. Or two of us and four of them. It was smarter to place Cindy into the them category.

Waiters and staff scurried around the patio retrieving cushions, closing and securing umbrellas. Guests quickly scooted indoors. The bank, not of fog, but of sand was half-way across the river. The hotel stood on the edge of the East Bank, first in line to be hit. But neither the men nor Cindy paid attention.

A waiter caught my eye, I shook my head. He shrugged and disappeared into the building.

The wind lifted my skirt. I smoothed it down. "What do you mean stay?" I asked in as conversational manner as I could. Damn, and after all Miranda had done for her.

"I asked, but they won't tell me. They found me at Miranda's."

"We finally put that together. Miranda and Max were friends." The Russian said.

"They had mutual interests," I hazarded. I couldn't figure it out. What were they doing here? And why?

Was it about the hippo?

Cindy smiled, pleased that part of a plan actually worked. But she quickly gave way to frustration. "But I couldn't find anything!"

She turned to the men standing behind her. "I couldn't find anything. How many times do I need to tell you that?"

The wind increased; bits of sand whipped against my cheeks. It was about to be too late.

I am one of those people who stays for the end of a movie, even if I stopped liking it halfway through. I finish every book I begin no matter how terrible (thank you for staying with me). I always want to know the end. I always want everything wrapped up. I want closure. I always finish what I start.

Maybe it was time to change. The sand escalated to exfoliation levels then quickly increased into wind-whipped grit coupled with dusty low visibility. The men swore. Cindy cried out as the sand blasted her face.

In that second, I made a choice. I ran. I even knocked over the chair for dramatic effect.

CHAPTER TWENTY-THREE

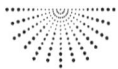

J ran to what I remembered were the lobby doors.

The wind helped push open the doors, they crashed against the wall. The total of my brilliant escape plan was to rush through the lobby and out to the street and lose myself in the gray, low visibility storm. I was hoping the storm would distract the men just long enough for my escape.

Once I pulled the doors closed, I straightened my dress and tried to look cool, difficult when you are covered in sand and already itching.

I saw the side exit just as a handsome young man approached. He seemed familiar, another model? Cindy's boyfriend? The new model for Chanel Men? Someone I met at the shows? He must have been a model. He looked like a younger version of the men, which did not immediately recommend him.

He tucked his phone into his inside jacket pocket. He glanced from side to side, with special attention to the patio door.

I nodded, trying to simultaneously acknowledge him yet

discourage his approach. As I hesitated, the hotel main entrance was being secured. The side door looked like it led to a parking lot. Better. I turned to that side exit. My new sandals slipped on sand-strewn marble floor. Sand really does get everywhere.

I had not discouraged the young man at all. He grabbed my arm and began to lead me to the side exit.

I automatically pulled back, but he hung on. He smiled revealing beautiful American teeth.

"Come with me" he said in English.

"Like the Terminator."

His smiled widened. "Exactly like the Terminator, come with me if you want to live." His accent was Italian but modified from study abroad, England or the States, the orthodontic work betrayed at least a few years spent in the States.

The far door to the patio moved and started to push in. I looked again at the Terminator wanna be. An indoor complexion, good suit, Saville Row. Understated striped tie. Young, very young and very handsome with dark swept back hair and deep brown eyes. We all have our biases, and a bespoke suit spoke of trust, responsibility and, I hoped, access to a get-away car.

I was not disappointed. He half escorted; half pulled me to a side door just as the patio doors bust open with a shout.

I heard Nic call my name, but I was already though the doors and out to a covered carport.

Sand blew under the covered porch and stung my eyes. I blinked, but before I could react, the young man loaded me into a waiting black limo. After buses with bad shocks, taxi drivers of death, trashed rentals, I appreciated the upgrade in kidnap vehicles.

I settled into the leather seat and stretched my legs. I absently brushed the sand from my hair then stopped, not wanting to get the car dirty.

"You have been through quite a lot." The young man slid onto the seat across from me. The car engine started. I glanced outside. The brown sand and wind obscured the view. But I could see gusts rushing down the side streets, buffeting pedestrians who held their scarves over their noses and mouths.

The doors to the carport opened, but before I could see who it was, the car pulled away. I was safe, at least for the length of the ride. Unless he was with our pretty boys.

I stopped fiddling with my skirt hem. Where was I and where were we going?

"We're heading to the airport." He said with extreme calm.

I looked down, ah, the plastic purse was still dangling from my wrist. Pulled out the phone.

"Charger?"

"On the plane."

"Of course. The plane."

I carefully brushed sand from my cheeks. Did I jump from one bad situation to one far worse? I was so tired I didn't care. "And you are?"

He leaned back. "I represent Holquist, Learnerd and Romano."

I buckled the seat belt even though there was no sign instructing me to do so. Habit. I had lived in this country long enough to know that traffic was always exciting. Even with zero visibility, the driver would regard stop lights as just a nod to the understood ideal of traffic control, not something you actually practice.

"We are the attorneys for Max Peters' estate."

"Ah." I had run into his people, I assumed they were his people, the day Max died. The lead lawyer had ordered me out; three young men, dressed in old-men suits (Italian to be sure, but off the rack), followed through, swooping in like vultures. I had no time to say goodbye let alone shed appropriate tears. They summarily pushed me out of the apartment, and I don't mean that metaphorically. They pushed. I was already packed, having just received word of my father's fall, but still, it was abrupt, a thirty-year friendship over in a blink. No one offered me condolences or even a thank you.

"We have been looking for you for three years." The young man said.

Like Sara Crewe in my favorite book, A Little Princess. "I was living in the apartment, not difficult to find."

"We were unaware of who you were at the time." He seemed contrite.

"What do you mean, you didn't know who I was? Max and I were friends." I looked at him pointedly. "Likely before you were born. I took care of Max for his last two years, fetched, carried, wiped. Where the hell were your people then?"

The panic and loneliness and sadness all surged back. What had happened? Did Max have a nice funeral, a strong send-off? I wanted to attend; I could have made arrangements so I could fly back to Venice. But no one contacted me with any information. No good deed goes unpunished, look at Cindy.

"They were looking for a man, Vic, Victor. So were we."

"They thought I was the help."

He looked embarrassed.

"Nice, thanks." My feet were gritty, and I wanted to brush them off as well, but it would have looked odd, or rude. I wondered why I cared.

"In the will, you were only named as Vic."

"Victoria Amelia Gardner." I corrected.

"We know that now, took a while. But clearly," he trailed off and looked at his watch. I wondered what a while meant

249

to him. For my nephews, a while clocked in at about ten minutes, often less.

"The law doesn't move very quickly." I observed. Only people with money to gain or money to lose move quickly. Vince and Vance moved quickly to sell our parents' house. Tiffany and Lucy moved quickly to sell Miranda's home. Did it always need to be about the money? Did Nic need the money? Did the damn Egyptian government just need more money? Couldn't it be about something larger? I didn't have the heart for this.

"Especially in Italy." He gazed out the window. He had not bothered to fasten his seat belt. The car lurched around a corner. He remained in place as if stuck to the seat.

"I apologize for the delay. Once we discovered our error, we worked to find you, but we ended up always one step behind."

"You've been following me?"

"The three years is almost complete. There were others interested, very interested in the estate. They wanted the money and if we couldn't find you, they would inherit."

"How interested?" All those boys, crowding into the apartment, drinking Max's wine, ordering food, pretending to care but actually casing the place for priceless objects. I failed to mention I replaced a number of those objects with fakes, the real items were too valuable to leave around. I had crammed a storage facility with all the extra baubles Max collected to decorate his lavish home, decorated in High Queer. The glass, the gilt, he didn't want to get rid of anything, just didn't want to have it right here, in the hall-way. It was the end, why argue with the man?

He smiled; his beautiful teeth lit up his face. "I apologize for that last incident; I didn't realize they would come at you so aggressively. It was a good thing I came to Egypt after all."

I watched him. "You don't get out much?"

"It was my first field assignment," he admitted. "Once I saw what you were involved in, I thought I could help."

"And you did, so why all this? You can send notarized letters, you know."

"Not to a dead woman's apartment, and there was no address for you in the states. The mail was returned."

I had moved directly into Mom and Dad's house. Okay, he had a point. I also admit that I was too involved in managing their Medicare, Medicaid, dwindling stock, insurance, etc., to consider that I never received any mail addressed to me.

"Call?"

"Blocked."

"Facebook?"

"Your account was inactive, I messaged you when I finally figured it out, but no response. I only found you now because you showed up on Instagram after Von Meiter's party. You know him?" He leaned forward.

"Do you know him?" I countered since I wasn't entirely sure Von Meiter wasn't a bad guy.

He leaned back. "Family knows him, of course."

"What is your name again?"

"Marcus. Marcus Romano."

"Of Holquist, Learnerd and Romano."

"Yes, my grandfather founded the company."

"Which explains why you can play James Bond."

He shifted uncomfortably. "But you are here."

Good point.

"Okay, okay, so I'm difficult to reach, I get that." What else was I supposed to think when I received an unknown phone call? I was not worried about the IRS sending the cops to get me if I don't pay up now. I was unconcerned that my Social Security number was in danger of being cancelled. I was not worried about needing an alert button. I was the freaking alert button, on call 24/7. I had some responsibility for this, but again, what did it matter? Max had enough money while he lived. Any extra I cheerfully loaned to Rachael and Francisca, and Nancy and Maria, and Claire to start college, to start a business, to start out in a new city. We all had our expenses.

"I actually inherited something from Max? Did he even have anything left to inherit?"

The limo bumped through a chain link gate and onto the tarmac. The side of a sleek corporate jet loomed up out of the swirling dust.

Marcus waited for the car to glide to a full stop. "We need to wait for the storm to calm. We will be fine here."

A few euros would be welcome. Maybe I could return to Venice once the boys were settled and Vince and Tina returned from their cruise. I could check into the Hotel Cipriani; they have a treatment called Journey Across the Lagoon I always wanted to try but never had the time. I could have a massage. It would be my reward after what I knew would be a month in the day care in the gulag. I was tired, I wanted to be indulged, not thrown into abandoned tombs. I was not out of it yet.

"He did have a little left." Marcus eyed me.

Remembering the plot of Bleak House, "After the lawyers' fees, after three years of research," I made scare quotes, "How little is little?"

"He left everything to you."

I closed my eyes. Everything. "A broad term, Mr. Marcus Romano of Holquist, Learnerd and Romano, everything."

He leaned his arms on his thighs. "Do you know anything about a storage facility?"

CHAPTER TWENTY-FOUR

*M*ax had lovers. Max had attractive hangers-on. Max traveled with an entourage. Who didn't? What was it like to believe, with all your black, black heart, that because you were loyal, even loving, to a sickly, aging queer, you would automatically be in line for a piece of the inheritance? And what was it like to discover that your richly deserved deserts were to be delayed, even interminably, by a pack of lawyers who insisted on the letter of the law? What was it like to be the victim of a system that required searching for a rightful heir?

And what would your reaction be when that heir suddenly showed up on Instagram draped in Bulgari?

How much were we talking about? The paintings and objets d'art I had stored would bring in something—maybe even enough for two days at the Hotel Cipriani. If the apartment had been kept intact, there would be much more. But I have learned to never underestimate angry, entitled people. I imagined Max's apartment had long been stripped down to the plaster.

Marcus assured me the apartment was intact. A relative term, especially since even the wallpaper was valuable.

As soon as the storm passed, we climbed into the jet and took off.

Marcus explained a bit about the family dynamics, his and Max's. I knew enough of Max's family to know why they were not named in his will. I was more interested in the Romano family.

"I wanted to show my father." It was all Marcus needed to say. Chris, at nine, told me he wanted to show his parents he could do things on his own. When I let him, it wasn't a disaster, but Tina was not convinced. I felt for this young man.

"Father will meet us at the airport. And the storage facility?" Marcus cut into my thoughts.

I gave him the name of the place on the mainland, surprised I remembered.

"Do you have the key?"

The plane bumped down on a short tarmac and screeched to a stop.

We climbed out onto the cool, sand-free tarmac where, yet another handsome, debonair Italian waited for us.

"My father," Marcus said under his breath.

Sig. Romano greeted me with a triple kiss. "You look lovely, Ms. Gardner."

I smiled at his gallantry, I did not look lovely, I looked like the final survivor of a British bake show. The senior partner of Holquist, Learnerd and Romano was an older version of Marcus with a shock of white hair that contrasted with his genuine Mediterranean tan. He bowed. "On behalf of the firm, I am delighted to finally meet you Ms. Gardner."

"Thank you."

He turned to Marcus. "But we are too late."

Marcus looked at his watch again. "We had an hour more."

His father shook his head. "We don't have an hour. They did it, they ran down the clock."

Marcus slumped against the car.

Poor Marcus, he told me he had tracked me for the better part of the week. He took that bumpy bus to Albania, he flew to Egypt, he brought me back. The prize. Minutes too late.

"They get it all then." Marcus said dispiritedly.

"No, they can now contest the will since we didn't find the named inheritor in time." His father corrected. "It will take…," he trailed off and Marcus perked up.

"Years."

"Likely." He turned to me. "But that does not help you, my dear."

I tried to process what I just heard. "They have been following the wrong person?"

"Vic, Nic, they thought he was the name in the will. The old man didn't have it all together. They assumed he was confused."

I smiled, "Max was many things, but never confused."

"The key?"

I nodded and Marcus escorted me into the limo. My flight was only hours away, I would give them the key and that was the end. Of the adventure.

The key was at the apartment, so we all had little choice but to rush back to the center of town, retrieve the key, and rush me back to the airport. The men appreciated the urgency, Sig. Romano asked for my flight to check me in. I leaned back in the plush seat and said my farewells to Italy as we rushed to a small dock and a captained speed boat.

I did not understand why the storage facility was, as they say, a thing.

"Didn't you find the key in Max's stuff?" I called over the wind. It was cold on the lagoon, Marcus handed me a blanket.

They shook their heads. "No key, the only reason we know about the facility at all is he mentioned it in his will and that you were the only person who could access it."

"That is far too mysterious. You can get a court order and open it. Simple."

"If we knew where it was." The men repeated.

"And now you do." I finished, the boat took us up the Grand Canal to the base of Miranda's apartment, I wound through the side alley and up to the apartment. In Miranda's apartment, I stepped over the spillage of Cindy's clothes from the guest room to the hall. I pulled out my suitcase detached the storage key and loaded it with my new clothes and all of Miranda's makeup. I kicked Cindy's clothes into the guest room. Picked up five glasses and put them into the sink and wiped down the coffee table. It was ready for a new owner. I hoped they would appreciate the light, the location and the history.

I took one last look in the bedroom. "I'm sorry, I didn't find your killer."

If Miranda's spirit was still around, it was silent.

On the ride back to the train station, my phone began pinging. I would have liked a farewell glass of wine, a toast to the water and the light. A toast to my days of being closer to myself than I had in years

"You are going to be rather disappointed when you see what Max is storing." I handed the key to Marcus.

"Samples." They said together.

"Good guess. And these are exciting because?"

"The fabric, the patterns, are enormously valuable. We have an offer from LVH for the original plans, designs and the patterns of Max's work. The sample books will help."

But they weren't as big a deal as the designs and patterns stored in Max's laptop. I knew the lawyers had the computer. They had everything. And everything would be given over to the boys. Max Peters' big moments had mostly occurred in the sixties, with those enormous bright Gucci and Pucci prints, Twiggy, Jean, short hair and shorter skirts. I knew his work was making somewhat of a comeback, I helped with a few deals with Target just before he died. But I don't even remember if he had signed off on any of it.

That comment, everything, had given me at least an hour of surprised speculation. If I had my own money I could pay for care for Chris, a housekeeper for Tina, and for me a room of my own, hell, my own apartment, maybe my own life.

"If I'm not inheriting. Why am I helping you?" I ask bluntly.

The father put his hand on my knee. "Sig. Peters was canny, we have inventoried the contents of the apartment, his bank accounts, and there are many discrepancies, income and items that are unaccounted for."

I smiled. "Who figured out the chandelier was a fake?"

"I did." Marcus piped up. "It was obvious, but the boys want it anyway."

"Did they clean out the apartment?"

"No." Both men said in unison.

I nodded. Good, that was good. I felt better knowing that at least the apartment, in my mind a shrine to Max, had not been violated.

I was indeed Cinderella after the ball, sans dress, sans one shoe and sans prince. Of my many messages, Nic was silent. Busy with Cindy, busy explaining to the pretty boys that he was not the target. Probably busy explaining that he did not have any idea where the hippo was, and it probably didn't much matter.

At least my ride back to service and obscurity was comfortable. The imposed digital silence was like a mini vacation, and Sig. Romano had upgraded and paid for a first-class seat home. I slept the whole flight.

When I wasn't crying.

I GOT a ping from Nic as I urbered to Vince's house, now my house as well. I would like to say that when I arrived, the boys leaped with joy, hugging me, showing the damage from both the trebuchet and the crowbar, telling me they loved me, and I should never let them go.

But they are teenage boys.

I glanced at Nic's message inquiring as to my whereabouts.

I dragged my suitcase up the walkway. The green lawn rolled out before me, something I'd make sure to organize every week. The roof needed some new shingles on the far west side. That crack in the walk needed to be sanded down.

The front door was unlocked. Matt needed to be more careful and lock it when they were home. I had missed Tina and Vince by minutes, they were relieved I was home. Actually, Tina texted that it was about time.

"I'm home!" I pulled the suitcase and left it in the foyer.

"Hi Aunt Vic!" Matt called from the family room.

"Hi," Chris echoed.

Dishes piled in the sink; mud scraped along the kitchen floor complete with the tracks of rolling luggage leading to the garage. It was almost like Tina had created as much mess as she could to illustrate the need. I got it; they didn't need to make me scrub the floor.

"Gentlemen, why are there dishes in the sink?"

The boys looked up from their game. "I found more poisons," Chris announced.

Completely awake at 3:00 in the morning, my small room closed around me. I hadn't realized it was smaller than the storage room in Miranda's apartment, albeit without the clutter and I admit, charm. I changed into sweats, flipped on the kitchen lights, and started to clean the mud off the floor. Hands and knees, like groveling. I was here because it was family, and family came first. Matt and Chris had been happy to see me, and helpfully unconcerned with my story, the sudden trip to Italy, the abrupt return; they took it in stride and ordered delivered pizza for dinner. Matt helped with the dishes, Chris made a pass at the floor, but he was still distracted by his poison theory.

I sat back and looked around. It wasn't my kitchen. It wasn't my living room. They weren't my children.

My phone rang and I hurried to answer even though a small sound like a phone would not wake the boys. It took two alarms, five shakes and cymbals to get Matt out of bed in the morning.

"Signora Victoria?"

"Marcus?"

"Si, yes. I am so sorry for the time."

"I was awake anyway." I closed the bedroom door but did not flip on the light. The bare walls were too disturbing.

"You are safely at home now?"

"Well, I'm safe. And thank your father for the upgrade; that was very kind of him."

Marcus paused.

"Marcus, is everything okay, did you get into the storage facility?"

Were they missing something? Had I missed something?

"I wanted to tell you the story myself. Are you sitting down?"

I was cross-legged on the single bed.

He launched into his story. I did not know why I needed to hear it, but again, unlike the hippo and Miranda's death, at least I knew at the start of this story that Marcus would deliver the finale. I settled back.

Marcus and his father hurried to the storage facility

immediately after sending me off to the airport. I didn't ask why the rush; it had been three years. But Marcus explained that they both wanted to be finished with the boys. They felt terrible for me, and terrible for Max.

"We did not relish the idea that all of Max's estate would go to these men. We thought we could find something that maybe Max hid that would help us delay."

Bleak House wasn't too far off the mark then. Run down the clock, spend down the estate in taxes and fees. Now that I was on their side, I cheered their efforts.

"And all you found were piles of sample books."

"And the genuine antique chandelier." He pointed out.

I tried to recall, what else had I stashed there? Chippendale chairs, inlaid mosaic tables, a hideous gilded German clock, three obscene Greek vases. First in, last out. The furniture was stacked and organized as best I could by myself. Had I rescued that Eames chair?

"Did you build those racks yourself?"

"Did they fall on you?" The racks were flimsy, the best I could do, and carry. I had tossed book after sample book onto the shelves, so many. Max was nothing if not prolific.

"No, no, we found all the books."

"Max was sure they would be valuable."

"Oh, they are." Marcus was now cryptic.

"Out with it, it's 3:30 in the morning here."

Once father and son began moving the books, papers fell. At first, they thought it was just sales receipts, instructions, scrap paper. Which would have been my guess. I had been too busy just loading the leaving to really scrutinize the contents. Why would I?

Marcus picked up one of the papers and really examined it.

"And?"

"A stock certificate for Max Peters." He said with awe.

That's right, we went public. Like so many IPOs—a strong start, falling off to reasonable, slower growth. Max was a sensation, for a while, but like most fame, we only got about fifteen minutes. Maybe sixteen minutes. I had honestly forgotten about the stock.

"Hadn't we sold out?" I asked.

"To LVH." Marcus confirmed.

"We then started opening all the fabric books, some of the papers were stuck but we think we found them all. You need to come back to Venice."

"What? Why?" And leave all this?"

"Max re-invested."

"That was smart." I was unfamiliar with the stock. I helped with household finances, leaving Max to gloat over stock prices. He indulged in a little buying and selling. Not much of course, what could he accomplish in the short time he had left?

"We discovered something else, something," He took a breath. "Fantastic. When can you get back? We will send you tickets."

"I don't understand."

"There was more, not just stocks for Max's own company but Apple, AOL (oh well), stock in AIG, stock in Yumm. The Apple stock alone totals 5,000 shares."

"That's quite a bit for the boys."

"It doesn't go to the boys."

"Marcus." I used my best adult, don't-mess-with-me voice.

"The stock is yours. And that's not all."

I was indeed glad I was sitting down. I could buy my own place. I could buy two places. I could hire professional help for Chris. I could probably afford two housekeepers plus a cook. I must have said it out loud. If it was real, if Marcus wasn't telling me a fairy tale. And what about taxes? Mom and Dad were always worried about taxes. Wasn't there a heavy tax in Italy? I would have to liquidate and pay the taxes. Maybe I was down to just one housekeeper, but maybe I wouldn't have to scrub the floor ever again.

That was an appealing vision, it was a very appealing fairy tale but difficult to believe. Why not just give me the damn stock? Why the mystery? I already knew the answer, because Max was Max, and it was Venice, and maybe he did not trust all his last-minute friends as much as I thought. Good for Max.

"We found his holographic will."

"Translation, please."

"Max left everything to you. You inherit it all."

I frowned. Forgive me, when I hear the word inherit, I think of poorly made copies of Victorian love seats and a 9,000-pound Encyclopedia Britannica set c. 1974. I think of crates of Depression glass and collections of expired metal license plates. I think of priceless collectables from the Franklin Mint and of empty acres of property located thirty miles from the nearest desirable school district or store. I picture enormous art that needs selling and a tiny hippo statue that needs hiding.

What comes immediately to mind is: problems.

"What my father doesn't understand is why was all his furniture in storage if he knew you would inherit the apartment and all the contents?"

Marcus clearly had not attended any parties that Max, or Miranda, for that matter, threw. As good Venetian citizens, they should know better.

I thought the apartment would have already been rented and occupied. You couldn't just leave an apartment on the canal, in Venice, just empty, could you?

"Could you?" I said it out loud.

"That's part of the estate. He owned the apartment."

"He owned the apartment?"

"Actually, the whole building. See? You need to return to Venice."

A whole building? I couldn't take it in. "I can just up and leave. We can do all this remotely, DocuSign and all that. I need to stay with my nephews. Tomorrow is a school day."

"The boys, what do you call them?"

"The pretty boys?"

"Yes, they don't know and are demanding to read the will and I assume collect the spoils. I have an appointment with them on Thursday. Don't you want to be there for the big movie finish?"

"The Hollywood ending?"

"That is it—the Hollywood ending. You must close up the apartment officially, list it if you want to sell. There are many papers to sign. We will send the ticket today."

He had made up my mind.

I did need to crate and bring home some of Miranda's paintings, that hummingbird by Church would brighten up my room… I shook my head; I was thinking very small. I could call Maria to help sell Max's apartment, but it would be nice to have one more look. . .

"When?"

"Fly back tomorrow. It will give you just enough time for espresso before we meet." He was firm, no longer the young boy, but the scion of an institution that did not take no for an answer.

My phone pinged, probably the ticket.

"Round trip."

"Of course." He assured me.

The boys rose early for school. I approached the kitchen bar with some trepidation.

"Great hair, Aunt Vic." Matt smiled through a mouthful of Cocoa Puffs. Where did the Cocoa Puffs come from?

"Thanks, say I have something to tell you."

"It looks like a heart attack." Chris burst into the kitchen, his pajama bottoms were stained and threadbare at the hem, he seemed halfway between bed and bath.

"Have you showered yet?"

"What?"

"What?"

He waved his phone. "Natural stuff can kill you. Looks like a heart attack."

Matt pointed to the box of cereal and took another big bite. I ignored him.

"Natural stuff can kill you," I said very slowly to not disrupt Chris's train of thought.

"Do you have a name?"

He studied his phone screen. "It says that Monkshood is a good sleeping pill. But too much can cause heart failure."

I grabbed another cup of coffee. Monkshood was poison, old school, but poison. I was again packed and ready to go, I just needed to get the boys to school and make them swear to text me every minute or so to tell me they were fine. If Matt can purchase his own sugar cereal, there were probably other untapped skills we could start to tap.

My bet was on Cindy. Pick up a natural sleeping remedy, no prescription, no paper trail. She needed to find the hippo. The Albanians were breathing down her neck, demanding accounting for everything. She wasn't really supposed to sell the articles; she was just supposed to stock them so the right people could pick them up. And Miranda was the wrong person. I shook my head. Did Cindy even realize she killed Miranda? Or had she talked herself into believe it was an accident? And did it matter? I had at least one answer.

"I'm not kidding." I lectured the boys: "Text me every half hour, tell me what you're doing, don't see anyone, and don't fire the trebuchet, at least not on my watch."

Matt's eyes were huge over the remains of his cereal. "You're leaving? You're letting us stay by ourselves?"

"You know where the fire extinguisher is, you know where the crowbar is. You can drive Chris to school. At least I think you can."

He nodded. "Charges were dropped."

I took a breath. "It will be good for you. And I will be back by Saturday, I just need to finish some business in Italy."

"Are you going to see Dr. Ratzenberg?"

I quickly kissed the top of Chris's head before he could duck away.

"Probably not."

Ah, Nic. Took him a while. Was he still in Luxor? The pretty boys had wasted no time returning, had Nic followed? I texted him on the way to the airport.

Where are you?

I'm fine thank you. Where are you?

Back in Venice. See you?

I calculated the timing. I could see him Thursday night, after my meeting with Marcus.

Meet me in the plaza.

Same place?

Same place, tomorrow at 11:00.

I'll be there.

I had heard that promise before. I took a breath and stopped the call but still held the silent phone. My heart was not beating, my face wasn't flushed.

When had I gotten over him? In the tomb? Over lunch? The day he dumped me? Two days ago, when I ran out on him? The day I realized that all during my time in the States, he never called, never asked about me?

One more thing to wrap up before my return to my nephews.

Another first-class flight, a personal pick-up by the same

captain running the same powerboat. I spent no time in the airport, and no time in line. Dressed in the Max Peters duster and jangling fake necklaces, I strode to the lagoon facing offices of Holquist, Learnerd and Romano banging my suitcase behind me.

The morning was bright, almost glaring, black gondolas floated along the quay, the walkway was empty of tourists. I lingered to savor the moment. I was back. It was unbelievable. Maybe I could return for a vacation. I could afford a vacation. I could afford many things, but I didn't want to count my money before I left the table. I would hear out Marcus first. I would find a way to make this real before I did or said anything.

I was greeted by an elegant woman with upswept black hair and a classic Chanel suit. "He is expecting you, Ms. Gardner."

I nodded as if I was accustomed to the attention and the courtesy. I was more used to getting in trouble and getting yelled at, but I could do this too.

Marcus greeted me with three kisses and offered me a seat to the right of his impressive carved desk.

"We are so glad you could come!" He grinned. As if it was my idea.

"Thank you for the first-class ticket."

"Get used to it."

I shook my head. A ruckus outside the door interrupted any lecture about thrift and preserving capital and living within a person's means. The door swept open and the three men, like the three Musketeers, if the Musketeers had been, close, crowded into the office. They were happily convinced they had won the battle. Judging from Marcus's expression, I had won the war.

They didn't even pause when they saw me. "And here she is, here for the bad news?" The Russian crowed.

"Following you to Egypt was the best." The three jostled for the best chair.

"Those Albanians were super helpful, gave us another seventeen hours."

"We are in your debt." The Italian bowed to Marcus who scowled.

I didn't move from my chair. I sat to one side so the boys would have an unencumbered view of their attorney.

Marcus shuffled a few papers, then set them down and glared at the men. "I understand you kidnapped Ms. Gardner and Dr. Ratzenberg and abandoned them in a tomb?"

Put it that way, they at least had the decency to look sheepish. Of course, now that I had a little more time, I did recognize them. All three had a wonderful run in 2015, their faces on just about anything that didn't move. They had posed with Cindy, for a five-page ad in September Vogue, they on the ascendant, she minutes away from her Jimmy Choo debacle.

Some people use fame to leverage their next move. Some just let it go to their heads and believe everything they are told. Like these characters. Not one of them looked like he had worked in years. Well, five years? That's about twenty-eight in fashion years. And I thought I had been absent from the business for too long.

"But we inherit, all the beautiful things, all the priceless carpets and that bed."

"I always wanted that bed."

"Fond memories?"

The adorable Italian elbowed the Russian. "It's a Biedermeier, who wouldn't want it?"

"We are counting on it!" They chorused.

I briefly considered giving him the bed, but Marcus shook his head. How did he know?

"Gentlemen. I apologize if you were under the erroneous impression that you inherited."

"We ran down the clock, we want to put in our claim."

"But that will take years to unravel." I protested. They had already wasted three years of their lives, don't waste another three.

But few people understand sunk costs. All three shook their heads. I couldn't help it. "Where are you living?"

"We have an apartment off-island." The Russian rattled off the address. They lived blocks from the storage facility. Well, wasn't that ironic?

I glanced at Marcus who was now glaring at me. I tightened my lips and sat back.

"There is no need." He pulled out the hand-written, holographic will, that according to he and his father, reversed the public will on record, and according to Marcus, was about to change my life.

Wordlessly, he handed it to the American who scanned it then howled in protest. The Russian snatched it from him and read it. The Italian made to tear it in half, but Marcus calmly removed the paper from his fingers and set it back on the desk.

"You see?"

"But we were his friends."

I must have snorted. Marcus was impassive. He was impressive, dressed in his bespoke suit, sitting behind a carved desk that weighed as much as a car. The family business surrounded him like a cocoon. Or, I considered Marcus, perhaps a shroud.

"Indeed. Max Peters had many friends."

Many pretty, pretty boys. I never wanted to know the details. I had my own people to contend with, I didn't need to worry about who Max was into. What old queen doesn't want young men around? But they were dessert. I was the main course.

"You could return to work?" Marcus offered naively.

It was their turn to snort. I almost joined them. No, it was too late. But they could try. Who did I know who could help?

They filed out quietly. What would happen to them? I made to rise, I could help, even after all the trouble they gave me. I could buy them a glass of wine, okay, a whole bottle and help them figure out their next steps. But Marcus stopped me.

"We still need to settle with you."

I sat back down.

Marcus pulled out a Montegrappa pen and dashed off long numbers with more zeros than I had ever imagined. He turned the paper to me.

"The rents alone will give you a basic income, if it ever comes to that."

He wrote down a few more numbers. "But the stock, the stock is substantial. Plus, the licensing."

I was still focused on the zeros. "This is all mine?"

"You'll need a stockbroker, a financial analyst and, of course, an attorney."

I smiled. People. I had my own people. I needed my own people. How incredible was this?

Marcus handed me a key. "To the apartment."

Wordlessly, I added the key to my key ring.

CHAPTER TWENTY-FIVE

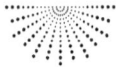

I banged the suitcase down seven blocks, over two bridges and into Max's, now my, building. I called the locksmith. Was it too late to come this afternoon?

"Never too late for you, signora."

After three years living surround by sensible beige and we-may-someday-sell-the-house white walls, Max's apartment was a shock. Most of the furniture was covered in dust cloths, even the fake chandelier was protected. But the silver and navy wallpaper was intact, the stately Biedermeier four-poster bed was still in one piece. All the windows and French doors leading to the patio were dim with grime.

The locksmith helped me remove the heavier cloths and he even climbed the ladder to remove the bags covering the chandelier.

"Murano." He said with approval.

I did not correct him.

The phone buzzed.

I tipped the locksmith with all the cash I had left.

The phone buzzed again. We are home. Ordering pizza.

Add some vegs

Friends over

Hell no, and I will check

I narrowed my eyes. For the time being, all I would do was clean and consider. Any rash act, like Tiffany and Lucy's immediate sale of Miranda's apartment and the sale of our parents' house was ill advised.

I sank onto the deep green-velvet couch and gazed at the sun reflecting off the canal. How many evenings? How many sunsets had I watched from this exact place? How many dawns? This time there was no call for a cocktail. Even if he shouldn't drink, Max did anyway. Because what the hell?

It was just me.

I rose and walked to the liquor cabinet. The phone buzzed again just as I reached for a very dusty of what was now well-aged scotch.

Ah, Tina.

The boys have soccer tomorrow remember to take them. And shop for healthy food, Chris needs more protein in his diet and do the laundry, their uniforms need to be bleached. Do that tonight. Did you clean the floor?

I contemplated my answer as I used the bathroom. The master bath was tiled in black marble: floor, walls and ceiling. I'm surprised it hadn't dropped into the lagoon. Double sinks, one for each hand. An oversize shower, a god send when Max couldn't easily leave his wheelchair. A soaking tub the size and dimensions of a sarcophagus.

Floor is clean.

There will be hell to pay when she found out I left the boys alone. But I would be back tomorrow. No harm, no foul.

I was not foolish enough to believe Nic would meet me alone nor was I gullible enough to retrieve the hippo and show up at the café carrying it in one of my classier purses, although I was becoming quite fond of the Hello Kitty purse. Both the hippo as well as Nic were loose ends. To his credit, Nic hated loose ends and ambiguity as much as I.

I didn't trust Nic because he was not in a trustworthy situation.

I even texted Max's address to Chris and asked him to stand by.

I showered and dressed with care, the legging/sweater combination was working, I could wear low-heeled boots, and look good while actually being able to walk without turning my ankle. I wound a Hermes scarf around my neck and headed out for my date.

A date.

The streets were lively and at this hour packed with more locals than tourists. Nonetheless, I had learned my lesson and watched my back and clutched Hello Kitty against my side.

I missed lurking Marcus. He seemed disappointed that the adventure was over. I would talk with him, maybe he wasn't cut out for the slow steady life in the confines of the family business.

I entered the square and took a breath. I loved it here at night. I loved riding a boat down the Grand Canal to the square. I wondered if the gondoliers still picked up from private patios. I could walk across my patio to the edge of the water and just hail a ride. The idea made me giddy. Maybe for my last ride I could try. Just once.

I paused at the Negor Amana and surveyed the café next door. I immediately spotted Nic. He looked damn handsome in dress shirt and slacks. He toyed with a glass of red wine and every other second glanced behind him as if he expected me to sneak up on him, which wasn't likely. I searched the tables. Ah, there they were. My favorite thugs, Oscar and Oslo. The blonde and the heavier bald man.

How disappointing that Nic was in this so completely, both the deep port as well as selling on the black market. He was a double agent, which is romantic in the movies, but complicated in real life. Dangerous. Some of us would say immoral. Some of us needed to remember we were not responsible for the state of Nic's soul.

I gestured for a waiter and handed him a handful of euros. I covered Nic's drink and sent a bottle of Montepulciano to Oslo and Oscar.

Nic's face lit up when he saw me. I smiled and resisted a glance at Nic's babysitters.

"You're all right." He stood and kissed me.

"Of course."

"When I saw you leaving with that man, I didn't know what to think."

"That I escaped?"

He sat down and gestured for the waiter who was already following me with my own bottle of Primitivo.

"I'm sorry," he said simply.

The waiter opened the wine and poured me a generous amount, he did not pour for Nic.

"For?" I sipped my wine. Yes, a woman could get used to this. But no one lived in Venice anymore. It was expensive, it was overrun with tourists, it was sinking into the sea.

He dragged his hands through his hair. "I didn't think it would come to this, all this." He waved his hands.

"Nic, you never know what it will all come to."

"They were just there to delay us," he admitted.

"They is rather unspecific."

"Those young men. At first, I thought they were following the hippo, but it turned out they were following you, or rather me. They thought I was you," he ended lamely.

I wasn't inclined to help him out. I sipped my wine and waited. Pigeons flew up around a small girl and she squealed either in delight or terror, sometimes it's hard to tell the difference.

After a long pause, he sighed and continued. "Those men. They wanted to delay me, well, you, it turns out. They didn't figure that part out until you had escaped." He smiled even in his agitation. "They were not happy that I was not Vic."

"I would have thought that Cindy would have told them."

"Didn't believe her."

"No, I don't imagine they did. And by the way. It worked."

"What worked?"

"Their plan. They were trying to run down the clock on Max's will."

He nodded. "Epic parties. But I wasn't a big participant."

If anyone did not swing both ways, it was hopelessly heterosexual Nicholas Ratzenberg.

"His will was being contested because the attorneys for Max's estate couldn't find me. Both the lawyers and the boys thought I was a man."

"Rather narrow-minded. Did it work?"

"Yes." I let him stew with that. I had other questions for Nic. I admired the surrounding buildings the proportioned arches lining the deep walkway that protected the store fronts from most of the elements. "Are you going to tell me what happened to Miranda?"

He closed his eyes, clearly in pain. "I found that out too. Cindy had given her something."

"Don't blame Cindy."

"Actually, I do. We all returned to Venice together. The boys were anxious to claim their inheritance and I think because they were so confident, they rejected Cindy and her help; they didn't even listen to her." It wasn't just the rich who were careless, beautiful people were careless too.

"Did she cry?"

"Of course, she did. Didn't work. Anyway, she needed a friend and I was the only straight man in the group. To get me on her side, she told me what happened." He cleared his throat and poured himself a half glass.

I sipped my wine. I had a pretty good idea, so I hurried the story along.

"And you? Did you intend to kill Miranda?"

My phone buzzed. It was Tina, with a lot of exclamation points and angry emojis.

"No!" His horror was genuine. "Miranda was fine when I saw her. She invited me in to discuss the hippo, but she never produced it. Cindy's visit must had made Miranda suspicious. And stubborn. According to Cindy, not only did Miranda not fall asleep after Cindy slipped her the natural sleeping pill, she had enough energy to escort Cindy from the apartment."

"I told her to never let Cindy spend the night again." I confirmed. "Glad she remembered."

He nodded. "Cindy was supposed to get the hippo and hand it back to our friends Oscar and Oslo."

"And you?'

"I needed it for my side."

"So to speak." My phone buzzed again.

"So to speak," he repeated. "All I did was put two Ambien in her wine. She fell asleep. I searched her place and found nothing."

"You should have tossed it. It would have looked more authentic."

He nodded, took a drink and leaned on the table head in his hands. "I was shocked when I heard. I must have been the last person to see her alive. I've been racking my brain on how two sleeping pills could kill her? Did they kill her?" He took my hands, desperate, unbelieving. I took pity on him, just this one last time.

"That natural sleeping pill? Was probably Monkshood. Not deadly necessarily on its own, but coupled with the wine and your contribution, well…."

"Cindy." He drained his glass and reached for the bottle.

"Miranda wasn't supposed to have the genuine thing, nor the ushabtis."

"Those were all fakes," he said with certainty.

"The ones you have, yes." I sipped my wine and watched him.

He narrowed his eyes. "You have the hippo still?"

"Of course."

"With you?"

I sensed a stirring from the other table. Customers were finishing their dinners and leaving the restaurant; simultaneously, a few couples wandered in for an expensive after dinner drink on St. Mark's Square. Because they were in Venice. Because it was romantic.

"Give me some credit, Nic."

"I give you a lot of credit, you got me, you stood up to the company men. You figured it all out."

"There isn't going to be an archeology dig museum, is there?"

He shook his head.

"Just a story to get the project through?"

"The hippo matters, Vic. An educational component always makes the process easier." He eyed me. "And it's better press. If the media discovers we are digging out a real archeological site, we won't be able to move forward. We are in competition with marine resorts, more building along the Red Sea. Luxor wants their piece of the tourist dollars. The powers in Albania want their shot at building luxury ships. It's important."

I remained silent. I knew that. I also knew that what we

considered precious and exciting, the locals viewed, for the most part, a nuisance. I waited.

He downed the wine and played with his tiny cocktail napkin. Finally, he looked me in the eyes.

"It's just business. We were planning to cover the discoveries, even move the hippo and other things to another site, away from the dock, like Amarna, where it probably came from in the first place. But then the Albanians got involved."

"Trafficking in stolen artifacts, not even large Belzoni-sized artifacts. Doesn't seem worth the trouble."

"When the hippo appeared in Venice, all hell broke loose, rumors, questions. We, they, were worried the artifacts could be traced back to the site."

We hadn't yet ordered dinner. Nic was too wound up in his story and I was too interested in hearing the big finish.

And here it was.

"I'm finished here. Those guys? They just want to make sure I don't talk. And I won't."

"Don't want your house burned?" I gestured for the waiter.

Nic snorted. "Funny girl."

The waiter arrived surprisingly promptly. I order another bottle for us and another bottle for the big boys. Once the waiter disappeared, Nic made his move.

"Come with me." He leaned in taking my hands. "We can live in the States; they won't pursue us there. We can buy a house, one that won't burn."

That ruled out California. The bottle arrived. Nic gripped his glass so hard I thought the stem would break.

"I have enough for a house. We can live out our golden years together. What do you say?"

When I was in my forties and camping with him in a tiny tent on the great big desert, there was nothing I wanted to hear more. Forty, when a girl's fancy turns to stability. He would have been a buffer against my family. He would be my most important obligation. When Tina called for free babysitting, I could cite my husband as the reason I couldn't. When Vince demanded I spend three years caring for our parents, I could use Nic as the excuse as to why I couldn't. What my family understood was husband and wife. They never considered Miranda and Max real partners.

But they were, they had been.

I sipped my wine. Out of the corner of my eye, the men at the other table opened the second bottle of wine. They were smoking and telling either jokes or absurd stories about their conquests and successes.

But now? Today? I would have a partner. I could buy any house I wanted and Nic could move in. I narrowed my eyes. The shine off the square cobblestones was like glass. Locals wandered across holding hands, the pigeons were finally quiet. The Basilica glowed golden against the night sky.

I would be cared for as well. Taking selfies on Senior Day (Tuesday) at Payless Drugs.

We would escape tonight, the hippo wouldn't emerge for years, not until new management at the hotel cleared out the un-claimed packages.

"What about your keepers?"

He glanced at the men, toasting. I turned and saluted them, which they seem to find mildly disturbing.

"I'll tell them you never had it, never found it."

"It's not the only hippo and those were not the only ushabtis."

He didn't look at me. "It's not my circus anymore. I've been fired, I don't have any authority, I…"

I put my hand on his. I had loved him. I gave up my exciting life with Miranda to follow him to the desert, and it had been glorious, wonderful and damn uncomfortable.

"Nic, I love you. I will always love you. But I'm not moving to the suburbs with you."

I had no idea that sentence could come out of my mouth. It was both thrilling and terrifying.

Nic left the café alone.

CHAPTER TWENTY-SIX

a hole in my heart. That's what Nic had excavated discovering nothing but emptiness. It would take some time, I knew that.

Did I trust him? No. Once those thugs woke up and coffee-ed out their hangovers, they would pay attention, again, to loose ends. I assumed Nic was flying to the States, if he were smart. But me? I was still here; I was still a loose end.

I checked in with the boys who took a series of videos on their video game progress. Chris admitted he accidentally let his mother know they were spending the night alone.

I glanced at the series of invectives from Tina. Some were fair enough. Others not so much. She even went as far as saying if I knew what was good for me.

I wondered what exactly was good for me?

My flight was scheduled for early evening. I had time to say goodbye to my friends and yes, pay them for their help.

Before I walked out into the late morning light to Rachael's gallery, I stopped by Miranda's place. We hadn't stopped deliveries, nor the mail. Tiffany and Lucy still needed to clear out bills and statements. One of my jobs was to gather up the mail and forward it to them. And of course, once I had my new credit card, it was easy to order things.

The apartment looked good. Cindy's clothes and suitcase were gone. The remaining painting were just right for the space. Maybe Tiffany and Lucy would sell the paintings along with the furniture. I certainly wasn't up for moving it. And with a place of my own, I wouldn't have to.

A text from Maria. The buyer wanted me out of the apartment by the end of the week.

No problem, I texted back.

I pulled the double drawer out from under the bed. I pulled out the toys, the whips and chains. That too was another life. I found a large orange Hermes bag and loaded the toys in. Should I need more, I could always take a quick trip to Amsterdam.

The box had been delivered a couple days ago. I opened it to reveal my very own William, the Met mascot. I dropped him on top of the bag. He looked too new. Hmm. I hated to do it, but I spent some time roughing him up. I put him back on top of the toys, better. Then I, oh so innocently, strolled to Rachael's gallery.

I was accosted only a block from the apartment.

They could have said "stick 'em up" for all the subtlety they displayed.

"Gentlemen." The men loomed over me, as they had this whole adventure.

Oscar growled, "Give us the bag, the hippo."

"What? You aren't here to thank me for the wine?"

They both growled. But I sensed it was a little forced.

I wanted to ask who was in charge, I wanted them to draw an org chart for me, who was on the top of their food chain? But we did not have that kind of relationship, bottles of good Montepulciano aside.

I did my best to look guilty. I even glanced at the bag dangling from my arm.

The blonde lunged and grabbed the bag so hard the handle snapped.

I looked horrified, or at least I hoped I did. They both dashed away before I could deliver the full performance.

"Does this mean we're over?" I called out, but they had escaped around the corner. This time they had not bothered with my purse. Thank the gods.

"THANK you so much for your help." I squeezed Rachael's hand.

"It's a pleasure, I'm so happy to be able to finally pay you back." Rachael squeezed back.

"Max was always good to his friends." I tucked the refused money back into my bag. She was right, it wasn't about the money, it was about leveraging, it was about making the people you care about happy and secure. Wealth. I suppressed a sigh, a lot of wealth is good, but security is better. And I had it now, I could do exactly what I wanted.

"Max?" Rachael looked puzzled.

"It was Max's money." I reminded her. He loved to give me money to help the girls. During his last year, he couldn't get outside much, he was too weak. But he could still type. He spent hours on the computer, I assumed it was gay porn and so didn't really want to inquire too closely. Now I know he was buying and selling stocks and issuing them in my name in order to reduce the estate taxes. For some, it's all about the taxes, in Italy that is rather more important than in the States, but still. I'll have to pay taxes. I was happy to. Compared to nothing, paying on something was just fine with me.

"You've forgotten," she accused.

"It's been a long three years. Sometimes I feel I've just been released from a Turkish prison."

She fumbled. "You said, return the favor someday. That's what you always said, to all of us."

I frowned. "Yes, of course, return the favor, but I never thought..." I trailed off. The Chagall was stunning; in the artificial lights of the gallery, it glowed blue.

"You never collected." She finished.

Naturally I never collected, that was never the goal. It is surprisingly difficult to help proud people. I knew when a girl needed a boost, a helping hand, a meal. Particularly a meal. The fashion industry is a cruel place, more so because the images are so lovely, so excellent. When you admire that beautiful girl on the cover of Sports Illustrated, know that the rock on the beach with the beautiful sea behind, is in fact, digging into what is left of the model's thighs, it's February and freezing cold, five people are circling her to make the best shot, the photographer is calling out instructions, the main one being, look natural. She had a leg cramp, is about to be knocked off the rock by the next wave and must smile enticingly.

Beautiful.

I always engaged models in conversation while the lighting was set up. Photo shoots require a lot of standing around. I found I could draw the models out. I was fond of discovering what they really wanted to do once their hunger for both food and meaning became acute. Classes, training, college, leveraging the modeling into something more lucrative, lasting and livable.

And how to make it all work was to simply say, you owe me, and I'll catch you later, keep in touch. Some did keep in touch and I'd update Max on their progress. Some came at the end to thank him for his generosity. He enjoyed their visits.

"Don't be absurd. I never ever thought to collect. We just wanted to help."

Rachael waved to the whole of her business. "You helped me."

"You were so interested in art in the other side of the business. I'm glad you found this as your passion."

She nodded. "It was Max's money."

"Of course."

"But it was your idea."

That stunned me. I didn't consider it my idea at all.

Rachael waited while I processed.

"I..."

"Don't explain, I didn't realize you didn't even know yourself. You are far too generous you know."

I nodded. "Can you do me one more favor?"

LIKE NIC, I do appreciate some closure; also, I didn't want to start my new life with anything hanging over my head. I texted Tiffany—Did the painting arrive?

I had time to eat one more pasta dish, more bread, another dredge of green olive oil, before Tiffany buzzed back. A terse yes.

There was enough silence on her end to tell me the sale of the property was now very critical indeed. No May-the-First Party for those girls. They never did have an eye for genuine art.

I WALKED into the hotel lobby where it all began. I was pretty mellow from the wine and giddy that for the first time since I landed in Italy, I was not followed. The desk clerk nodded, and I approached just as a group of tourists tumbled down the stairs banging their enormous bags behind them.

"Paula! Come back and take this. God, woman, what did you buy? Lead statues?"

I turned and watched Paula and Henry stagger into the lobby. Paula carried two Princess Cruise canvas bags, each stuffed to overflowing. She pushed and pulled her bags to the desk, lining them up like soldiers on parade. Henry brought up the rear guard and added to the collection. Five bags, two tourists.

Paula nodded to me but did not greet me. She didn't recognize me. Henry gave me a second look, but dutifully stepped into the line behind his wife.

I gave the clerk my old room number and she retrieved the bulky package. I took one last look at the couple. I would be leaving in an hour. One piece of luggage. One painting.

Rachael helped me package the hippo and ushabtis and route the package to first Rome, then Iowa, back to London, each time the package would be re-wrapped with a new label. I decided to donate the hippo to the Petrie Museum of Egyptian Archaeology in London. I was a fan of Amelia Edwards and she was a fan of Petrie. That seemed right.

I slotted my key into the apartment, the new lock turned with a satisfying click. As I stepped inside, Nic texted that UCSB had offered him a temporary position filling in for an on-sabbatical professor. I wondered if Chris had anything to do with that. Nic was, after all, his hero.

No, I would not like to visit, I texted back.

No.

I walked out to the patio; the water lapped against the low wall. It would be a bitch during the high tides. I'd need to replace the sandbags, reinforce the wall; the upkeep would be tremendous and all consuming. It was impossible and stupid to even think of it.

I texted Chris, not caring about time zones.

Mom is really mad. Uncle Vance is coming over. He's mad too.

And what? Make me return? Withhold my share of the inheritance? I turned my face to the Italian sun. Never speak to me again?

You'll be just fine, I texted Chris.

I'll visit your home, he texted back.

I blinked. He was right. I was home.

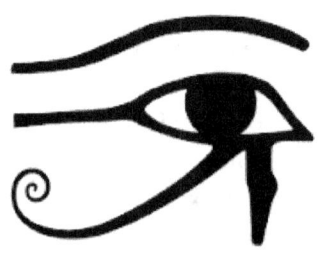

ABOUT THE AUTHOR

Catharine Bramkamp is a professional writing coach, bringing her clients from idea to published book to promotion. She produced 200 episodes of the writing podcast, Newbie Writers Podcast, has written 20 novels and 3 books on writing. She believes that adventure is possible at any age, as long as there is wine with lunch.

Website – http://www.Catharine-Bramkamp.com
    Sign up for the newsletter!
    Contact me directly @Cbramkamp@gmail.com

https://www.linkedin.com/in/catharinebramkamp/
    https://www.pinterest.com/cbramkamp/
    https://www.instagram.com/catharinebramkamp/
    @cbramkamp